A Choice of Darkness

A Work of Fiction
By
Jon D. Kurtz

D1714555

Text Copyright © 2013 by Jon D. Kurtz

Cover design by Jon D. Kurtz.

Editing provided by Jeanne S. Yaggi.

V3

ISBN-13: 978-1494363352
ISBN-10: 1494363356

A Choice of Darkness is dedicated to two groups.

First, words fail me as I attempt to describe the meaning of family to my life. They have and continue to provide me with a source of strength, joy, and pride. Though I give, it will never compare to what I have received.

Second, this work is dedicated to the men and women of law enforcement and the criminal justice community, who willingly travel into the darkness in order to light the path for those innocents lost among the shadows.

"Nobody ever did, or ever will, escape the consequences of his choices."
Alfred A. Montapert

"There are dark shadows on the earth, but its lights are stronger in the contrast."
Charles Dickens

Chapter 1 (Monday)

Demons

Warmed by the sun's bright rays, Thomas Payne scooped up his wife and tossed her into the foamy surf. Briefly submerged, she resurfaced with a sputter and a playful splash. Her flirtatious expression instantly transformed into a smile. Prompted by her gaze, Thomas turned in time for the breaker to strike him square in the face.

Knocked underwater and dragged along the gritty bottom by a fickle Mother Nature, he humbly righted himself with a cough and sheepish grin. His amusement quickly faded at the bizarre scene playing out before him. Beneath a now overcast sky, the once moderate waves had morphed into large, powerful swells. Thunder cracked and lightning flashed.

Bewildered, he cast his eyes over the water and sand to find he stood in solitude. Alone with the now cloying smells of the sea, desperation blossomed. Only the fleeting scent of his wife's perfume slowed its bloom. As if to provide direction, the fragrance prompted him to scan the horizon, where he glimpsed a head bobbing among the waves, pulled along by an unseen current.

In desperation, Thomas dove into the choppy water and swam with herculean effort toward the receding figure. With each breath, he lifted his head to ensure he remained on course. Astonishingly, though he swam hard, the gap continued to widen until Lynn's figure receded and disappeared as though never having existed.

At that moment, Thomas experienced a sensation of great loss. Frozen by grief and subjected to the relentless pounding of the water, he floundered. Strength and hope drained from his body. Exhausted, he stopped treading water and stopped caring; he gave up. He relaxed and accepted their fate. Embraced in cottony arms of resignation, he descended into the darkening depths, longing to join his wife.

Disoriented, he found himself alone, sitting up in bed, drenched in sweat rather than seawater. The bedside clock indicated 4:32 a.m. Since Lynn's death from cancer five years ago, bad dreams visited regularly. Accustomed to these unwelcome callers, Thomas recognized the adrenaline coursing through his system signaled the end of his night's rest.

His recourse, place one shaky foot onto the soft-carpeted floor and then another. By habit, he levered his well-muscled six-foot frame off the mattress and trudged into the bathroom to begin his day. As he passed the mirror, he saw his dark hair, though short, shot off at crazy angles and the whites of his normally clear green eyes blazed with ribbons of red. Hands on the sink, he looked at his reflection, breathed deeply, and whispered for the thousandth time, "Why did you have to go?"

Reticent to continue down the well-travelled, but hazardous, road his thoughts now occupied, he began his morning routine. As usual the steamy spray of the shower invigorated him. It loosened and sloughed away the salt water residue of his dreams, carrying them down the drain and into the sewer from which they had come.

With the aid of the water and habit, his mind spun up to a respectable rpm, allowing him to turn his focus away from the demons of his night, to the monsters which inhabited his day. A warrior of the first magnitude, Thomas J. Payne battled beasts for a living. An agent with the Pennsylvania Bureau of Criminal Apprehension (BCA) for two decades, he had witnessed the savagery and engaged in combat with that most dangerous of creatures: man.

A seasoned investigator and supervisor, he had conducted and overseen a wide range of inquiries, including numerous cases of homicide. His combination of innate intelligence and highly honed work ethic made him an exceptional investigator, one well respected within his department and the law enforcement community.

An hour later, shaved, dressed, and fed, he made his way to the office. As expected, his morning ritual tempered the nighttime blues. The tenuous truce with the beasts occupying his sleep seemed to be holding.

Now alone in the office, nightmare all but forgotten, he found himself energized by the significance of the day. Today, Monday, January 1st, marked the first day of formal operation for the Major Crimes Task Force (MCTF) and Thomas' first day as commander.

A child of frustration, the task force had been conceived in the backrooms of state government. Created from the political need to appear tough on crime, the governor tasked the director of the BCA with creating a statewide entity able to investigate, what he considered, noteworthy crimes. Specifically, his administration established the MCTF to investigate two child murders that had occurred over the past month in the city of Harrisburg. Since lawlessness in one's capital city cast a pall over the local electorate, it fell within the aforementioned category of noteworthy crimes.

An anomaly from an organizational perspective, the task force took its official guidance from the director of the BCA. In reality, its commander would often receive informal direction from the governor's office. Having two bosses with, in some instances, two sets of goals had already left Thomas feeling as though he lived in two worlds, but belonged in neither. As example, this morning, he struggled with finalizing a PowerPoint presentation for the governor and his staff regarding the city's homicides. His unanticipated conundrum: how much confidential information could he release to a non-law enforcement audience?

Caught in contemplation, he nearly missed the subtle movement near his doorway. An intimidating, but familiar figure, Robert "Robby" Franklin strode into his office. A member of the

4

fledgling task force and Thomas' oldest and closest friend, Robby stood six foot two, slightly taller than Thomas but built equally as solid.

Friends since high school, Thomas and Robby shared a love for sports and physical conditioning. Though forty, they maintained excellent fitness through running, lifting weights, and mixed martial arts. Conversely, while Robby had preserved the free-spirited nature of his youth, Thomas had become more thoughtful following his wife's death.

Noting he had Thomas' attention, Robby remarked, "If I were a lion, you'd be lunch."

"If I were lunch, you'd have indigestion. Plus, I knew you were there. Your big head blocked the light coming in the doorway."

"That might hurt if I wasn't sure my head was perfect for my body," retorted Robby. "How many times do I have to remind you—best of both worlds, baby."

The comment made Thomas smile. A racial mix of black and white, Robby viewed his blended ethnic heritage as a blessing. Consistent with his personality, he focused on the positive, made the best of his gifts, and shared them with others.

This attitude had never been more apparent than after Lynn's death. Considered part of the family, Robby grieved her passing as he would a sister. Yet, he became the rock on which Thomas relied to get through the long debilitating cancer treatments, the viewing and funeral, and the aftermath. Moreover, while that aftermath continued to drag on, he remained at Thomas' side.

"By the way," he added, returning to a critique of his friend's insult, "that head comment was beneath you." A beat later, he asked, "Hard time sleeping again?"

"No more than usual. I'm just crunched for time with this presentation." replied Thomas, brushing away the comment as he returned to his computer monitor.

"I'm starting to get the feeling you don't love me anymore," protested his friend with a wounded look. He supplemented the comment with a wink and, "You know I still love you," which quickly transformed with the addition of, "Yeah, the manly, rugged kind of love one brother in arms has for another," as he realized someone listening might misinterpret his wisecrack.

Focus elsewhere, Thomas barely glanced up before stating, "On that note, I'll get back to work, while you go off to examine your feelings."

Again, Robby attempted to look wounded; however, he failed miserably. Obviously anxious to continue the conversation, he summoned a more professional tone and declared, "Assuming your briefing is about the city's homicides, we should talk about a few things before you go."

Robby's change in demeanor had the desired effect. While often a joker, his investigative insights usually proved valuable. Interest piqued and now fully engaged, Thomas responded, "Okay, you've got my attention."

Noting Thomas' curiosity, Robby began, "First, leave the crystal ball at the office. At this point, we don't have enough information to justify a full assessment."

Agreeing, Thomas replied, "I've been hesitant to push the PD for updates. They don't need me pestering them for reports. On a more specific note, the governor's people are bound to ask about the blankets. The media seems hell-bent on making a connection between them and the emergency response community."

Synthetic yellow blankets commonly used by EMS, fire, and police personnel had covered the bodies at both homicide scenes. Thomas admitted, "I don't discount the theory, but it's caused serious trust issues. The city's even had a few mini riots as a result." He thought out loud, "It'll send police-community relations back to the Stone Age if the media turns out to be right."

"Speaking of the blankets," Robby interjected, "targeting kids and displaying their bodies under blankets is pretty bizarre. Assuming he's as screwed up as it appears, understanding his motivation might be a tall order." For humor sake, he quickly added, "Unless we can find someone who's just as screwed up and perverted to interpret his behavior. Like, maybe one of our local politicians."

Though Robby enjoyed rare form this morning, Thomas' ambivalent stare signaled defeat. Resignation evident, Robby sighed, "Man, you're tough. I'm giving you my best material." Rewarded with a mute glare, he performed a quick about-face and before sidling away, proclaimed, "I need to find a more responsive audience. My talent's wasted here."

As he reached his desk, he yelled, "Let me know when your funny bone grows back."

Though distracted, Thomas had heard Robby's observations. Additionally, his friend's parting comments managed to bring a slight, if not noticeable, smile to his face. One of Robby's strengths, the ability to know when and how to lighten the mood, often provided respite from the demands of the job.

Robby's efforts reminded Thomas of the dedication and self-sufficiency of his new team. They required little direction and no prodding. Each of the five investigators had worked tirelessly to absorb the case information since arriving the previous Monday. Eager to unlock the unit's potential, Thomas returned his focus to his work, blissfully unaware of the fate train bearing down upon him.

Chapter 2

Birth from Death

Fifteen minutes later, Thomas stretched and rubbed his stinging eyes. Hands behind his head, he reflected upon the specific events leading to the creation of the task force. Roughly a month before at the beginning of December, someone had dumped a child's body along a dirt road on the outskirts of Harrisburg near the city's southern border with Steelton Borough. Two weeks later, mid-month, the dreadful scene repeated.

While the first homicide had stirred the waters of community sentiment, the second resulted in a tidal wave of anger and finger pointing that quickly inundated the offices of the city's mayor. Already burdened by a budget crisis and dwindling resources, he reached out to his party mate and friend, the governor, for advice and assistance. The governor saw an opportunity to help when Agent Thomas Payne from the BCA requested an audience.

The visit had nothing to do with the city's homicides. Payne simply needed to complete the final interview in a Terroristic Threats investigation involving the governor. Much like those before him, this governor served as the chief lightning rod for the failed and unpopular policies of the entire government.

Five months earlier Thomas had been monitoring an anti-government website on which he had observed increasingly paranoid ramblings. He interpreted one particular rant as a call to arms. In response, he intercepted an extremely unhappy and well-armed veteran on his way to Harrisburg to right a perceived wrong. In the process, he saved the governor from the monotony of the man's marijuana and mushroom enhanced philosophy, and, more importantly, possible injury or death.

Confident in Thomas' expertise and judgment, it took little time for the governor to switch from interviewee to inquisitor. Thomas initially sidestepped the issue, which he thought more appropriate for his director, but the governor insisted. In the uncomfortable glare of the spotlight, Thomas provided a brief history of law enforcement services in the Commonwealth. The most important point, with over 1200 police departments, many comprised of four officers or less, most agencies couldn't afford to commit resources to a lengthy criminal investigation.

Pushed for a solution, he had opined that a small, dedicated team of investigators with statewide powers of investigation and arrest could prove effective against major crimes. Rather than use the current BCA model of providing temporary crime scene, forensic, or investigative assistance, this team would become an integral part of a complicated local investigation. With a long-term commitment, they would be more easily accepted by local investigators and, in turn, dedicate more energy to reaching a positive outcome.

After the interview, Thomas left the governor's mansion with the satisfaction of having completed his interview. Conversely, he suffered the disconcerting feeling he had been used and might have stepped into the proverbial steaming pile of dog crap. In either case, he needed a shower.

Not surprisingly, early the next morning he received a brusque command to report to the director's office. This confirmed his fear that the large pile existed, and he had stepped in the middle of it. A severe ass-chewing in his future, Thomas regretted not owning a pair of bullet resistant underwear.

Twenty minutes later, Thomas weaved his way through the phalanx of the Director's minions and entered the inner sanctum. As the door closed behind him, the office's current occupant, Arnold Green, a short, thick man in the autumn of a long and successful career with the BCA, stood and without offering a greeting bellowed, "What in the hell are you doing talking to the governor?"

The terse comment wasn't unexpected. Thomas had worked for the director at various stages of their careers. Renowned as much for his sporadic tirades as his proficiency in running a large police agency, the director tended to nurture the gruff persona. However, while abrupt and, at times, rough around the edges, Green had long ago earned Thomas' respect. Accustomed to the style or, some might say, lack thereof, Thomas knew the director's rant would quickly diminish.

With this in mind, Thomas took a breath, measured his words, and responded, "Director, I was in the governor's office yesterday conducting an interview for another investigation. After we finished, he started asking me questions about the city's homicides."

Thomas waited for a response which failed to materialize. In frustration, he added, "With all due respect, sir, what was I supposed to do, plead the fifth?"

"Thomas, you're a bright boy. Did it ever cross your mind to couch your answers, even a little?" Green vented. With exasperation-tainted acceptance, he quickly added, "As of this moment, you're detached to implement this new task force. You'll need to scavenge for your own office space. Vehicles and equipment can be procured through the normal BCA channels."

"Yes, sir," responded Thomas, unwilling to prolong the beating.

Mindful of the precarious position Thomas had been in, Director Greene finally lightened his tone and commented, "Listen, Thomas, you're a good investigator, but you may have bitten off more than you can chew on this one. You'll be in the unenviable position of reporting to two masters: me and my boss, the governor. Also, you should be aware of the politics of the decision. The governor's receiving pressure from the city's mayor, who happens to be a member of the state Democratic Committee. Therefore, as you might expect, the governor's receiving pressure from the party. Being relatively new, he wants to look tough on crime. How does he accomplish that? He sets up a state-level task force to solve these heinous, media-hyped crimes and assigns a well-known criminal investigator to run it, that's how. An idea whose seed was planted by that same investigator, I might add. It's a win-win for him because he's taken action. It's only a winner for us if you solve the crimes."

"So, if I can leave you with one thought," Greene continued, "you'd better be able to deliver."

Back in the here and now, Thomas' desk phone rang, abruptly ending his reminiscing. Engrossed in his daydream, he had failed to note the inevitable passing of time. From the display, Thomas recognized the caller as Margaret "Maggie" Bennett, the task force's office manager, secretary, receptionist, and den mother.

Despite her tiny five-foot frame, Maggie spun like a compact tornado from morning until night. A force of nature exhibiting an occasional sharp edge, the widowed mother of two young children recently had turned thirty years old. A difficult transition made harder by the absence of her husband, she, nevertheless, bore the challenge mightily with the aid of some good-natured teasing from the task force members.

Receiver in hand, Thomas mocked, "Payne's Elder Care. Today's specials include half price walkers and free denture cleaning. How may I help you?"

"You can start by marking the board to show you're in the office," she replied tersely.

An example of her need to know every aspect of what occurred in and around the office, Maggie had implemented the dreaded "board." She insisted task force members entering or exiting the office move the little red magnetic circle to the appropriately labeled "in" or "out" column. As the task force began to take shape, the members quickly learned moving the magnet took far less effort than moving Maggie.

First verbal jab countered by Maggie's stiff right, Thomas immediately laughed and pleaded mea culpa, "Sorry, Mags. I was in a hurry to finish this briefing."

Aware of the pressure her boss faced in his new position, she softened and replied, "I'll let it slide this time, but don't let it happen again. I just wanted to remind you of your appointment in the governor's conference room at 8:00 o'clock."

"Don't you mean oh-eight hundred hours?" Thomas interjected, throwing a verbal right cross of his own, which he regretted immediately.

"Oh-eight hundred, oh-eight thousand, or oh-eight million, that isn't the point," she retorted. "You have to be in the conference room and set-up in let's say…oh…four minutes, wise guy."

Momentarily in shock, Thomas nearly fell out of his chair trying to eject the thumb-drive containing his presentation from the computer. In the same position for two hours, his feet had fallen asleep. On pins and needles, he grabbed his suit coat and hobbled through the office. The last words he heard after limping around the metal slab, which passed for a front door, came from Maggie, who stated dryly, "I guess it's a good thing you never marked the board after all."

Chapter 3

Shadow of the Wolf

As the new week and New Year dawned, the man's eyes, normally sightless and dull, shone with the singular anticipation of a heroin addict clutching two crumpled twenty-dollar bills. Fourteen days, 336 hours, or 20,160 minutes from his last trip into the darkness, he yearned to explore. He longed to exchange expectation for the knowledge only visible through the wise, scarlet eyes of the wolf.

It hadn't always been this way. Once, he had been a boy, as innocent as any other. But that had changed abruptly when his mother unwittingly welcomed a wolf into their lives. A carnivorous creature cloaked in human form, it feasted upon the unsuspecting. Adding to its own wickedness, this wolf brought with it an immoral traveling companion, a sinister darkness. Hungry as well, it craved more than flesh and blood. It feasted on innocence and compassion.

While the wolf destroyed bodies, the darkness consumed souls.

A young child when first introduced to the wolf and the darkness, he endured four years of torment as the unscrupulous duo fed upon him and his mother. Then, one night, the darkness, with its greedy nature, destroyed the wolf and, along with it, his mother. Left alone, he found himself unprotected and vulnerable to the shadows.

Wrongly assuming all adults served as carriers of the darkness, he elected to trust no one. He distanced himself from others, including those willing to provide the support he so desperately needed. Inevitably, his flight forward brought him full-circle. By destiny or whim, he caught up with and came face-to-face with that which he most feared. Yet, instead of peering into the terrifying eyes of an immortal enemy, he saw, not the wolf of his youth, but his own wretched reflection gazing back sadly.

Confronted by the familiar face, he accepted his fate. He embraced the darkness, allowing it to flow over and empower him. After more than fifteen years, he ended the standoff with the angels of his better nature. He chose to take up residence in the void once occupied by a loathsome creature. And in doing so, he shed the skin under which he hid and became the wolf.

His transformation had occurred six months before on a sultry Texas City night. He recalled the stink of the ocean brine and chemical cocktail swirling off Galveston Bay as he walked to work on that evening in June. Few other cues penetrated the heat and humidity knitted into the oppressive blanket covering the area. Senses parboiled, he ignored the ramshackle houses to his right and the decrepit chain link fence to his left. The simple act of placing one foot in front of the other demanded all his effort.

Focused on getting to work and into the air conditioning, he nearly missed the feeble voice. At his normal pace, the crunching gravel beneath his feet would have obscured the sound. Riding invisible currents of air from the inky blackness beyond the fence, he heard a cry for help.

Drawn to the weary melody, he crawled through a break in the dilapidated barrier and awkwardly picked his way past rocks and underbrush. Eventually, his eyes adjusted to the lack of light away from the street, allowing him to see what lay before him. There at the base of a small hill near the edge of a derelict quarry sat a small boy.

The child appeared unable to stand. His legs splayed beneath his body like those of a young deer. No older than ten, he wore grimy black shorts and a stained white undershirt. Against his chest, he clutched a small furry figure.

Elated upon discovery, the little boy recreated his misfortune to his distracted rescuer, who stared open-mouthed into the vast darkness. Transformed into a cloudy looking glass, the seemingly infinite void of the pit provided his first glimpse at the beast haunting his dreams. Examining his own image, he finally understood the message: to see as the wolf of his youth, he must become the wolf.

Guided by his revelation, he acted without consideration of cost or consequence. He sought answers that had eluded him since childhood. When he finished, the boy laid still and quiet.

Following his impromptu actions, the man, not long ago a boy himself, took stock. Panic blossomed under the increasing weight of his actions. He scuttled away, kicking and clawing to gain separation from his deeds. His spastic movements had two results. First, he found himself at the top of the hill, winded and with holes in the knees of his uniform pants. Second, he observed his lunch bag and a small stuffed bunny rabbit amongst the rocks and dust below, but no boy.

Into the darkness he peered, trying to make sense of the scene before him. And the answers came. Not his intent, the boy's once supple and growing body now lay distorted at the bottom of the pit. In turn, the man, who looked for answers, found more questions.

Opening act in his journey of self-discovery complete, he sensed the answers he sought would not be found in the familiar dirt and unwelcome memories of his native Texas. He picked up stakes and, on impulse, moved north, settling in Harrisburg, Pennsylvania. With four distinct seasons and mountains, it seemed the direct opposite of his homeland. Driven by tortured memories of his past and dreams of a fulfilling future, he left behind his barren existence in search of a fertile garden in which he could exchange his caterpillar reality for butterfly dreams.

Back in the present following his brief inspection of the past, the man's desire built as he counted the minutes until nightfall.

Another extended Monday work shift had arrived and with it opportunity. Camouflaged by the black of night and his uniform of blue, he would move as a wraith among the living and strike again.

Two weeks removed from his last hunt, his manic mood swings had resolved and his confidence had returned. Hooked to the well broken-in diesel engine of the shadows, he sensed his destination, a terminal of discovery, nearing. The price of the ride no longer mattered as he provided his well-worn ticket to the conductor. No amount was too great to finally understand the obscenity that was his life.

Chapter 4

Beginnings

Ensconced behind her desk, Maggie watched Thomas hobble out the door, struggling with his coat. She marveled at the recent changes in her life. Two weeks before, she had been well into her tenth year as the office manager for the Dauphin County District Attorney (DA). This had been where she first met Thomas. Initially professional acquaintances, their relationship changed drastically as a result of a series of tragic events, now five years in the past.

It began with the death of her husband David. Homeward bound following his second shift job, his vehicle had been struck head-on by a truck operated by a depressed and intoxicated driver. The drunk failed in his quest to commit suicide, but succeeded in killing her husband, best friend, and father of her two children. For months following the crash, she withdrew into herself, hiding beneath a two-sided coat sown of anguish and rage.

Ignorant to any crisis beyond her own, Maggie slogged through her days. She knew nothing of the tragedy unfolding in the lives of Thomas and his wife Lynn. Diagnosed with stage III breast cancer, Lynn was in the fight of her life. Six months later, brutalized and weakened by cancer and cure, she lost the war and slipped away.

Lynn Payne's passing struck a chord in the nearly emotionally bankrupt Maggie. It stirred cold memories of that night when her life changed forever. Strangely, she yearned to reach out to Thomas, but bound in her emotional straitjacket, she found herself incapable of acting.

By chance, not long after Lynn's funeral service, Maggie bumped into Thomas at the courthouse. Each provided a token greeting and then regrets for the other's loss. Thomas, with the freshest wound, had turned first to walk away when Maggie found herself, uncharacteristically, reaching out and hugging him. An awkward silence followed but didn't last. Soon sitting on a nearby bench, they talked for an hour. Other discussions followed, and an extremely close, although platonic, relationship developed.

Initially convinced her need to speak with Thomas emanated from a desire to help him, Maggie now recognized self-preservation as the true motivator. She had been wearily paddling through a sea of torment and pity and had reached out to grab the first lifeline to come within her grasp. It didn't matter that it drifted behind a floundering ship.

Over time with Thomas' help, a sense of balance had returned to her life. Sorrow remained; however, its sharp edge had been tempered. She nearly smiled, but guilt set in as her thoughts shifted back to Thomas. An exceptional listener, he empathized, dissected her feelings, and offered sage advice. Unfortunately, he remained hesitant to follow his own counsel. He circled the wagons and kept the Indians of a personal life at bay. He seemed satisfied to simply endure.

Now five years after Lynn's death, Maggie understood that Thomas' actions and inactions afforded him a means to limit the painful memories he associated with joy and happiness. This revelation had come with its own personal embarrassment. During one of their discussions, she found herself half-heartedly flirting with a clueless Thomas. Initially hurt, the sting quickly subsided as she recalled her own experience in purgatory.

Today, as she had done each day for the past week and a half, Maggie agonized over Thomas' unwillingness to remove his mask. The thought reminded her that two weeks had elapsed since he had come to her with the proposal to manage the task force office. Though initially hesitant, Thomas' enthusiasm, persistence, and their friendship, solidified by mutual despair, sufficiently tipped the scale. Truth be told, she saw this as an opportunity to help him as he had helped her.

On board and fully committed, Maggie threw herself into her new job. She shooed Thomas away to search for personnel, while she went about populating the office. The first big challenge turned out to be locating office space outside the limited confines of the BCA's headquarters building.

Her search led her to a renovated area in the basement of Pennsylvania's capitol building. An imposing green domed structure located in the center of Harrisburg, the capitol's upper levels contained the coveted offices of the political elite of state government. Although not nearly as fashionable, the basement boasted sufficient space and, most important, immediate availability.

Like most one-hundred-year-old structures, numerous renovations had transformed the lower levels into a mish-mash of offices, equipment rooms, and meandering hallways. In consideration of its layout and in recognition of its non-human population, it received the apt nickname of "the rat maze." This particular moniker had come to her attention on her first day in the building, when a middle-aged custodian provided her a tour, spinning fantastic tales of his battles with hoards of monstrous, angry rodents. Painting a picture of infestation on a grand scale, the short, overweight knight offered protection and his undying service to the fair Maid Maggie.

The memory of her grungy Galahad caused her to cringe and turned her attention back to the search for office space. In short order, she had identified an appropriate sized space and lucked into a surplus of good desks, chairs, and modular cubicles recently orphaned by an unforeseen swing of the budget ax. With functionality the priority, she placed her desk near the front door, so she could double as receptionist. This led Thomas to kid the design reflected her need for control. Though she vehemently denied the assertion, at least to his face, she supposed the comment contained a measure of truth.

With the office now nearly complete, she cast her view over her accomplishment. The main office contained a forty by forty foot exposed bay area housing the investigators' cubicles. Around the perimeter, four enclosed rooms provided separate space for the task force commander's office, a conference room, an evidence locker/room, and an interview/interrogation room. In total, they had laid claim to approximately twenty-five hundred square feet of prime subterranean real estate.

Pride evident in her smile, Maggie's thoughts turned to the audible click of the electric lock on the front door, which normally heralded the arrival of a coworker. Today, not one, but all four of the remaining members piled through the door. They laughed and joked as they partook in that most customary of police activities, the verbal abuse of one of their own.

Maggie's gaze moved to the butt of the joke, a dejected mountain of a man clutching a malfunctioning keycard. She giggled as she listened to the conversation. Apparently her unhappy colleague had chosen to wait in the hallway for another member to arrive, rather than interrupt her and incur her wrath. Their difference in size, he stood a foot and a half taller and outweighed her by two hundred pounds, combined with his deference to Maggie had become an ongoing office joke.

Maggie considered the group dynamic. She marveled at the speed in which the diverse group of individuals had bonded. Along with Thomas Payne, Robby Franklin, and her, their new informal family included Stanley "Stan" Brown, the defective keycard owner, Veronica "Ronnie" Sanchez, Raj "Doc" Patel, and Bill Travis.

Once, in an attempt to describe the task force members to her father, a recently retired, yet ever curious police sergeant, she found herself resorting to a verbal picture. "They're like M&Ms, different on the outside but the same inside." She had added, "You already know Thomas and Robby Franklin. Then, there's Stan Brown. He's brown like his name and bald. He's also huge. Think six foot six inches and three hundred pounds. Doc's Indian and off the chart's smart. He owned a tech company before coming here. Bill Travis is the youngest at twenty-five. He's nice, but a little immature. Last," she finished, "is Ronnie Sanchez. She's a few years older than me. She's spent the past few years undercover."

At this moment, Maggie appreciated how much her life had changed. Five years ago, thoughts of the future made her tremble with uncertainty and fear. Now she felt hope. Constructed from the once scattered puzzle pieces of her old world, her future, though much different than she might have anticipated, now seemed a semi-complete mural of optimism and possibilities.

With this thought in mind, she turned to the newly arrived task force members, smiled sweetly, and said "Good morning, all."

Then, without skipping a beat, she barked, "Don't forget to fill in the board!"

Chapter 5

The Big Game

Thomas slowed as he approached the large brass plaque designating the "Governor's Conference Room." He had just run up four flights of the ornate marble staircase at the southern end of the main capitol building. Winded from the exertion, he quickly composed himself and entered just as a nearby clock chimed eight o'clock.

To his chagrin, the empty room stood in stark contrast to his expectations. The silence that greeted him caused his blood pressure to rise. At this very moment he should be exchanging pleasantries with the governor, his chief of staff, or, at the very least, his deputy secretary for public safety.

Perplexed, he wondered if he had gotten the time or place wrong. It had happened before. He recalled once walking into a meeting of unfamiliar faces, due to a last minute switch. Fortunately no one had noticed his misstep. The mid-level bureaucrats in attendance never looked his way. Their attentions had remained steadfast, divided between the words of their chief executive and the inside of their eyelids.

His mind filled with possibilities. The most likely, the others were simply running behind. Fifteen minutes later, twice teased by the sound of clicking heals in the hallway, resignation set in. No one was coming to the "big game."

Confused and annoyed, Thomas reluctantly gathered his belongings and prepared to return to his bunker in the basement. As a defense against his growing indignity, he let his mind wander. He contemplated the large handwritten sign on the inside of the door, "Please ensure this door is shut and the lights are out." In a rebellious moment, he considered ignoring the edict, but then thought better of tempting fate. With his current luck, an armed response team waited outside, aching to enforce the decree.

Compliant with the request, he extinguished the lights, securely closed the door, and crossed the wide hallway to the white marble railing of the balcony. Hands on cool stone, mind elsewhere, he absentmindedly stared over the side to the main hallway, three open floors below. Distractedly, he watched the lone security officer sitting behind a grey metal desk and the occasional state worker or politician walking purposefully to carry out the will of the people.

To his surprise, in this mix, he caught the unmistakable profile of Mark Murphy, aka, the governor's deputy secretary for public safety. After meeting Murphy for the first time, Robby Franklin had described the deputy using a fruit analogy. According to Robby, Mark Murphy looked like a pear. Of average height with a small head and shoulders, he possessed a disproportionally wide lower body, which led to the undeniably accurate comparison and, ultimately, to his nickname of "Murph the Smurf."

Thomas watched as he waddled past the marble staircase and the brass doors of the elevator that provided access to the upper levels. The deputy secretary seemed to have business elsewhere. Smoldering flame of anger now fanned, Thomas' customarily solid self-control crumpled as he shouted, "Hey, Mr. Murphy."

At that moment, Thomas' tiny sliver of the world froze. He must have yelled louder than intended as anyone within earshot halted and looked around, including Mark Murphy. Embarrassed, Thomas consoled himself with the thought that he hadn't yelled, "Hey Smurf" or something equally as derogatory.

In vain, Murphy searched for his mystery pager, leading Thomas to call again in a more subdued manner, "Mr. Murphy, up here. May I have a moment, please?"

Prior to the deputy secretary's response, Thomas hurried to the steps taking them two at a time. He descended the final landing, scrutinized by Murphy, who squinted in his direction. The man's round face remained blank until Thomas moved closer and recognition bloomed.

"Ah, Agent Payne, so good to see you," he said, plastering on a smile. "How is everything going, or, should I say, what's the latest on locating office space and investigators?"

"To be honest," replied Thomas, surprised by the deputy secretary's question, "the office is up and running, and everyone's in place. They have been for nearly a week."

The response elicited a peeved look from Murphy, who quickly shifted gears and said, "Oh, well, that's wonderful. Is there something I can do for you today?"

"Did we have a meeting scheduled for 8:00 o'clock this morning?"

The question caused Murphy to pull out the ever-present smartphone in order for him to check his schedule of meetings. After a quick review, he related, "I see a meeting for today was scheduled two weeks ago, but it appears to have been canceled last week. Didn't you receive notification?"

"No, sir, I didn't," replied Thomas, biting his tongue as he felt the collar of his dress shirt tightening.

"Well, I'm sure my secretary would have called your office or, at a minimum, sent an email," stated Murphy, doing his best to look surprised. "You might want to check with your secretary. Maybe she misplaced the notice."

Thomas saw through the smoke and mirrors immediately. Moments before, Murphy hadn't even been aware the task force office existed. However, he overlooked the poorly constructed dodge, unwilling to belabor the issue, and related, "In any event, I completed a presentation as requested regarding the two unsolved child homicides in the city. I can provide a briefing at your or the governor's leisure."

"That won't be necessary," responded Murphy with little thought. "The issues surrounding that matter have begun to resolve, and the governor is currently focused on more pressing matters. Now, I'm late for a meeting, Agent Payne. Is there anything further?"

The abrupt change in tone, which fueled his mounting feelings of anger and humiliation, caused Thomas to blurt, "What the hell are you talking about? In the past four weeks, two little kids have been murdered. There's no viable suspect, and it's unknown if more deaths will follow. From my perspective, nothing's been resolved." Payne immediately wished he had been smoother. He took consolation in having, at least, tempered his language. Dropping an "F bomb" in the capitol didn't seem wise.

For his part, the deputy secretary staggered as if struck. His face showed a healthy measure of fear and then changed to a look of acceptance. He spoke as if providing instruction to a dense student, "Look, agent, I've heard you're very good at your job. You must be to open an office in less than two weeks. But here's the reality. The governor was under acute public and political pressure two weeks ago after the second homicide. The media and the community somehow connected the local police or emergency personnel with the killings. Riots started and the Mayor was crying for help. The answer was the MCTF. Since we announced its creation, the hue and cry has abated."

"In the meantime," Murphy continued, "other priorities have arisen, such as the economic crisis and the jobs picture. We no longer have time to meet and discuss an ongoing investigation. What we do need is for you to solve the crimes, so the governor has one less issue populating an already full plate. Hell," he added, "just make sure a similar homicide doesn't occur again, and you'll be able to call it a win."

With that, the deputy secretary for public safety turned on his heels and doing his best penguin imitation, continued on his original course. Over his shoulder he offered, "Call my office if you need anything."

Experiencing a moment of light-headed Déjà vu, Agent Thomas Payne recalled his discussion with Director Greene. He unexpectedly felt a surge of respect for the man who had for so long successfully navigated the perplexing political waters of state government. He suddenly wondered if he possessed the ability or desire to do the same.

Chapter 6

The Gallows

Robby Franklin sat at his desk in cubicle city, casually discussing the recent homicides with the other members of the task force. "In one study, covering was explained as a means for the killer to hide his shame," he imparted.

After a thoughtful moment, Stan Brown's deep voice rumbled, "I worked a case once where the killer later told me he turned the body onto its stomach so he didn't have to look at the face. It made the victim seem less human, depersonalized the event."

The discussion continued with each member chiming in with the exception of Raj Patel, who listened from the periphery. Patel, who preferred to be called "Doc," hesitated to comment lest he prove himself the fool. Though he possessed advanced degrees in mechanical and electrical engineering from MIT, Murder Investigation 101 had not been included in his studies.

An honors graduate and successful businessman, Doc had established a thriving technology start-up. Ten years later, he sold his company, resulting in a hefty payday and unemployment. In the wake of the sale, he found himself searching for life's next great challenge. He drifted aimlessly until fate brought him and Thomas together during an investigation involving one of Patel's ex-competitors.

Over a seventy-two hour period, Doc assisted Thomas in translating "technese" into plain English. With his help, they quickly exposed and captured a thief. A victim of his own success, Doc's search for meaning began anew.

Two weeks ago, following a three-month hiatus, Payne surprised him with a phone call and, more important, an offer of employment. His decision required little deliberation. The bug had bitten. Doc had never felt as alive as when he helped track down his first criminal.

Now he found himself sitting among seasoned investigators. Their discussion had nothing to do with bits and bytes. He feared he didn't belong. Though welcomed with open arms, he felt like an intruder.

His silence had not gone unnoticed. A sensitive and caring person, Ronnie Sanchez looked directly at him when she asked, "Do we make the same jump as the media in assuming the blankets are somehow connected to the ER community?"

She waited for a reply from Patel, but he dropped his gaze leading her to probe, "What do you think, Doc?"

Doc looked up immediately. He seemed to shrink from the eyes riveted on his actions. Hesitantly, he answered, "Uh, well, I didn't really think about it."

He could have kicked himself as soon as the words spilled out. He did have thoughts relevant to the discussion. His anger gave him strength leading him to offer, "Don't they have other uses? Can't you buy them at most home stores?"

"Good point," Ronnie complimented. Not ready to let him off the hook, she inquired, "Any chance Overlord can help track the blankets from manufacturer to owner?"

Bolstered by the kind words and the reference to the software package he had created specifically for the task force, Doc responded with increased poise, "Overlord can analyze and compare information from any database, including data in narrative format. So, provided the opportunity, I'm sure it can help." Now eager to discuss a topic in his area of expertise, he added, "With the new reporting module and Overlord's ability to cull through disparate information, what used to be inaccessible or took hours to manually compile should take nanoseconds."

Ready to provide further insight, Doc stopped when the familiar click of the front door caused everyone to look in that direction. In walked Thomas Payne who provided perfunctory greetings as he passed Maggie's desk and the members' cubicles. He marched directly to his office, visibly shaking his head as he closed the door behind him.

Usually levelheaded and even-tempered, Thomas looked like a man walking to the gallows. Robby, who had noticed the unusual behavior, glanced toward the others only to find each looking back at him. Their expectant gazes said it all.

With a resigned breath, he accepted his position as the chosen interrogator, stood, and walked slowly toward the boss' office. At first hesitant to barge in, Robby reasoned that if the task force stood any chance of survival, the members had to watch each other's backs. That included sharing the burdens. Additionally on a more personal note, if someone planned to hang his longtime friend, he wasn't about to let him go alone. Now more confident in the appropriateness of his mission, Robbie strode to the closed door and knocked.

The rapping stirred Payne from his musings. His mind had been trying to process the morning's events. Through refocused eyes, he witnessed Robby standing off to the side of the door peering through the glass panel and vertical blinds that served as the front wall of his office. Tempted to ask for a moment to himself, he reconsidered when Robby placed his hands and face directly against the glass, sealed his lips on the smooth surface, and exhaled the air from his lungs into his mouth, causing his face to take on the appearance of a blowfish. Not satisfied he enjoyed Thomas' full attention, he waggled his tongue before disengaging.

Unexpected and inappropriate, Robby's performance caused a small breach in the clouds darkening Thomas' mood. He waved Robby into the office, hiding the smirk lying just below the surface.

As the door cautiously opened, he broke down and laughed, "There's something seriously wrong with you. You'd better be planning to wipe that off."

Contemplating the smeary hand and face imprints on the once spotless glass, Robby countered, "I'll get to it as soon as you tell me what's going on."

Thomas paused to study his friend's face before replying self-consciously, "I don't hide my feelings very well. Lynn always said I wore my emotions on my sleeve."

Momentary silence ensued, until Thomas continued in a more somber tone, "I got blindsided this morning. I felt like I walked through the wrong door or something. One minute, I'm in the capitol building, the next, the *Twilight Zone*."

Thomas explained in detail about the cancelled meeting, his chance encounter with Murphy, and the resulting conversation, ending with, "I'm getting the distinct impression the task force was the trend du jour and has served its purpose. What's more, if I had to guess, I'd say Mark Murphy's fingerprints are all over the sudden change."

"I can see it all now," he said, pausing as if looking at a picture. "The governor gets pressured to assist the city, and Murphy scrambles to help. Then I offer them the perfect out, an investigative task force legitimatized by the BCA. My naiveté's put us all in the barrel," he decided as he pushed forward with his scathing self-critique.

Thomas recognized he had pulled the members of the task force from secure positions and familiar routines. Now he wondered how long he would have jobs for them. He particularly felt for Ronnie Sanchez. While the others had jumped at the opportunity to work on the new task force, she required a harder sales pitch. In fact, she initially declined his offer.

Ronnie had spent the first eleven years of her thirteen-year career conducting sexual assault and child abuse investigations. She had once been considered the best in the agency at her job. Then, two years ago, her presumed career path took an unexpected turn when she accepted a long-term undercover position. A one-eighty, she left her coworkers stunned over the sudden switch.

For the next two years, she lived the job from morning until night. Raised in a house by a mother and father from Cuba, she found it easy to gain acceptance in the local Hispanic community. It didn't hurt that she genuinely cared for people, helped those in need, and put even the most obstinate people at ease with her combination of beauty and grace. In the end, her investigation led to the arrests of numerous felons for crimes, including racketeering, burglary, assault, and an unsolved gang homicide.

Thomas had closely followed her investigation and understood the resulting prosecutions would lead to notoriety. Cover blown, she would be looking for reassignment within the agency. He could think of no better place for her talents than his new task force.

"Unfortunately, that was then and this is now," thought Thomas adding to his self-abusive musings. Now he wondered if Ronnie and the others would suffer due to his political inexperience and lack of vision.

The thought, like a slap, brought him out of his trance. "Sorry, I spaced out for a minute."

During Thomas' internal debate, Robby Franklin had sat patiently allowing him his pensive moment. "Thomas, can I tell you something you might not wanna hear?"

From the tone, Thomas divined the direction of the conversation. He also recognized he probably needed the offered perspective. With a nod, he sat back for his semi-annual scolding. This led Robby to say, "You've heard it all before, but for some reason it never sinks in."

After a long pause, he began, "Since Lynn's death, you've put everything you have into the job. You have no other life."

"I hope you're going to take this conversation somewhere new."

"My point," Robby continued, refusing to be goaded, "work is your anchor, and you don't like someone rocking your boat. Now you're in charge of a new task force in a new office with new people. You have two bosses, one who's a politician, not a cop. All these changes have pushed you outside your comfort zone, and you're overreacting to things that have little bearing on the job."

Robby stopped to allow the concept time to settle. During the break, he noted the look of skepticism growing on Thomas' face.

"Let me ask a simple question," he queried, cutting to the chase. "How does what happened this morning change our job?"

With an incredulous look, Thomas responded, "What?"

"Well, I guess that's better than 'duh,' but the answer is, it doesn't affect our job at all. We're not here to serve the governor or his lackey Murphy. It's not even about you, me, or the others in the task force. It's about the victims and their families. With emphasis, he added, "That's why we all signed on."

Simple words, they forced Thomas to reconsider his pal's comments. For the second time that morning, he felt shame bloom. Robby's comments, like cold water to the face, had forced him to refocus. His environment had indeed changed, and he needed to change with it. He needed to evolve or, in this case, devolve into the Thomas Payne from before Lynn's death, the one who never stumbled on such triviality.

Through the break in the cloud cover, Thomas hit upon the truth he had failed to fully consider. Task forces came and went like leaves on a tree, some due to political whimsy and others to budgetary shortfalls. Those factors he couldn't control. However, he could, and would, ensure this task force didn't die off due to his shortcomings.

With renewed zeal, he pushed himself away from his desk, stood steadily, and with a look of determination, said to his comrade, "You speakum a great truth, Kimosabe. Let's get to work."

The words and the change in demeanor caused Robby to smile. He responded with feigned surprise, "After all these years, I get to be the Lone Ranger instead of Tonto. I was starting to think it was some kind of racial thing."

Thomas laughed as he made his way around his desk. Quietly, he passed his loyal friend, patting him on the shoulder in wordless thanks. Then, he strode with confidence into the main office bay announcing for all to hear, "Meeting in the conference room…two minutes. Bring your notes and be prepared to comment."

Chapter 7

Monday's Matinee

Ironically, as Thomas Payne returned to his office following the cancellation of his morning presentation, the man, who once feared the wolf that he had become, enjoyed a presentation of his own. However, his didn't require a computer, software, or even a projector. As with his earlier thoughts of his first face-to-face meeting with the darkness, he needed only his memory.

In a physical sense, he navigated the growing Monday after New Year traffic in mid-town. Daytime and a cold January rain surrounded him, but he took little note of the weak sunlight or the misty drops playing across his windshield. The sights, sounds, and smells enveloping him miraculously fell away, replaced by dark and dry conditions from the past.

As his mental presentation clarified, he felt the energy increasing in his body just as it had on the early December evening of his recollection. In the post-dusk hours after a long day of work in and around the city, he found for the first time that he not only had the means and motive, but also the opportunity. At that point in his life, he had killed only once before and that had occurred by accident.

Since arriving in Harrisburg back in July, he had wrestled with his thoughts and bided his time. He waited and watched. Then on that dark and chilly evening now nearly four weeks ago, he chanced upon a young boy slipping into an abandoned building along Cameron Street.

For months he had worked among these rundown old buildings, yet he had never really taken their full measure. He had glossed over the once venerable soldiers just as a farmer looks past the individual stalk of wheat in a field. As a result, he initially failed to see their purpose. Currently unsuitable to house a proper business, any of the timeworn, commercial structures would serve his needs.

Eagerly, he turned at the next cross street and parked around the corner. He knew no one would think twice about seeing his vehicle along this road. A common sight like the old buildings in the neighborhood, its façade cloaked the danger within. Hidden in plain sight, he shut down the engine and allowed the darkness to take control.

He waited, examining his surroundings. Finally, confident in his seclusion, he crossed the street to the corner building. On the sidewalk, he stopped as if tying his shoe. Once more, he surveyed the area. Satisfied, he slid noiselessly into the dimly lit area behind the long-standing structure.

At home among the shadows, he wove his way north through trash and weeds, pausing only when he reached the third building, his destination. Similar in design to the first two, the third differed in that it boasted a large rear parking lot and loading dock. An additional distinction, its boarded lower windows exuded a sinister air, a kindred spirit to the man skulking nearby.

At this point, the man's excitement increased. His mind lost patience and fast-forwarded. Now he stood in the shadows after quietly entering the building through the same partially boarded window as the child. He heard and then saw the boy coming toward him. Dark and dank, the space received sufficient light through the high, uncovered windows to create a silhouette of the boy as he navigated around a hulking piece of machinery, moving toward the exit. In his right hand, he clutched a long, slender object.

Suddenly, the child stopped. He seemed to sense something amiss in the intervening space. He looked into the shadows, but saw nothing. Finally in a moment of resolve, he hustled through the gloominess toward the window and the perceived safety of the manmade light beyond.

He never made it.

With unaccustomed viciousness, the man pounced, denying the child time to savor the relief of reaching the window. Mind and body on fire, the man watched each punch and kick. Powerless to stop or slow his actions, he felt detached as though viewing the scene through the bulging red eyes of someone, or something, else. In the end, the child lay still, beaten senseless.

Winded, the man paused to savor the same power and control felt by the wolf of his youth. Yet somehow it seemed insufficient reward for the pain he had caused another. There had to be more.

Confused, he scanned the stout old warehouse. His thoughts raced, searching for that which he must have missed. Memories of his youth flooded back, the slaps, the punches, and the kicks. He felt the hands closing around his windpipe.

Then he remembered.

The beatings had caused pain, but the choking had evoked visceral terror. Fingers or forearm around his throat, even now he gasped for air. How could he have forgotten?

And the boy stirred.

Memories vivid in his mind, he straddled the woozy form, placing his gloved hands around the tiny neck. Slowly he tightened his grip. He eagerly examined the pleading eyes in the shadows. He took the boy to the very edge, hoping to gain further insight.

Mimicking the wolf of his youth, he convinced himself he could obtain answers without death. However, the outcome proved inevitable. The bronco bucked, and he feared losing its saddlebag of answers. In response, he bore down harder.

Initially unnerved, he soon found himself observing in a clinical manner as the thrashing slowed and eventually stopped. Different than he had imagined, the struggle ended, not with a bang, but more of a disappointing pop. The child's body simply ceased working. No fireworks display, no long goodbye, and no answers.

As he considered this information, the projectionist suddenly shut down the reel of his mental movie. A child sent to bed before the end of his favorite show, his anger flared. Engrossed in the presentation, he had hoped to detect some hidden morsel previously missed.

Now, once again driving on the slick city streets following his impromptu matinee, he took stock. He conceded that he could continue to search recent memories, but recognized his best chance of finding answers lay in the future. And the future would arrive as soon as the sun disappeared over the horizon.

When darkness fell upon the land, he would fall upon his next victim. He would murder again. Once thought unnecessary, death had become an integral part of his journey.

Chapter 8

The Voyage Begins

Thomas' pronouncement caused the previously apprehensive mood of the task force to change to one of excitement. The investigators collected files and notes while Maggie made her way back to the boss' office. With a light knock, she walked in and offered, "Anything I can help with?"

"Not unless your superpowers include the ability to catch killers."

With a frown, Maggie scolded, "Not really what I meant. You seemed a little down when you got back."

"Thank you, but I'm good," sighed Thomas. "Robby talked me off the ledge."

She studied his face and noting a change, she granted, "Well, I'm glad it worked out. Now as far as the meeting is concerned, the conference room is set-up, the coffee's hot, and Doc's energy drink is cold."

"Just one?" laughed Thomas, noting the use of the singular. "They're like chips to him, can't drink just one."

"Not anymore," she corrected. "He's on a strict one can a day limit." In response to Thomas' quizzical look, she explained, "More for my sanity, than his health."

"Not a bad idea. We need marathoners, not sprinters."

Maggie agreed with a nod of her head. She turned to leave, but not before adding over her shoulder, "I'll let you get to work now that I'm satisfied you're okay."

Her parting comment brought a grin to Thomas' face. Maggie's motherly behavior always reminded him that someone cared. The thought buoyed his spirits as he collected his case notes and walked toward the conference room.

He entered and immediately noted five sets of expectant eyes focused on his movements. The members' attention and the quiet, led Thomas to make a decision. Calmly, he set his paperwork on the table and picked up a plastic bottle of water.

"I'm not normally one for ceremony," he revealed, walking toward the concrete basement wall. "But after the past few days, a tiny bit might be in order. Ladies and gentlemen," he offered, tapping the bottle against the hard surface, "I officially welcome you to the new home of Pennsylvania's Major Crimes Task Force."

The spontaneity of the simulated christening was followed by a few jolly "here, here's," a simple "yeah," and one "amen, brother" from Stan Brown. It also led Robby to comment dryly, "It's just not the same without champagne."

Not to be outdone, Bill Travis laughed and added, "Business as usual for the state, man. Champagne results on a bottled water budget."

Laughter ensued, but eventually faded. In its aftermath, Thomas turned thoughtful and stated "Before we start the case study, I wanna go over a few side issues. One has to do with me, the other with you. First, I'd like to ask your forgiveness for my moodiness this morning. To be candid, I got distracted by some petty political bullshit."

"Better you than me," pronounced Stan Brown. "That's one reason I have no desire to be a supervisor. I'd rather deal with rapists and murderers than politicians." His comment caused everyone around the table to nod vigorously in agreement. They all understood the down-side of being in charge.

Briefly, Thomas considered expanding his comment, but realized enough had been said. His apology had been made and accepted. "Okay, that's it for today's confession, now on to you guys."

Before he could continue, Ronnie interrupted, "Not that I want to correct you, but being Catholic and all, I don't know if that qualifies as a confession. It's more a miracle. A man willing to admit he did something wrong. It would have to be investigated by the Vatican's Miracle Commission, but it's a shoo-in."

Her comment caused the room to erupt in laughter. In an effort to fire a salvo of his own, Thomas pointed out, "At least we know Ronnie's awake."

He overlooked her casual "humph" in return and turned more seriously, "Back to my second point. I'm amazed every time I think about the talent sitting in this room." Thoughtfully, he offered, "We have the potential to accomplish so much."

Ready to provide examples, Thomas searched the room for victim number one. "Just to illustrate," he began, choosing the most prominent member, "before logging fifteen years with the BCA, Stan spent twelve years in the Army. Part of his service included working with their CID." He referred to the Criminal Investigative Command, once known as the Criminal Investigative Division. "He's recognized both nationally and internationally as an expert at assessing crimes and profiling criminals. His talents will be particularly useful in instances, like the Harrisburg cases, in which we can't speak to a victim. Maybe as important," he said, twinkle returning to his eye, "Stan's the perfect number one man for a dynamic entry."

Amidst growing snickers at being placed into the "fatal funnel" of door crashing, Stan responded, "Oh, no, here we go again. Abuse the token big guy. Y'all know this is discrimination. In fact, I want the number for my union rep. No one's usin' this brother for a shield."

The comment caused everyone to laugh harder and allowed Thomas to move on to Robby Franklin. "I've worked side by side with Robby for a long time. He's relentless once he's picked up the scent. Also, while Stan has great connections in the city, Robby's tied into many of the outlying areas. And, as you've seen," he added, "he knows how to reel me in when I get too far away from the dock."

After Robbie, Thomas found himself looking at Ronnie Sanchez. He recalled anew her reluctance to join the task force. "While Ronnie's been undercover for the past few years, her true expertise is in sex crimes and child abuse. When it comes to interviewing women and children, no one does it better."

His statement caused a flash of sadness to cross the woman's pretty face. Thomas quickly shifted his gaze to Doc, unwilling to dwell on his observation. Unfortunately, the scrutiny seemed to make the dark complexioned, thirty-year-old man uncomfortable as well. Not necessarily bad in a team environment, it appeared some of the members didn't care for the spotlight.

In Doc's case, Thomas knew the man would eventually feel more comfortable with his new job and his new coworkers. He had proven himself once and continued to do so each day. Now wasn't the time to make him more self-conscious. To the point, he said, "I think all of you know Doc's strength. Simply put, he's *the* master of technology." The brief words caused the computer genius to relax, providing Thomas the opportunity to add, "One thing you may have overlooked, though, is his shrewd, analytical mind. I think you'll see in short order he has more to offer than hardware and software."

Thomas next moved his gaze to Bill Travis, who straightened in his seat. "Last, but not least, is our youngest member at the ripe old age of twenty-five. If you haven't already noticed, Bill has the unique capacity to recall the minutest details of a crime scene or information in a report. It should come as no surprise that the department psychologist claims he has a near eidetic or photographic memory."

"Is that *all* the shrink said?" interrupted Stan.

Bill had just begun to object, when Stan added, "Scratch that question. We probably don't have enough time left in our careers to cover it all."

The comment caused Travis to drop his head in an effort to symbolically protect his blue eyes and glasses from the sharp barbs raining down upon him. His mop of wavy brown hair failed to hide the reddening of his ears. Verbally brutalized, yet enjoying the attention, he looked up at Thomas with a crooked smile.

Thomas waited for the banter to die down. He sensed this to be a good transitional point. "Okay, enough fun for one day," he interjected. "Time to get down to business."

Like flipping a switch, the atmosphere in the basement conference room turned serious as the members readjusted themselves in their seats and began leafing through case files. The abrupt swing from humorous to serious, common to law enforcement, did not go unnoticed by Thomas. The day and the mission had just become real, and Thomas thought, "Time to see just how good these people are."

Chapter 9

Simply Number Three

With five calls under his belt by 9:00 a.m., the man robotically worked his way toward his sixth. Luckily, today's assignments had required little thought, allowing him to focus his energy on the evening's possibilities. Conversely, it also permitted the familiar pessimism of his early years to intrude upon the perfection of his daydreams. So, as had become the norm, the darkness stepped in and took over. With its malign, yet confident, nature, it hid his worries behind soothing reflections of the recent past.

Once more, magically transported into the night, he basked in the warmth of memories. Earlier he had re-experienced his first and second kills, one an accident, the other not so much. Now, it seemed only right his thoughts move on to number three. "Number three?" he thought to himself.

He contemplated the question. At some point, he had begun to number his explorations. Since he had made this particular memory two weeks ago, he had relived it so many times he now simply referred to it as number three. The others, in a comparable fashion, had become numbers one and two.

He disliked the simplistic labels. They mocked his actions by minimizing their importance. In a similar manner, the crude descriptions degraded his victims. Though a lesser means to a greater end, he still had no desire to depreciate their value to numbers on a ledger.

Initially thought provoking, his mind quickly tired of the extraneous conflict. Urged on by the darkness, he decided to move to more important matters. He would work on the numbering problem later because, right now, his mind insisted he return to the past, to...number three.

As a result, the man, once again, saw the boy meandering up the deserted, uneven sidewalk under the false shelter of bare trees. Alone, the child remained oblivious to his environment and the danger posed by the wolf hiding in the nearby shadows. At his tender age, he didn't understand the true nature of monsters.

On that night, like most others following the start of winter, the human traffic along the streets had diminished as the sun dropped below the skyline. Gripped by cold and blanketed in darkness, adults instinctively sought to hibernate behind insulated walls, awaiting spring or the next work day, whichever provided the greater pull in their mostly ordinary lives. Children, on the other hand, allow curiosity to trump intuition. World to themselves, they wage imaginary battles wielding swords made from sticks or ride plastic sleds down make-believe Himalayas.

In their land of fantasy, children often fail to take note of the gradually increasing cold or the encroaching darkness until it is upon them.

In his mind he saw himself pull the vehicle up to the curb. He watched the boy's initial look of concern transition to uncertainty and then recognition. The clearly marked, familiar vehicle and the friendly face of the driver caused him to relax. He dropped his guard. The man had hoped for this reaction, because for once in his life, he had laid the groundwork leading to this moment.

Fresh from training, he, like most rookies, had been assigned responsibility for calls in this lower income neighborhood where children freely roamed the streets. During his first week, he had identified the same style of absentee parenting practiced during his childhood. With familiarity came comfort and, in this case, opportunities.

As a result, he had taken every chance to talk to the youth as he worked the area. It hadn't been difficult. He found it easy to talk to kids. Unlike grownups, they didn't judge him. Connected in a way he would never be with other adults, he knew they offered answers.

"Need a ride up the hill?" offered the man, sensing a ripe harvest.

Initially conflicted, the adventure proved too great a temptation. With a child's innocent and trusting nature, the boy climbed into the front seat. Expectantly he settled himself on the warm vinyl padding. He never heard the electric door-lock spring shut. Though made of plastic and thin steel, it sounded strangely like a vault door as its dense metal rods slam home.

Eager for the excitement to begin, the boy watched as the man's once smiling face clouded with rage. Too late in recognizing the danger, he could do nothing to ward off the furious attack. Before his mind could fully process the magnitude of his error, he was rendered unconscious.

Out of breath, the man realized that, like the last time, his desire remained. The darkness hadn't been fed. He needed room to explore.

Mind clouded by emotion, he forced himself to think. Somewhere along the periphery of his thoughts, he recalled the abandoned building in which he had discovered the last child. Situated at the bottom of the hill and cloaked in the shadow of the ordinary, it provided an ideal laboratory for his experiments. With the most basic framework of a plan in place, he put the vehicle into drive and slowly worked his way back to Cameron Street.

In minutes, he had parked in nearly the same spot, took the same path behind the buildings, and entered the warehouse through the same poorly boarded side window as before. Now in the darkness, and the darkness in him, he laid the boy onto the dirty concrete floor that served as his test bed.

Thoughtful, almost wary, he watched until he noticed the first stirrings. Calmly, he straddled the prone figure, sitting on the boy's waist to limit movement. Then, with a cool and detached motion, he placed both hands around the child's twig-like neck and squeezed. Each second that answers evaded him, he increased pressure.

He felt the muscles and tendons of his arms straining. He studied the boy as the reality of his situation struck home. He watched the face, but mainly the eyes. He felt the movement of the struggling body, smelled the fear. He tried to miss nothing.

When his memory reached this point, he found the familiar ache had returned. An interesting contrast, thoughts of his explorations usually increased his need, but, at the same time, allowed him a means to focus the energy. Not unlike a fissure in the Earth, which gradually releases gases and prevents an eruption, his daydreams often provided a vent for his desires.

Unfortunately, on this occasion no venting had occurred, and his cravings had reached a peak. Release felt both necessary and imminent. So strong was the physical sensation that it interrupted his reverie.

Suddenly, he found himself back in the present with the darkness percolating in his veins. His desires now so intense, he wondered if he could wait for evening. The shadows called to him, screamed at him. He heard them proclaim him "wolf." And like the wolf, he needed to feed.

As if by Providence, at that very moment, he caught sight of a little boy running across an empty lot. Unable to take his eyes from the small figure as it raced through the debris-scattered field, he considered the possibilities and the problems. But, as he had done his entire life, he glossed over the difficulties in favor of the prospects. In his present state consequences held little sway over his actions.

Locked on target, he turned the vehicle. He needed to reach the other side of the field before the boy. Though darkness did not yet bathe the land, he had waited long enough. The time for action was at hand.

A fire-and-forget missile traveling at supersonic speed, only an act of God could force him to disengage.

Chapter 10

A Day in the Life

A few miles south of the capitol building, Al Jefferson plodded through what seemed like a fifty-pound backpack-carrying day. On this first Monday of the year, he contemplated the number of garbage cans he would have to sling to pay off his misguided sports bets from the too short holiday weekend. Adding to his discontent, a light rain had blanketed the area since he boarded the back of the truck at 6:00 o'clock that morning. Four straight hours of feeling hung-over, wet, and cold had put him in a sour mood.

Pity party in full swing, Al considered the events which had led to his current position in life. A star athlete in high school, he had expended minimal energy on academic pursuits, yet made average grades, due to his innate intelligence. Written about in the papers and talked about on radio and television, a bright future appeared certain.

He had been offered numerous full scholarships to play football, but had chosen a small local college that promised immediate playing time. Lined up to become the next BMOC (big man on campus), he failed to anticipate the effect his growing drug problem would have on his plans. As a result, his aspirations of football and higher education floated away into a pharmacological haze.

During what he thought of as his "wandering period," he lost weight, friends, and in the end, respect for himself. On a vicious downward spiral, Al Jefferson's rocket ship of fame, inevitably, crash-landed. Arrested for armed robbery, he copped a plea that netted him a two-year stint at the State Correctional Institute at Graterford, north of Philadelphia.

To say the facility at Graterford resembled a crumbling nineteenth-century psychiatric hospital wouldn't be a stretch. But, in spite of its outward appearance, the institution offered an array of innovative programs for those prisoners desiring to better themselves and, eventually, reintegrate into society. In Al's case, he received not only detox assistance and counseling, but also an opportunity to take some basic college level courses. Viewed a model inmate, Al earned an early release after eighteen months.

Discharged a free man, other than a yearlong probation, Al quickly found a criminal record disqualified him from not only good paying jobs, but also any paying jobs. For some reason, employers hesitated to hire felons. Consequently, even though he made a concerted effort to locate employment, his record always stood in the way. Under the pressure of constant rejection, his confidence suffered, as did his willingness to remain drug free.

Luckily, or, as he now thought, by the hand of God, he met a girl who believed in him. Smart, well-spoken, and pretty, her initial interest provoked suspicion. Someone willing to waste affection on an outcast convict, no doubt, hid a secret.

On their second date, he discovered the skeleton in her closet. Sheri Henry unapologetically believed in God. She attended church on Sundays and volunteered to help those less fortunate. Though she rarely forced her beliefs on him, she lived her principles, which made Al uncomfortable. Each week she invited him to church but never pushed. Finally, on one particularly beautiful spring Sunday, Al agreed to accompany her to the service.

A short walk from her apartment, the old structure that housed the Community Baptist Church sat on a small hill, sandwiched between residences. Built with large grey stones, it exhibited a weathered white steeple above the entrance. Two tall, thick wooden doors at the top of six wide granite steps offered entry. Near enough now to touch the railing, Al felt fear.

For her part, Sheri noticed Al's hesitation. She attributed his reluctance to unfamiliarity. She would have been astonished to learn Al's vacillation actually stemmed from his sense of familiarity. The old dark structure reminded him of his time in Graterford.

Once in the vestibule, Al's fear increased exponentially. Bewildered and frightened, the sound of the big wooden doors closing behind him mimicked the sound of his old cell door locking shut. Strange voices resonated off the flat surfaces reminding him of the unceasing noise made by fifty incarcerated men confined to a small secure space. He breathed hard as the walls closed in.

Then, unexpectedly, as more members of the congregation began to arrive, the walls seemed to slowly withdraw. By ones and twos and as family units, the people entered, engaging in animated conversation and friendly rituals. At no time did anyone choose to look down upon him or judge him.

From that first moment, the members accepted him as they would a lost son. In fact, on that first visit to the House of God, he met a man who worked as a foreman for his current employer. The man offered to hire him on the spot. He could recall the surprising turn of events to this day.

In the close confines of the church social hall, the man had overheard a private conversation between Al and Sheri regarding Al's employment difficulties. At an opportune moment, he slid in next to Al stating, "I didn't mean to eavesdrop, but this is a small church and nothing stays secret for long." He hesitated upon seeing Al's suspicious look, but persisted, "Maybe we can help each other. I'm in need of a few hardworking, honest men, and it seems you're looking for a job. You seem to be in good shape. Can you start next Monday?"

At first, amazed with the offer and then ashamed, Al reluctantly explained about his past and, in particular, his criminal record. Embarrassed, he dropped his eyes and turned to walk away. He stopped in his tracks when the man responded, "Look, man, I know who you are. I followed your football career. You had a gift."

He paused and continued, "You frittered that gift away. But God always has a plan. No better place to decipher that plan than in His house." With a wink and a smile, he added in a conspiratorial nature, "None of us mere mortals is perfect. I myself may have had a few scrapes with the law in my younger days." A testimonial Al learned later to have been an understatement.

The foreman waited patiently as Al pondered the proposal. Eventually, he pushed, "What do you say, brother? Willing to give it a try?" He laughed and added, "The job don't pay all that well, but you get to snack for free all day long."

The rest they say "is history." Al married the girl, conceived two healthy children, and lived a comfortable, yet meager, existence. Off drugs, other than alcohol, he had few vices, barring the occasional bet. As Al compared his current life to his past, he offered a brief prayer of thanks to God.

Now near ten o'clock, the truck had reached the outskirts of Steelton on North Front Street. Only one business remained for pick-up before break time. As the big truck pulled off the main road and into the parking lot of the small manufacturing complex, Al's thoughts shifted to a hot cup of coffee, a large sugary donut, and his need to relieve himself. Lost in his thoughts, he never noticed the yellow blanket in the high grass next to a dumpster.

By habit, Al jumped off the truck, lifted the smaller plastic cans and deposited their contents into the truck's hopper. He had just levered himself back aboard when his driver yelled back, "Hey Al, you forgot that big yellow piece of plastic over there."

Irritated, Al hopped back down off the truck with a grunt. He wondered how many times a day he stepped up and down. The thought made him tired and punctuated his need to pee. Focused on his bodily functions, he nearly missed the small pale hand protruding from beneath the bright synthetic material.

As he would later tell the police, standing near the crime scene with a jacket tied around his waist to cover the large urine stain on his pants, "I thought it was a doll or something until I lifted the blanket. Then I remembered those other bodies. They were found down this way too. I couldn't believe it. I just couldn't believe it."

Chapter 11

Initial Profile

Back across town, the members of the task force continued to arrange their notes as Thomas began the initial case review. "The first victim was discovered on Tuesday, December 6 at approximately 0730 hours. His name is Jesus Miguel Rodriguez, a Hispanic male, age nine. He lived in the Allison Hill section of Harrisburg City with his grandmother, mother, two siblings, and numerous transient relatives."

He scanned another file before continuing. "The second victim was discovered two weeks later on Tuesday, December 20 at approximately 0800 hours. His name is Jamal Cedric Wilson, a black male, age eight. He also lived in Allison Hill but with his mother and four siblings."

In an effort to personalize the victims, Thomas paraphrased using the boys' names. "Jesus' body was located at the southern-most end of the city, off an access road leading to an electrical generation plant. He had injuries to his head and upper body indicative of a beating. He was found lying on his back with his ankles crossed and hands on his chest. He was covered with a yellow synthetic emergency type blanket. Discovery was made by a plant worker."

"Jamal," Thomas related, moving back to the second victim, "was located in the same general area but farther south. He was found along another access road, this one serving as a secondary entry point to a facility leased to the Department of Transportation. Body positioning, injuries, and use of the blanket are consistent with the first homicide. Discovery in this instance was made by a local man walking his dog near the river."

Pump now primed, Thomas asked, "Thoughts?"

The first to speak, Stan Brown offered, "The similarities between the crimes are too numerous to be coincidental: antemortem injuries, strangulation as the cause, body covering, and on and on."

Thomas interrupted, "The media says we have a serial killer."

"We might," responded Stan. "But, a word of caution: Don't get caught up in the media hype. More important than any label is motivation. A person that kills another person has a reason: profit, anger, power, etc. The same goes for a person that kills multiple people. That's where our focus should be. Second, the media sensationalized the connection between the blankets and the ER community. It's way too early for that. Anyone can buy those blankets."

"Now, back to your original comment," Stan guided. "Past studies define a *serial killer* as someone who murders three or more people in three or more separate events. Some even drop the number of victims to two. In either case, the description is based on quantification of victims. So to answer your question, I think by either definition our perpetrator is a serial killer, because I don't believe these were his first kills."

At this point, Thomas noticed confused looks dawning around the room. "Care to enlighten?" he asked.

In answer, Stan rose from his seat and began, "First, let me start by saying most serial killers work alone." Like a professor in a classroom, he moved as he talked. "A blitz style of attack was utilized in both crimes, which points to a disorganized personality acting spontaneously. The killer seized an opportunity and tried to quickly incapacitate the victim to reduce risk. The blitz attack is part of the MO," he explained, referring to the modus operandi. "Another part of the MO is body disposition. In this case, it appears the bodies were dumped at locations away from the incapacitation or kill sites."

He took in a deep breath before he clarified, "While the blitz attacks point to a disorganized personality, the transporting and dumping of the bodies indicates an organized train of thought. In essence, the offender is leaving mixed signals. While at first this seems confusing, it's common for a disorganized offender to learn to be more organized in some aspects of his crimes as he gains experience. So, I believe it's likely there was an earlier crime or

crimes that didn't involve a separate location for body disposition."
To complete the thought, he said, "The mixed indicators point to a
young offender who committed one or more similar acts prior to
these two homicides. His MO is evolving as he matures and gains
experience. He's no longer totally disorganized but moving on the
spectrum to a mix of both personality types."

"Also," he went on after a few seconds, "another interesting
aspect is the personation."

"You just lost me," interrupted Doc with a mix of frustration
and embarrassment.

Stan smiled and glanced in Doc's direction. He granted,
"Personation is a confusing concept." He seemed to search for the
right words before he explained, "MO refers to actions and
behaviors necessary to commit a crime. Personation is ritualistic
behavior that isn't essential. It normally only has meaning to the
actor. Some examples here are the positioning of the bodies and the
use of the blanket." One circle of the room now complete, Stan
dropped into his chair and finished, "Since both actions have
repeated, they might also be signatures we'll see at other crime
scenes associated with this offender."

As he fell silent, Bill Travis took advantage of the
momentary lull to interject, "If Stan's right, which I think he is, we
can make some assumptions about our killer." Travis, while
nowhere near as practiced as Stan Brown in the homicide arena,
nevertheless, possessed considerable knowledge from his study on
the subject. By rote, he began, "First, as indicated, most serial

killers operate alone. In addition, most are male. To expand on Stan's observations, if we consider this individual more disorganized than not, current wisdom would have us searching for a young adult male, possibly in his late teens but most likely early twenties. He'll have average to low intelligence and be introverted. He'll have some grudge against society due to a perceived wrong done to him in his youth. He may be employed, but his job will be menial in nature."

After rattling off the information, Bill added as a postscript, "At least that's what I've read."

"What do you think, big man?" asked Thomas, looking at Stan.

"It's a good starting point," he responding, shifting in his seat. "But as I cautioned, don't get stuck on labels or past indicators. No two actors have the exact same motivation, act the same, or look alike." He paused briefly and allowed, "However, as far as past studies, Bill's comments are on the mark."

Stan then looked over at Travis, winked, and probed, "What other interesting facts do you have banging around in that computer you call a brain?"

The comment caused Travis to laugh and Ronnie Sanchez to go pale as she begged, "I thought we weren't going there."

Now laughing, she took the opportunity to add her own observations, "Some other common points are the age and sex of the victims. Also, both are boys of color."

Stan cut in, explaining, "The killer's most likely looking for young boys, but race normally isn't a big factor. Since he doesn't seem to be a detailed planner, his victims are likely just in the wrong place at the wrong time." He hesitated and added, "Also, consider the target environment. The Allison Hill area, normally just called The Hill, is mostly populated by people of color."

"Which brings up another point," he thought out loud. "The disorganized personality feels most comfortable in a familiar area. Typically, it's where he lives, works, or plays. That's a dynamic to keep in mind. Jesus and Jamal both lived on The Hill. At the bottom of The Hill is Cameron Street. Between one and two miles south off of Cameron near Steelton Borough are the dumpsites."

As facilitator, Thomas offered, "That seems like a break. The killer's provided us with a relatively small search area."

Stan considered the statement before answering, "That's a fair observation, but here's the rub. Most people have multiple comfort zones. If he lives in the area, he may work or play in others."

Stan paused to let the members digest the information. Satisfied with the looks of understanding, he added, "Another point to consider, because of the close proximity of the victims' residences to the dump locations, I think we'll find the perpetrator made initial contact and killed them within this same general area. This kind of killer normally doesn't spend too much time with the body." Nearly finished, he looked down at the table and haltingly provided, "But that could change as he gains experience and confidence."

The comment sent a communal chill through the room. Other heads dropped until Robby Franklin irreverently broke in, "Then somebody needs to shake up his confidence a little. Let's give the psycho-bastard something to worry about."

His words led to a shared sigh as if the building pressure in a boiler had triggered its relief valve.

Unfortunately, unknown to Robby or the others, three stories overhead, Deputy Secretary for Public Safety Mark Murphy's pressure spiked dangerously into the red zone. Behind his big desk, his eyes burned into the screen of his smartphone. His hands shook. He had just received an email from a media source. Short and to the point, it read, "Another child's body found in Hbg."

Chapter 12

Political Positioning

Finally able to control the involuntary movements of his hands, Deputy Secretary Murphy ran the combinations through his head. Another body would wipe clean his hard work to make the governor look tough on crime. The governor's approval numbers would probably take a hit. Then his mind struck upon the most relevant point of all: Shit ran downhill, and he lived near the political base camp.

At times like this as he gazed at walls adorned with framed photos of meetings and parties with the rich and famous, he realized just how important the trappings of a successful political career had become. Not that the success was his, but he contented himself with his choice of the right horse. He had sensed long ago that he didn't possess the personality to perform as a frontline politician. Voluntarily, albeit resentfully, he hitched his wagon to the man who would eventually become governor. Feet now firmly planted on the elder statesman's coattails, he refused to allow the deaths of a few street urchins to get in his way.

Fortunately, Murphy always prepared for contingencies. Long ago he had determined the appropriate spin for such an occurrence. Now he just needed to put the plan into action.

Confident in his strategy, he picked up the receiver to his desk phone and rang his secretary. She answered immediately, and he stated, "Please contact the Major Crimes Task Force office. You'll have to get the number from the main switchboard. Have the commander, a BCA agent by the name of Payne, come to my office immediately."

For the next few minutes, he contemplated tactics, until the call back from his secretary interrupted his scheming. She offered, "Mr. Secretary, I spoke with Maggie at the task force. She said Agent Payne was in a closed door meeting and couldn't be disturbed except for an emergency." Murphy insisted she refer to him as "Mr. Secretary." She added, "I told her I'd check with you and call her back."

Without comment, Murphy absentmindedly hung up. A brush-off by a secretary would normally have infuriated Murphy, but not today. He decided a personal visit was in order. It would emphasize his disappointment in the unit's failure and help distance him from any fall-out.

He rose from his chair feeling almost giddy. On his way out the door to dispense a tongue lashing, he sarcastically called back to his secretary, "I'll be in an important meeting. Call if there's an emergency."

He giggled at his play on Maggie's response. Self-involved as usual, he missed the mumbled words of his secretary as he left the room. After a year working for the man, the words spilled from her mouth, "What an asshole!"

Blissfully ignorant, Murphy continued on his merry way to the task force office which, he had discovered to his embarrassment earlier, actually existed. He still felt the lingering bruise on his ego. In his mind, ignorance and power didn't go together, and he thought of himself as a very powerful man.

Not one to prod a fresh wound, he cast the bothersome thought aside. Breathlessly, he marched down the three flights of stairs to the nondescript metal door with the electronic scanner. Now in what he deemed the dirty bowels of the capitol building, he swiped his identification. A red light and the sound of a buzzer resulted, making him feel like a losing game show contestant.

After his third attempt to enter failed, he noticed the ringing phone attached to the wall by the door. He picked it up and tentatively answered, "Hello."

The efficient tone of a young woman filled the receiver, "This is Maggie. May I help you?"

"Yes, young lady," he replied curtly. "Deputy Secretary for Public Safety Mark Murphy to see Agent Thomas Payne. Please open the door."

Unbeknownst to Murphy, Maggie already had eyes on him. As part of the security system, Doc had installed miniature cameras along the hallway leading to the task force office. In addition, a certain secretary had called to alert her to "Secretary" Murphy's imminent arrival. Judged to have jumped through sufficient hoops, Maggie electronically buzzed him into the office.

While they had never met, she had heard stories of Mark Murphy, none flattering. Still, to see him up close for the first time reminded her of a past comment she had passed over as petty. Now she realized its appropriateness.

The man's body did, indeed, look like an egg. He swayed as he walked. The scene reminded her of a popular 1970's child's toy, which caused her to think, "He wobbles, but he won't fall down."

Unaware of her thoughts and quick to disarm, Murphy immediately moved around Maggie's desk and presented his hand, "Good morning, I'm Mark Murphy, the governor's deputy secretary for public safety. I don't believe we've met."

Maggie took the proffered hand and, doing her best to remain professional, responded, "Good morning, Mr. Murphy. I'm Maggie Bennett, the office manager for the task force. It's very nice to meet you." She added sweetly, "Can I get you some coffee or something else to drink?"

"No, thank you," replied Murphy. "I need to speak with Agent Payne on a matter of great urgency."

"Your secretary called earlier, but said she'd call back with details," countered Maggie. "If it's really important, I can interrupt the meeting."

"Maggie," Murphy stated, looking down his nose, "would I have come all the way down to the basement if it wasn't imperative?"

Maggie ignored the condescending comment. She had noticed his subtle move toward the main office. "Mr. Murphy," she stated, standing and intercepting him by the arm, "may I give you the ten cent tour? You're the first dignitary to visit the office," she added flirtatiously.

The offer caused Murphy to pause. He had time for some pleasantries before Agent Payne's beating. With a slight nod, he responded, "That would be very nice, Maggie, thank you."

"I'll just go announce your arrival first," she stated.

As she excused herself, she thought to add, "Please wait here, I'll be right back."

To her surprise, he remained at her desk as she made her way to the conference room. Reluctantly, she knocked on the door.

Ten seconds later, the door cracked open and Robbie whispered, "What's the password?"

Maggie disregarded Robby's attempt at humor and pushed through the door. In a business-like manner, she informed Thomas, "Mr. Murphy's here to see you. He indicates it's very important."

She added, "I'll show him around and then have him waiting in your office."

Thomas took the hint from her demeanor. Apparently Murphy would not be put off. With a resigned sigh, he directed, "We need to take a break anyway. Let's reconvene in about thirty minutes." He also offered, "Good discussion so far. We're making progress."

With that, the task force members abandoned the conference room for the security of their cubicles. As for Thomas, he had no illusions of making it to safety. He couldn't help but think the fox had already entered the henhouse.

As promised, Thomas found Mark Murphy waiting, not-so-patiently, in his office. He wandered about freely, observing, touching, and, somehow, lessening Thomas' personal mementoes. Surprised by the unusually mean spirited thought, Thomas resolved to act professional even though he didn't trust the man.

Following an awkward greeting, Murphy took a seat, relaxed, and then casually dropped the bomb, "They've found another body in the city."

The ease of the comment initially knocked Thomas off guard. However, another body seemed to fit their preliminary profile of the offender. Regrettably, in this instance, he took little solace in the notion. He had sensed momentum during the morning's discussion and hoped his team would have sufficient time to act before the killer.

"Do you have any details?" Thomas asked after regaining his feet.

"No, I received the information from the media," Murphy responded harshly. "I was hoping you might have the particulars."

With no recourse, Thomas admitted, "I've heard nothing about another body."

Murphy seemed to gain strength from the admission. "Agent Payne, we've taken important resources and diverted them here at your suggestion. What I've seen so far today isn't giving me confidence in that decision. And," he emphasized, looking at his watch, "it's only 11:00 a.m."

Thomas again flashed back to the comments of Director Greene. Clearly, Murphy looked to position himself in such a way that when the bus arrived, he would be safely on the sidewalk as it ran over the task force. Aware that what he said wouldn't matter, he still questioned, "To what are you referring, Mr. Murphy?"

"Well, it's obvious your communication with the local departments is less than adequate. Had it been, someone would have contacted you immediately."

Unable to dispute the truth in the words, Thomas allowed, "Communication is always a problem, particularly when we're in assist mode. Most departments try to handle every situation on their own until it's crystal clear they can't. Add to that the logistical and operation problems inherent in a new task force, and I think you can see why communications aren't perfect yet."

"I'm not sure you can blame everything on being new," Murphy responded, unwilling to concede. "Something as simple as the cancellation of this morning's meeting was apparently missed by your staff. Then, when I tried to contact you just now, I got the run around."

"So you see," he stated, driving in the final nail, "I have serious concerns this task force might have been a mistake."

With his points made, Murphy relented, "But, let's not dwell on that right now. The task force does exist, and I need you to find out what's happening in the city. I can't have the governor blindsided."

No longer having the desire to debate with the manipulative bureaucrat, Thomas simply replied, "I'll make contact with the city police right away. When I find out what's going on, I'll let you know."

"On that note and knowing you understand my concerns," responded Murphy as he stood, "I'll take my leave."

Without as much as a goodbye, Deputy Secretary Murphy strolled out of the task force commander's office. He sauntered through the central bay and out the main door, taking the time to interrupt Maggie by commenting, "Thank you again for the tour, Maggie. It's been a pleasure."

As he wobbled around the corner and out of sight, Maggie bit her tongue as she uncharacteristically thought to herself, "What an asshole!"

Chapter 13

Game Day

Thomas pondered how best to respond to the information provided by Murphy. He couldn't help but feel the devious bastard possessed more information but wanted him to struggle. He cringed, thinking he might be getting paranoid. Then he smiled when he recalled the words of novelist Joseph Heller: "Just because you're paranoid doesn't mean they aren't after you."

More relaxed, he put in a call to the city's chief of detectives Captain Jack Malino. A trustworthy man and hands-on commander, he would most likely be on scene. Two rings of the cellphone later, Thomas heard, "Agent Payne, I wondered how long it might take for you to call."

"Using your sixth sense now, Jack, old boy?" Thomas quipped back.

"Man, right about now I wish I had a sixth sense. It might help me figure out who's killing these kids. Sadly, I have caller ID, and I don't have to be very bright to figure the reason for the call."

Thomas noted the frustration. He quizzed, "How bad is it?"

"It's another little boy. I don't think it can get much worse. My only personal solace," Malino said in a slightly more upbeat tone, "is the body's actually south of the city in Steelton Borough. It's just over the line."

Thomas waited a beat and then asked, "Would you like company?"

Malino went thoughtful. Momentarily he answered, "Thomas, we're only assisting, but let me talk to the chief from Steelton. I'll call you back in five," he said prior to hanging up.

Now in wait-and-see mode, Thomas walked into the office proper. He expected to have to gather the troops, but found them already at their desks. They resembled puppies anticipating their daily walk.

Without fanfare, he informed them of the recent events just outside the city, leading Stan Brown to say, "I've known Jack Malino for quite a few years. He's a sharp guy."

Payne responded, "We've worked together in the past, and I've gotten the same impression. In any case, right now he's our best contact. Let's hope he doesn't forget to call back."

But good to his word, Malino rang back with a minute to spare and related, "I spoke to Chief Smith. He's fine with you guys coming down. Drive south on Cameron out of the city. You can't miss us." Then, more seriously, he threw in, "I wouldn't bring too many cars. It's a zoo down here."

"I understand," acknowledged Thomas. "And I appreciate your getting us in. I know you didn't have to do that."

"We don't always see eye to eye with you state guys," responded the captain after a pause, "but I'm not too proud to accept help when it's offered, particularly in this case."

"I just hope we can be of some help," Thomas said as he signed off.

Thomas clipped his phone on his belt and looked to the task force members. "We're in," he declared. "The rest of the meeting can wait. We can only take one car, so I want Stan, Bill, and Ronnie with me. Robby, stay here. When I get preliminary information, I'll call you, and you can relay it to the director's office. By then, I should have other assignments away from the scene."

To Raj Patel and Maggie Bennett, who stood on the periphery, Thomas said "Doc, I need you to get all the existing Harrisburg police reports into the computer system. Maybe Overlord can find some needle in the haystack. Maggie, since the deputy secretary seems to have taken a shine to you, you can call him after Robby calls the director."

"Guess who's taking one for the team," Maggie responded with an affirmative, yet resigned, nod.

Ready to move out, Thomas noted tension in the room. The racehorses had been brought to the gate. With no need for further comment, he stated, "Okay, grab your gear. It's time to earn your pay."

Within minutes, Thomas and his three chosen investigators found themselves heading south out of the city. A mile from the crime scene, traffic snarled and slowed to a crawl. Even with the windshield and grill lights operating and an occasional chirp of the covert siren, the quantity of vehicles, as well as the antiquated design of the roadway, thwarted their progress. As they inched along, Ronnie gave note to their frustration, "A woman in a wheel chair just passed us on the sidewalk."

Thirty minutes into the ten minute trip, they spotted the first police checkpoint, manned by a junior patrol officer. Baby-face hidden beneath a plastic covered campaign hat, he took one glance at their badges and serious looks and waved them through. As they passed, he sneezed and wiped the moisture from his glasses.

Once beyond the hastily erected barrier, Thomas quickly located an open spot and parked amongst the army of emergency vehicles. Now within the protection of the outer perimeter, the task force members exited the car and began a survey of the scene. Approximately one hundred yards away, inside a secondary area marked off by yellow police tape, two forensic unit members, wearing disposable overalls and booties, methodically walked the ground. The tape defined the inner perimeter, which housed the actual crime scene.

Stan pointed toward a grey haired man of average height and weight walking in their direction. "Here's Jack," he noted.

With a wave, Jack Malino made his way to the group. As he reached Stan, he offered a hand and stated, "Good to see you, big man. How's the family?"

"Great, Jack, how about yours?"

They traded quick pleasantries before Stan made further introductions. Not one to stand on ceremony, Malino got right down to business. "The victim is a four-year-old white male, tentatively identified as Jeffrey Englehart. His family lives a few blocks south of here in Steelton. The mother's here now. The forensics team's filming and photographing the scene as we speak, so we'll have to wait to view the body. The coroner already conducted his initial examination." He pointed toward a nearby unmarked police vehicle and added, "Since we can't get into the inner perimeter yet, I have a few preliminary photographs I can show you of the body and scene."

With that, Malino walked to the car and opened the driver's door. Detaching a laptop from his center console, he returned and said, "Let's get under some cover, where we can stay dry. I can also introduce you to the chief."

As a group they moved toward a large canvas tent, which had been erected to provide protection from the cold rain. Next to the only table stood a tall grey-haired man wearing cowboy boots and a grey rainproof duster. He looked over as the group entered.

With a grim expression he greeted the new arrivals, introducing himself as Chief Lenny Smith from Steelton Borough. Immediately turning toward Thomas, he stated, "Jack filled me in on your task force. He said you're just beginning to look at their homicides. I'm grateful for any assistance you can provide."

As Chief Smith spoke with the members of the task force, Captain Malino booted up his computer. He searched the files until he located one specific photograph. Satisfied, he spun the laptop for everyone to see. The digital image showed a yellow synthetic blanket standing in stark contrast to the dark green grass it covered. The tiny hand peeking from beneath its border left no doubt as to the object it concealed.

Without comment, he clicked to another slide, which showed the same figure partially uncovered. As indicated previously, the body appeared to be that of a young male child. Fully clothed to include a winter coat and hat and positioned on one side in the fetal position, the body exhibited no obvious signs of bruising or injuries.

He had just reached to press the next key when Bill Travis interrupted, "Captain, is that the original position of the body?"

Malino thought and responded, "I believe so."

He turned to the chief who agreed, saying, "To my understanding, no one touched anything except to check for vitals or move the blanket."

In anticipation of the answer, Travis stated, "You said this boy lived south of here in Steelton, not the city."

"That's correct," answered Malino, unsure of the agent's line of questioning.

Undaunted, Travis continued to fire away, "Looking at the picture, I didn't notice any head trauma. Did anyone check for visible injury?"

"The coroner didn't mention any," replied Malino, searching his memory.

The comment caused Bill to turn towards the other members of the task force. This led to a brief sidebar, which ended when the Chief asked, "Something bothering you boys?"

Thomas looked at his team. Confident with their discussion, he offered, "Chief, I think we need to discuss a little problem."

A long-time law enforcement member, the chief knew the word "problem" could mean many things to many people. Also, a fairly good judge of character, he felt Agent Payne wouldn't use the word to describe a hangnail. So, when he asked, "What kind of problem?" he feared the worst.

When Thomas answered, Chief Smith looked as if someone had hit him across the forehead with a baseball bat. He didn't speak immediately. Conversely, Captain Malino spoke, but he sounded like a prisoner in the midst of a waterboarding as he sputtered, "What do you mean by two killers, two people working together?"

"No," Thomas replied. "We think the person who committed this crime and the person who committed the two in the city are different."

Chief Smith inquired, "What makes you think that?"

Thomas glanced to his right and nodded for Stan Brown and Bill Travis to explain. In detail, they laid out their suspicions. When they finished, Captain Malino turned thoughtful and noted, "I have to admit I glossed over most of the details. To be honest, I was just relieved it happened outside the city for a change. But the more you guys talk," he added, "the better I like your theory. Assuming your take is accurate, where do we go from here?"

"Well, since you asked," Thomas responded, "I think your departments should follow SOP." He referred to standard operating procedure. "Complete the examinations of the body and scene and canvass for witnesses. For my part," he directed to Chief Smith, "I'd like to offer the services of the task force to test our theory."

Going thoughtful, Chief Smith responded, "What do you have in mind?"

In response, Thomas first donned his "we are here to help look." Aware of over-stepping, he offered cautiously, "We can conduct the victimology," referring to an investigation into the victim's background, lifestyle, and risk to be victimized.

Thomas could see the wheels turning as the chief considered the ramifications of the proposal. With a sigh, Chief Smith asked, "What if you're wrong?"

"Well, that's the beauty. If we're wrong, you've lost nothing. You've continued to follow SOP, and we'll document our findings for inclusion in your report. On the other hand, if we're right, you won't be wasting time looking for the wrong killer."

Again, Chief Smith took a moment before resigning himself to his course of action. "Okay, Agent Payne. I don't have the personnel to spare on anything fancy, and we need to speak with the family anyway. So, run with it. But," he added immediately, "I'll expect to be kept up-to-date on any information you obtain."

"That goes without saying," Thomas responded, internalizing his relief at having navigated the dangerous waters of interagency relations.

With a tentative plan in place, the chief bid them good luck. As he and Malino moved off to speak to their investigators, Payne called his team to follow him back to their vehicle. Once safely ensconced inside, he utilized the group talk feature on his phone to contact the members still at the office.

With the entire task force listening, either in person or on the phone, Thomas succinctly began to break down duties, "Robby and Maggie, you'll need to relay information to DHQ and the deputy secretary. At this point, we have a deceased, four-year-old male. The cause of death is unknown. The body was discovered around ten hundred hours, covered with a yellow synthetic blanket. The investigating agency is the Steelton Bureau of Police. As you might expect, the city police are involved as well. I've spoken to the on-scene commanders of both departments, and, as of now, the Major Crimes Task Force has been asked to assist. You can pass along we'll be conducting an initial victimology."

He paused for breath and then moved on, "Maggie, if Murphy asks you to explain the term *victimology*, just tell him it's like conducting a background investigation on the victim. Most likely, he won't ask because he won't want to sound clueless."

Amidst chuckles, Thomas revealed, "Now here's the rest of the story which goes nowhere else. We've seen some indications this isn't the work of our previous killer. In fact, it appears the scene may have been staged to look as if it were the same killer."

Thomas looked to Stan who took over the discussion, "There are a number of differences apparent upon cursory observation of the scene. First, this victim is a white male and younger than the other victims. Second, though this may be a stretch due to proximity, this victim resides in Steelton while the others lived in the city on Allison Hill. Third, the first two victims were carefully displayed on their backs in repose. They were centered under the blanket with no body parts exposed. We've been told this little boy was found on his side with a hand visible. Fourth, the blanket is similar to the others but appears to be of a coarser material and a slightly different shade of yellow. It's most likely from a different manufacturer than the first two. Last but not least, there are no visible injuries to the head or neck. While our original killer's process will change, I don't think he'd abandon the blitz attack this soon, if ever."

To emphasize what he considered the most important point, Thomas tacked on, "Criminals usually stage a scene when they're in the victim's sphere of family or acquaintances. Now you know why we need to talk to the family. So, to break down assignments, Ronnie and Stan will speak with the victim's mother."

He focused on Ronnie, "You know what to look for. Get her to open up. If she's the biological mother, she'll provide the clearest picture of our victim's life and final days." He nearly added, "And it'll be hard for her to hide her emotions," when he noticed a wistful look cross Ronnie's face.

With no time to examine her mood, he turned his attention to the phone and said, "Robby, when you're finished at DHQ, I want you to pick up Bill and me here at the scene. Once we've located the stepfather, we'll speak with him. We'll all talk again after completing the interviews. At that point, we can determine our next course of action."

As they prepared to go in different directions, Thomas looked around the car. "I don't have to tell you the importance of cleaning this up quickly, so saddle up and get it done."

As he opened the car door and handed the keys to Ronnie Sanchez, he briefly looked for any signs of the earlier sadness. Observing none, he added, "I'm counting on you. Good hunting and be safe."

Chapter 14

A Lunch to Remember

The man reached the far side of the trash strewn lot before his prey. Though he had briefly lost sight of the boy during his mad rush, he now saw him crawling through a broken section of rusty chain-linked fence. In position to intercept him before he crossed the next street, he wheeled to the curb.

Electrified with possibilities, the man screwed a smile onto his normally expressionless face and sprang from his vehicle. He passed the grill just as the boy reached the sidewalk. Nearly face to face as the intervening space dwindled, he could almost smell the child.

He had just raised his hand to wave and say "hello," when a harsh voice off to his left startled him. Alarmed, the man turned as if caught doing something wrong, such as abducting a child. A heavyset black woman of about fifty approached pushing a cart. Though she struggled to walk, she maintained a laser focus on the child.

Under her glare, the boy reacted with an angry sigh and a scuff of his bright red kicks on the sidewalk. By the look on his face, he had been the one caught doing something wrong. "Be right there, Granny," he answered sweetly, a smile now plastered on his lips. Then under his breath, "Goddamn busybody!"

Off to accept certain punishment, the boy finally noticed the man standing nearby. He appeared ready to speak, but instead turned, and shuffled toward his waiting grandmother. He hadn't gone two steps before she chastised, "Why aren't you in school and don't even think 'bout lyin' to me! You know I'll know if you lyin'. Don't make me hit you upside that thick head o' yours."

Temporarily finished, she turned a distrustful eye to the man, who suddenly realized he had frozen in place. Forced into action, he made as if to check the front tires of his vehicle. Seemingly satisfied, he returned to the driver's seat, put the transmission in drive, and sped off. He hazarded a glance at the pair as he passed them on the sidewalk. Deep in discussion, they paid him little attention. Both seemed preoccupied with her hand as she made good on her threat.

"Fuck me," he said to himself out loud, recognizing just how close he had come to getting caught. He tried to calm himself, but he couldn't stop sweating. Adrenaline surged through his body. As a result, he continued to drive, oblivious to his death grip on the steering wheel or the grinding of his teeth.

Half an hour later, he pulled off the road into a parking lot. Nerves slightly less frayed, he finally let loose of the wheel and began the familiar job of tweaking his memories. With the help of his companion, he slowly composed himself. In the end, he fixated on one fact: he had taken no overt action. Therefore, no harm occurred, no foul transpired, and, most important, no suspicion befell him.

Once again, his brain had shuffled its limited resources in order to minimize the damage caused by his impulsive actions. At this point, he should have realized he needed to plan better, but he didn't. Accustomed to rash behavior, he just accepted it as normal and prepared to move on.

Now, as he sat in a nameless parking lot in his idling vehicle, he felt something beyond frustration or desire; he felt hunger. Another sign of his imprudent nature, he had slept through the alarm this morning and had no time for breakfast and no time to make lunch. Not that he could have packed a meal even if he had time because his kitchen cabinets stood bare except for accumulated dust and one crunchy cockroach carcass.

Temporarily pushed aside, his worries now took a backseat to his physical needs. He contemplated options. He could run into a convenience store and nuke a pre-packaged burrito or order a sandwich to go. However, the thought caused the already churning acid in his belly to erupt, quickly losing any appeal. Unable to decide, he simply went back to work.

Another half hour later, his rebellious stomach, aided by the sight of a familiar green and white sign, finally gained sufficient foothold to force his hand. The sign belonged to a diner he had visited regularly with his coach during his training period. He hadn't been inside in months.

A loner, he shied away from regular haunts and friends. However, today this diner offered two important things, food and familiarity. The food he trusted would fill the hole in his intestines. More important, he hoped the restaurant's familiarity might provide some comfort. With this in mind, he pulled off the street and into a nearby parking spot.

Spurred on by hunger and a need to forget, he summoned his courage. He left his vehicle behind and walked through the heavy wood and glass door. Once inside he felt the welcome blast of warm air. The delicious aroma of breakfast and lunch food caused his mouth to water.

Finally, the man moved beyond his sense of smell. In that moment, he perceived the attack on his ears. Dishes banged, pots crashed, and people shouted. The noise seemed so loud it vibrated his skin. Even the volume of the television hanging from the wall seemed to suck the air from his lungs. Sensibilities already bruised, he turned to flee.

However, just as he reached for the door handle, a cute young waitress touched his arm. With a smile, she advised him to take a seat. He capitulated and did as she asked. As had become common in his life, an outside stimulus had triggered an unexpected reaction.

A minute late, the same waitress hustled back with a placemat, napkin, utensils, menu, and a glass of water. He marveled at her dexterity. She noticed his look.

"Sometimes I feel like an octopus," she kidded.

The mental picture caused him to grin, involuntarily exposing two missing teeth. Suddenly aware she could see the gap in the side of his smile, he closed his mouth. Self-conscious of the imperfections in his appearance, the embarrassment caused him to blush.

"I'll give you a chance to look at the menu," she said, acting as if she hadn't noticed his discomfort.

He watched her walk away from the corner of his eye. Distractedly, he picked up the menu, holding it like a newspaper. His actions mirrored those of other patrons. The difference, while they reviewed lunch choices, he sought refuge behind the laminated paper from the always prying and judgmental eyes of others.

He had just started to relax behind his self-erected fortification when a conversation on the television caught his ear. He heard an anchorwoman discussing him or, more correctly, the "Cradle Killer," his moniker du joir. "What a stupid freakin' name," he thought with exasperation, unable to make the connection between his actions and the portrait painted by the press.

Focused on the screen, he strained to catch the words over the din in the restaurant. He heard the reporter say, "Breaking news from the city of Harrisburg. Another body has reportedly been discovered off of South Cameron Street. This is the same general area in which the bodies of two young boys were discovered under yellow blankets on two separate dates last month."

As the face of the anchorwoman faded away, he could see a uniformed police officer standing behind a barricade. Then the news station showed grainy video of what looked like men in space suits walking inside an area surrounded with police tape. Evidently frustrated, the anchorwoman complained, "As I've said, police officials have been closed lip to this point. We hope to have more details in the next hour or so."

As he considered the scene on the television, his mind began to wander. He knew he hadn't committed this crime or, at least, thought he hadn't. He really couldn't be sure of much anymore, other than his desires. Still present, but now simmering, they fell in line behind his hunger and thoughts of nearly getting caught.

Unnoticed by his meandering mind, he lowered his paper and plastic barrier, exposing his face and dark eyes, which now stared off into the distance. Intent on his own thoughts and visions, he failed to feel the small ball of spittle forming at the corner of his mouth. Eventually a heavy droplet, it hung precariously until it joined the river on his chin, dropped down the waterfall, and in due course, become a small pond on the table.

Though they remained open, his eyes no longer saw. For better or worse, the darkness had, once more, taken control. Gradually, he found himself reliving and examining his past explorations. Only this time the shadows painted a picture of unqualified success.

A selfish and vigilant partner, the void often caught rebellious thoughts in their infancy. On those occasions, like now, it simply invoked its most powerful weapon. It lit up the cinema of the man's mind and cast the traitorous thoughts aside.

Streamed in high definition, he saw himself back in the warehouse. A small figure lay at his feet. In this version, he could see a streetlight in the parking lot blinking on and off. It caused a disco ball effect in the mostly obscure room. This continued for a few seconds before the light went out, increasing the blackness that surrounded him. As always, the darkness reminded him of its power.

Suddenly disconcerted to find himself in a diner, he wondered why a waitress, her face filled with concern, kept shaking his shoulder. Then it came back to him, and he slowly turned his glazed eyes and slobbering mouth toward her.

Her breath caught as she stuttered, "You scared me. I, I came to take your order, but you wouldn't even look at me. I thought you were having a seizure."

Frightened and more than a little embarrassed, the man hastily ordered a burger and fries. As the waitress moved away, he quietly eased himself out of the booth and toward the bathroom. In the long hallway beyond the tables, he passed by the men's room and burst out the sheet metal back door.

He had blanked out. It had happened before, but never in public and never with such alarming speed and power. Once enjoyable, his dreams seemed to be taking on a life of their own.

Confusion and doubt caused his head to swim. For the first time in his life, he became aware of a sound that filled him with dread. Unknown to him at the time, he was hearing the noise from the storm whirling in his own mind. A sound no one else could hear.

To him, it seemed the tangible precursor to a true meteorological event. Unseen as of yet, he sensed it cutting a path of destruction as it grew and spiraled unchecked. He remained frozen in place, listening and looking. Only the genuine cold of the day penetrated the fog of his thoughts, prompting the noise to level off and slowly fade to nothing.

In the deserted alley not far from his vehicle, braced by the cold, head-clearing wind, the man made a decision. He needed to recapture the equilibrium he had found since arriving in Harrisburg. Though queasy from the battle waged in his mind, as well as the lack of food in his stomach, he resolved this could only occur if he finished what he had started. He needed to reconcile with the darkness, for it alone provided hope of finding answers and, along with them, peace.

Chapter 15

Round One

With Thomas' parting words, "I'm counting on you," ringing in her ears, reality hit home. Ready or not, Ronny, once again, found herself waist-deep in the swamp of violent crime with the bent and broken psyches of past victims tugging at her ankles. Unsettled, she nearly turned to flee, when a large and pleasantly reassuring hand touched her shoulder and a deep voice inquired, "Need some help navigating, little lady?"

Pulled from her musings, she turned to face Stan Brown. Thinking, "More than you know," she nevertheless mumbled, "having some trouble finding the mom."

"Maybe we should ask them," Stan offered, pointing to the nearby building where Chief Smith and Captain Malino stood under an awning.

Using his size, Stan cut a swath through the mob to the raised portico from which the Chief and Captain surveyed the operation. Normally their gold "BCA" lettered raid jackets would have been given deference, but theirs were just three more letters in the alphabet soup crowd. As they neared the platform, Chief Smith caught sight of them and called out, "Did you find the mother?"

"She seems to have disappeared," answered Ronny.

In response, the Chief fished a black, portable radio from inside his duster. He spoke briefly with one of his officers before indicating, "Ten minutes ago she told my chief detective she needed to get away from here and went home."

Ronnie hazarded an inconspicuous glance at Stan who had turned toward her at the same time. Neither spoke, as the chief obtained an address for the mother. Back at their car, Stan asked, "Penny for your thoughts?"

"Cheapskate," she replied. "But since we're probably thinking the same thing, this one's on the house. I've been at scenes where we literally had to drag the mom away from the body. She left him on the ground with the garbage."

"Makes me think," interjected Stan, as Ronnie piloted the car from the scene, "like our theory might not be so thin."

Five minutes later, Ronnie pulled in front of a typical older two-story home covered in dirty white aluminum siding. Four crumbling concrete steps and a sidewalk bisected the hilly yard leading to the covered front porch. As she stared at the structure, Ronnie could feel her heart move into her throat. Only the movement of her partner exiting the car broke the invisible bond holding her in the seat.

Near the front door, Ronnie heard the sound of a television talk show blaring in the house. She could feel the bass in her belly, which suddenly began to roil. Though she felt her composure waver, she asked, "Ready?"

"Always," responded Stan with sufficient confidence for the pair.

Buoyed by his poise, she rapped on the pitted aluminum screen door and then the wooden interior door. She wondered if the knocking would breach the sound barrier created by the television. Almost thirty seconds passed before the volume dropped and shuffling footsteps came toward the door. Cautiously mindful of potential threats as the door opened, they found themselves facing a plump young female in a grey sweatshirt and undersized black spandex pants.

Dazed look in her red eyes, the woman remained silent, prompting Ronnie to initiate introductions and add, "Mrs. Englehart, we're very sorry for your loss."

No response followed, leading Ronnie to ask, "Would it be possible for us to come in and speak with you?"

The question seemed to catch the woman off-guard. She hesitated as if debating with herself, then opened the door. In a hoarse voice she whispered, "Come on in."

Without a glance back, she turned and led the way through the house. As she walked, Ronnie noted the same shuffling sound she had heard just before the door opened. Upon closer examination, she saw the woman swing her legs gingerly, barely picking her slippers off the ground. She reminded Ronnie of a weary cross-country skier.

In the first room, the investigators observed a clean, almost sterile, environment. Light furniture of the rent-to-own variety faced an old projection television situated against a far wall. Their reluctance host guided them through another room and into the kitchen at the rear of the house. With a feeble wave, she directed them to sit at an old, but spotless, metal and linoleum table. Everything in its place, nevertheless, something elusive bothered Stan about the space.

For her part, Ronnie failed to note anything out of the ordinary. She could feel her body tightening and her breath begin to catch. She willed herself to relax, hoping no one had noticed her reaction. "Just another day at the office," she thought nervously.

Fortunately, the notion of failing at her task spurred her on. She forced the words to come, because with the words often came strength. On unsteady legs, she started, "Again, Mrs. Englehart, let me say how sorry we are. I know this isn't the easiest time to talk, but it's necessary."

The woman bowed her head in acknowledgement and then responded quietly, "My name is Jennifer. Jennifer Spence. I remarried last year. Jeffy's my son with my ex."

Now engaged, Ronnie's tone became more deliberate, yet remained concerned. She asked the seemingly reserved young woman, "Well then, Mrs. *Spence*, is there anyone you'd like us to call to be with you?"

Jennifer remained silent, then stated, "My neighbor Gayle was here for a while, but I sent her home. I didn't really think about calling nobody else." She quickly added, "I guess I'm in shock."

"That's normal. We could call your husband if you like, even a clergy member if you have someone."

The young woman considered the offer. She sighed, "I guess I should tell Mouse you're here."

Curious about the owner of the nickname and the phrasing of the response, Stan inquired, "Who's Mouse?"

"My husband. Everybody calls him Mouse."

"Where's he now?" probed Stan further.

"Why?" challenger Jennifer.

Surprised by the reaction, Stan simply replied, "Well, we'll need to talk to him at some point."

"He doesn't know no more than me," she directed. "We woke up around 6:30 this morning for work, and Jeffy was gone."

"Gone?" Ronnie explored.

Jennifer clarified, "Jeffy's special. He's autistic."

During the response, Ronnie noticed the woman's unsuccessful attempt to relax, the darting eyes. She nudged "Go on, Jennifer."

She started slowly. Gradually increasing speed, Jennifer related, "He doesn't act like other kids. Once in a while, he gets up at night and wanders around. A couple times he went outside. He loves the stars. This morning, when I couldn't find him, I figured he must've gone out again."

She ended abruptly, breathing hard, and studying her hands, which she clenched above the table. Ronnie saw her eyes welling with tears.

In an attempt to lighten the mood, Ronnie observed, "You keep a nice home, Jennifer, very clean and orderly." Expecting a reply, but receiving none, Ronnie persisted, "How do you keep everything so clean?"

Jennifer wavered and tears began to build. Finally she responded quietly, "I don't have a job right now, so Mouse says it's my job to keep up the house."

With each word her anxiety rose, leading Ronnie to interject, "How about if we start with the easy stuff? Maybe you could just give us some contact information for your husband." She added in a friendly manner, "We can have someone go in person to explain the situation with your *beautiful* little boy."

Her calculated words had an immediate effect. Jennifer looked up and down and suddenly the reservoir restraining her tears crumbled. A natural act, Ronnie took the young woman in her arms to provide comfort. As she soothed, "That's all right. It'll be all right. We'll figure this out. I promise you," Jennifer Spence could no longer contain the sobs boiling from within.

Ronnie glanced at Stan as she slowly rocked back and forth. "I'll get the contact and biographical information for the family while she calms down. Call Thomas. Tell him what's going on."

With a nod, Stan turned away from the drama and made his way back to the living room. Out of earshot of those in the kitchen, he used his cell phone to contact Thomas. He explained the situation, ending with, "It's clear by her reactions that something's eating her up. We barely sat down, and she started to cry."

Still at the crime scene in Steelton, Thomas maintained, "Maybe it's just the shock hitting home."

"I don't think so. Her verbal and non-verbal cues tell me she's hiding something."

About to remark, Thomas' attention shifted to the sound of an arriving vehicle. Noting the impatient, throaty rumble of exhaust from Robby Franklin's car, he held up a finger as an indication for Robby to wait. Meanwhile, he saw Bill Travis jog from the cover of the tent and hop into the small vinyl back seat of the police vehicle.

Refocused on the call, Thomas wrote down the basic biographical information for Carl "Mouse" Spence and his wife, Jennifer. He listened as Stan cautioned, "Boss, it may take us some time to figure out what she knows. She seems ready to crack, but they always rally. As for the stepdad, you'll have to get a quick read on him when you meet."

Before he hung up, Stan added, "I will say this: most relationships have a dominant personality, and she ain't it."

Payne remained pensive for a moment before walking to the waiting car. He jumped into the front seat and instructed, "Head to Middletown. Do you know where the Lumber Store is on North Pine?"

"Not exactly," responded Robby, "but I know the general area. It shouldn't be hard to find."

South on State Route 230, it took fifteen minutes to reach their destination, a white block warehouse and storefront. In accordance with their hastily conceived plan, Thomas and Robby entered the store to interview Spence, while Bill remained behind to provide Doc with sufficient information to conduct a background on the man, and, hopefully, obtain leverage for the interview.

As he entered, Thomas smelled the pleasant fragrance of freshly cut lumber. His eyes took in the showroom and settled on an older gentleman sitting at a desk behind a long wooden counter. The tag on his red golf shirt indicated "Manager."

As Thomas moved in his direction, the man looked up and asked pleasantly, "Can I help you, fellows?"

"Yes. Sir," Thomas replied, displaying his badge and identification. "I'm Agent Thomas Payne with the Bureau of Criminal Apprehension. This is Agent Franklin. Would it be possible for us to speak with Carl Spence? I understand he works here."

Now concerned, the man behind the counter queried, "Is he in trouble or something?"

"No, sir," answered Thomas. "There's been a death in his family. We need to pass along the bad news."

The gentleman mulled over the information and responded, "I don't envy you that."

"By the way," he added, offering his callused hand first to Thomas, then Robby, "I'm no sir. My name is Earl, Earl Winters. I

manage and own this place. Mouse's only worked here for about a
year. He's back on one of the saws today."

"Would it be possible for us to speak with him some place
private?" inquired Thomas.

"Sure," replied the owner. "We have a small conference
room you can use. If you'd like, I can have the foreman bring him
right in."

"That'd be perfect, Mr. Winters. We really appreciate it,"
responded Thomas. He quickly inserted, "Please don't tell him why
he's coming to the conference room. It's best if we break the news
to him gently."

Winters motioned for them to come around the counter. He
led them down a freshly carpeted hallway to a bright, modern area
with offices and a comfortable conference room. After he left to
find Spence, Robby asked, "You taking the lead?"

"For now," answered Thomas, looking around the room. "I
wanna get a good read on his personality and get some behavioral
references before I decide on a strategy."

After his brief survey, Thomas asked Robby to close the
window blinds in order to prevent outside distractions. He then
positioned two chairs near the head of the conference table where he
and Spence could converse in close proximity without any
intervening barrier. Satisfied with the layout and order of the room,
the agents talked quietly and patiently waited.

Less than five minutes later, Winters returned with a tall
young man at his heels. About Robby's height, but rail-thin, Carl

Spence had long dark hair that hadn't seen a bottle of shampoo in days. Dressed in a brown wool sweater, dirty jeans, and the obligatory steel toed shit-kickers, he hesitated before walking through the doorway.

His vacillation didn't go unnoticed. Thomas strolled over and introduced himself and Robby. As Winters left them alone, Thomas took that moment to say, "Mr. Spence, please take a seat. We have some bad news."

"It's Jeff, ain't it?" blurted Spence.

Remaining poised, Thomas responded, "Yes, it is."

"He's dead, ain't he?" interrupted Spence again.

"I'm very sorry to have to tell you, but yes, he is."

With a course of questioning in mind, Thomas wanted to save the specifics of the death for later. Politely, he asked, "Mr. Spence, before we get into the details, would it be possible for me to get some personal information from you?"

Suspicion obvious in his gaze, Spence appeared ready to refuse, but relented, "Well, if ya have to, but I wanna know everything that happened."

Without delay, Thomas dove into the personal background of Carl Spence as Robby observed. While the conversation focused on him, Spence seemed confident and comfortable. At one point, he asked Thomas to call him Mouse.

"Everybody called me Mouse when I was a kid," he informed, "because I boxed at the YMCA in Baltimore. I was damn good, but I always had a mouse around one eye or the other."

Jon D. Kurtz

As witness, Robby understood the reason for Thomas' initial personal line of questioning. He intended to set Spence at ease and plot a baseline or reference point for his normal behavior. Like a warm-up before a game, the baseline set the stage for that which followed.

Sufficiently relaxed, Spence seemed almost surprised when the questions turned to his marriage and interaction with his stepson. In addition to surprise, he also displayed the first signs of anger.

Not quite ready to alienate his subject, Thomas decided to take a break. He offered, "Did you get any lunch today?"

Spence indicated he had eaten before noon, but could use a drink. This prompted Thomas to ask, "Robby, can you run out and grab us all sodas?"

Robby acknowledged and walked with Thomas, who opened the door. As the door shut, Thomas whispered, "Get with Bill. See if he got anything back from Doc yet. Also, check in with Stan and Chief Smith to see if there've been any further developments. I need more if I'm going to push this guy."

Now alone with Spence, Thomas lighten the conversation, inquiring about the young man's boxing career. Spence happily embellished his feats in the ring. This continued for almost fifteen minutes until Robby returned carrying three cold bottles of Coke.

He apologized for being away so long and handed Spence a bottle. Then, he placed himself between Spence and his interviewer. Along with a bottle, he passed Thomas a small piece of paper containing writing. A quick glance at the words brought a smile to Thomas' face.

The stage of proceeding with caution had just come to an end. The time had arrived to add some wood to the fire. He intended to smoke out a rat or, in this case, a Mouse.

Chapter 16

The Truth Hurts

A quick moving summer thunderstorm slipping through the Spence's kitchen, the sobbing lasted for five minutes before it faded to an occasional hiccup. As the clouds passed, Ronnie continued to hold Jennifer. So as not to interfere, Stan remained in the living room listening, while surveying his surroundings.

The first floor consisted of the living room, a small dining room, and the kitchen which ran the width of the back of the house. Near the front door, worn carpet ran up the steps to the second floor. After examination of nearly the entire first floor, he finally realized what had troubled him earlier. He saw no signs that a young child lived in the house, no toys, no small articles of clothing, and not one picture. He pondered the unusual situation until he realized the crying in the kitchen had ceased.

Still at the table, Ronnie released her embrace, but persisted in holding Jennifer's left hand. While she knew the contact would provide the younger woman comfort, she also recognized it could act as a conduit, transferring to her the same feelings that had forced her to flee sex crimes for undercover work two years before. Fortunately, well-practiced at repressing her emotions, she locked the unwelcome feelings away and endured.

"We need to talk about it," she stated, lifting the young mother's chin and looking into her brown eyes. Jennifer tried to look down, but Ronnie held her gaze, "Whatever the problem, I can help you."

Jennifer's eyes darted down as she mumbled, "Nobody can help me."

"Why do you say that?"

"I don't know," responded Jennifer softly. "I'm just so tired."

She tried to pull away, but Ronnie gently grasped her right hand. Now holding both hands, Ronnie invited, "Why are you so tired?"

Compelled by proximity or some unexplained tie, Jennifer made a decision. She began, "It hasn't been easy. We've only been married a year."

She stopped abruptly, but Ronnie remained silent.

With a deep sigh, Jennifer continued, "I don't usually drink. Mouse came home drunk last night. He brought a bottle of rum. I should've known better."

"Why?"

"Let's just say Mouse and booze don't mix so well." Thoughtfully, Jennifer finished, "We drank and then fooled around some."

"When was this?" prodded Ronnie.

"Around eight," answered Jennifer after some consideration. "Mouse got home late from work. He went to the bar with his friends." She stopped then added quietly, "I don't remember a lot."

Moving her chair even closer, Ronnie continued the extraction, "Tell me about it."

For the next thirty minutes, the young mother wove a sometimes-convoluted tale of drinking and sex. It ended with her in bed, passed out. As her story unfolded, her recollection appeared, at times, exceptionally clear and, at others, exceedingly cloudy. Normally, follow-up questions received answers, such as, "I don't remember" or "I'm just not sure."

While some time since Ronnie had interviewed a woman in this situation, her training and experience flooded back. She continued to suppress her anxiety, while discerning obvious signs of deception. Most interesting, she noted Jennifer's sustained focus on herself and failure to mention her son during the discussion. Pointedly, she asked, "Where was Jeffy while all this was going on?"

With the mention of her son's name, Jennifer's eyes widened, and her breathing came faster. She took a moment to compose herself before replying, "Mouse made me put him to bed." She added quickly, "I would never drink around Jeffy. I swear."

Worried she might lose the bond she had been building, Ronnie innocently slid her hand up Jennifer's left wrist. As she did, the young mother gasped and pulled her arm to the side. The sudden movement caused her sleeve to ride up, exposing the bottom of a large, fresh bruise.

Unwittingly provided with another small bit of the puzzle, Ronnie caringly, but directly, inquired, "How long has he been abusing you?"

For a moment, Jennifer looked as though she no longer recognized Ronnie. Then her eyes cleared and filled again, this time with tears of shame. She realized this other woman had brushed aside her web of lies and half-truths. Defeated, Jennifer Spence revealed the real story of her and Mouse's relationship.

She started with, "When we first met, he was a gentleman." Her voice trailed off as she reminisced and then continued, "The first time he did anything was right before we got married. He was at the bar with his buddies. When he came home, he wanted to screw, but I was too tired. He got mad, so I let him. I ended up with bruises all over and could hardly walk the next day."

The discussion of battering at the hands of her husband soon transformed into a story of child abuse. As it turned out, Mouse Spence hid his true personality well, at least until stripped bare by alcohol. Ronny had heard this same story many times before. It brought back the words of a mentor, "A duck remains a duck even if it yearns to change into a swan, and an angry, controlling, manipulative piece of shit will remain a piece of shit, no matter what."

As the tale unfolded, Stan moved closer to the kitchen. He listened with great interest. The purge lasted for nearly twenty minutes. Near its climax, he felt his cell phone vibrate in his pocket.

His first reaction was to let it ring, until he saw the name on the caller ID. "Hey, Robbie," he answered, moving away from the kitchen.

Out of earshot, he continued, "You aren't going to believe this."

Their conversation had occurred during Robby's soda run. After he had linked up with Bill Travis at the car, Robby had contacted Stan for an update. The information he obtained from both ended up on the piece of scrap paper now in Thomas' hand.

"Mouse," said Thomas feigning embarrassment. "I hate to prolong this, but is there a bathroom nearby?"

Forcing a laugh, Spence pointed to the hallway and said, "Next door on the left."

While the information on the paper appeared positive, it also brought to mind further questions. Thomas felt he needed more detail. Right or wrong, he extended the already long intermission, placed Robbie in charge, and headed straight for the car to speak with Bill Travis.

Once in the passenger seat, he pulled out the note from Robby. "Give me the skinny," he said, handing over the note.

Bill viewed the block printed words, "Husband beats wife and child; past history; and husband angry - kicked boy."

Succinctly, he explained the information gleaned from his inquiries and that passed on by Stan. Though more detailed, the picture of the events leading to the child's death remained blurry. Conscious of the ticking clock, Thomas hastily formulated and explained a new game plan. "Contact the lead investigator from Steelton. Strongly suggest he meet us here ASAP. This conversation is about to get interesting."

Thomas returned to the conference room, hoping the long interruption hadn't short-circuited the flow of the interview. Surprisingly, his absence provided him a bonding moment with his new best friend as Spence took the opportunity to comment on the long bathroom break by sarcastically remarking, "Everythin' come out okay?"

With a laugh, Thomas eased back into his questioning. He had nearly run out of fluff when a knock on the door interrupted the conversation. Thomas looked at Robby and asked, "Can you get that?"

By Thomas' wink, Robby understood the knock had been expected. He exited without fanfare. Once outside with the door closed, he met with Bill Travis and a short, heavyset man in a tweed coat, introduced as Detective Nick Benson of the Steelton Bureau of Police. Not yet privy to Thomas' evolving plan, Robby listened as Bill explained, "Detective Benson will become the second man in the interview. You and I get the exits in case our Mouse decides to bolt from the hole."

Satisfied with their roles, Robby moved off to the left, Bill to the right, and Detective Benson entered the conference room. A quick study, Benson assessed the situation and introduced himself, first to Thomas and then Spence. He noted a cloud of suspicion drift across Spence's face, leading him to extend his hand and offer, "My condolences for your loss."

Obviously uncomfortable, Spence wiggled around in his seat and asked, "What's goin' on? Am I in trouble?"

"Mouse, you said earlier you wanted to know everything," answered Thomas, intentionally avoiding the second question. "Since Steelton PD is the primary investigating agency, I asked Detective Benson to stop in with an update from the scene. If you're uncomfortable, one or all of us can leave, including you. In fact, we'll take you home, if you want." He paused for emphasis, "But we really could use your help."

Thomas could feel the conflict. He sensed the discomfort as the young man considered the appearance and implications of walking away. Boxed in a corner, Spence stated, "Well, anythin' to help, but ya know, you're takin' a long time to ask a few silly-assed questions."

In response, Thomas turned serious and agreed, "You're right. I'll try to be more efficient from now on."

For the next hour, Thomas poked and prodded Spence. He had him provide a timeline of activities for the previous day. He

asked him what he felt happened to his stepson. Thomas often
dropped back and had Spence answer the same question again,
adding to the young man's growing frustration. As the interview
continued, Spence's reactions went from friendly to angry.

As he recalled the events of the previous day and evening,
Spence mechanically explained that he had arrived home around
8:00 o'clock after an evening of "beers with the boys." Horny, he
brought home a bottle of rum to loosen his wife up. He indicated
she had been a "little shy" lately. After putting Jeff to bed, they
watched the football game and drank. Spence stated they got sloppy
drunk and went to bed to have sex.

When they woke in the morning, they found Jeff had gone
outside. Already late for work, he left while his wife looked for her
son. Spence ended by saying, "I was really screwed up, man. I ain't
too clear on the details after I got home from the bar."

As Detective Benson sat quietly, Thomas let the thoughts
sink in. He again inquired, "So, what do you think happened to
Jeff?"

"Well, ah," he started, "I told ya before, I don't really know.
I didn't think much at first. I thought she'd find him playin' in the
yard. When I didn't hear anythin', and then you showed up, I got a
bad feelin'." Quickly he tacked on, "I got to thinkin' about that sick
fuck out there killin' little kids. It's the same guy, ain't it?"

Payne cocked his head to the side. He looked directly at
Spence and asked, "What makes you think Jeff was murdered?"

Spence seemed taken aback. Thomas could see the wheels turning.

"Ah, uh, well," he stammered. "The murders have been all over the news, ya know. That's just the first thin' I thought of." Now annoyed, he raised his reddening eyes and spit, "Ain't it about time you guys do your fuckin' job and start lookin' for the guy that did it."

Without hesitation or emotion, Thomas persisted, "I never mentioned murder. All I ever said was we found Jeff's body, and he's dead."

At this point, the room fell silent. The scene had been reminiscent of a bullfighter in the ring, move in, move out, charge, and retreat. With the bull prepared to lunge, Thomas readied his sword for the final thrust.

"Can I tell you a story?" he offered.

Without pause, he began weaving the tale, "A husband is unhappy about having to work the Sunday right after New Year's. So following work, he blows off steam with his buddies at the bar. Feeling romantic, he buys a bottle of rum to take home to his wife. When he gets home, he finds his autistic stepson still awake and decides the young boy might interfere with his plans. So he gets angry and makes his wife put the little boy to bed."

"How does it sound so far?" posed Thomas.

Spence seemed to wake from a trance and simply responded, "Hum."

Thomas continued, "When his wife comes back downstairs, the husband plies her with liquor until his desire consumes him. She's not as responsive as he might like, so he gets a little rough and takes her on the floor by the couch. He's so excited he doesn't even take off his pants and boots. After what seems like an eternity, he tires of the floor and decides he wants her to perform oral sex as he sits in his favorite chair with his pants still around his ankles. Now, she isn't real cooperative, so he smacks her around a little before she performs her duty."

Again, Thomas paused for affect and inquired, "Sound reasonable?"

Other than a mute glare, Thomas received no response. He pressed on, "About this time the little boy, having heard the commotion, comes downstairs in his pajamas. The husband's concentrating and doesn't notice until the boy's standing next to the chair. Startled, drunk, and angry from lack of sexual release, the husband pushes the wife down, pulls his pants up, and plants a size twelve into the little boy's sternum."

Thomas paused momentarily and then resumed, "The mother's drunk, bruised, and battered but witnesses it all. She attempts to stop the husband, but he grabs her by the wrist and drags her to the bedroom. He throws her on the bed and takes out his sexual frustration. It requires time, but he finally achieves his desired result. At this point, his wife's no longer coherent, partially due to the alcohol and partially due to the physical abuse she's endured."

The grand storyteller, Thomas saved the most important chapter for last. He took a deep breath and finished, "The wife and stepson had gotten used to the abuse, just another day in hell for them. Only this time, the husband went too far. At some point, he went back downstairs to find the little boy had turned blue and wasn't breathing. Still drunk, but sobering fast, he recalls the news coverage of the 'Cradle Killer' and seizes the opportunity."

With that, Payne took another breath and tested, "What do you think of my story, Mouse?"

During the interrogation, Spence had remained still, looking at the floor. Now his entire body shook as he mumbled, "No...No...No...We was just drinkin'. We was really messed up."

Without emotion, Thomas tapped in the final nail, "Mouse, we have a signed statement from your wife indicating she saw you kick the boy. She has old and new bruises on her body. The coroner took a preliminary look at your stepson's body. He has old bruises and a new injury to his chest. It looks like a boot print. He has newly broken ribs and, most likely, damage to his internal organs. We also located an old police case from Maryland where you were accused, but not convicted, of abusing a girlfriend. I can go on, but I think it's time to read you your rights."

With that, Thomas allowed Detective Benson to provide Spence with his rights. As he finished, Spence asked, "Am I goin' to jail?"

Benson looked at Thomas, who stated, "I don't see any way around it."

Spence lowered his head and offered, "We was really messed up. I didn't do nothin' wrong."

As handcuffs jingled, reality seemed to set in. Spence entreated, "If I admit I might have done somethin', can ya let me walk outa here without the cuffs? I don't want nobody thinkin' I'm a criminal."

Thomas overlooked the irony of the statement and answered, "You have the right to an attorney, but if you wanna confess, I think we can leave the cuffs off until we get in the car."

With that assurance, Mouse Spence signed a rights waiver and confession. It stated simply, "I was really messed up. I kicked Jeff in the chest. I got scared, dressed him, and drove him to Thompson Machining. I put him under a blanket."

Confession in hand and Spence in tow, Thomas and Detective Benson rose to leave. They expected their charge to follow suit, but he remained seated with a look of exhaustion and defeat on his face. Only after Detective Benson took him by the arm, did he rise to accompany them. Good to their word, neither officer handcuffed him, but Benson did continue to grasp his right elbow.

They had just entered the hallway leading to the main office when they bumped into Mr. Winters. With a look of concern, he asked, "Everything okay?"

Detective Benson turned to respond, but stopped as Spence, reaching into some hidden reserve of energy, suddenly drew away and made a mad dash for the back door. He would still be running today if not for Robby Franklin, who faithfully remained at his post. Aware the agent stood between him and freedom, Mouse Spence fell into a boxing stance and fired off a hard right hand. A rudimentary tactic, Robby blocked it down with his lead left hand, immediately following with a devastating right elbow to Spence's exposed nose.

Bone connected with cartilage, wounds opened, and blood flowed freely from the smashed membrane. As a result, Spence's fabled boxing career came to an abrupt end on the floor outside the conference room. A witness to Mouse's futile attempt to flee, Winters, who simply wanted to know if everything was all right, remained composed and responded, "I guess not."

Later that evening, a local television network would pronounce, "Steelton police, with the assistance of other law enforcement agencies, have solved a case involving a stepfather killing his four-year-old autistic stepson. What had initially been thought to be the work of the 'Cradle Killer' is now a simple case of drunken rage."

Apparently, the significance and ramifications of the domestic abuse and killing of a young, innocent child paled in comparison to the actions of the "Cradle Killer." The subtleties of casting his battered body into the garbage or the eternal damage done to his mother's soul had gotten lost in the limelight cast by, what the media perceived as, a greater evil.

In a discussion with a friendly journalist a few months later, Thomas would be informed, "A killer in the hand is nowhere near as interesting as one hiding in the bush."

This would lead Thomas to consider with disgust the untenable state of a society which rates its murderers, comparing their malevolent handiwork as they might compare other's accomplishments.

Chapter 17

Wolf at the Door

After his aborted lunch, the man trudged through the rest of his extended workday in a stupor. Though his desires remained, their embers had been largely damped by the morning's events. By 8:00 o'clock in the evening, he returned home to the solitary darkness of his apartment where he contemplated his misfortunes.

He had embarrassed himself at the restaurant. More importantly, he had failed to capture his prey, leaving him no closer to the answers he coveted. On top of this, the afternoon news reporters blamed him for the less significant actions of another. In a sour mood, he felt a regression to a time when his existence mirrored the rain that had fallen on this ass-bite of a day: monotonous, uncertain, and destined for the gutters.

He had spent the remainder of the day working, trying to reconnect with the darkness, and looking for opportunities. In the end, he failed on all counts. Like a ninety-year-old man gazing into an empty bottle of Viagra, his confusion and fear had left him unable to perform.

Now, back in his cut-rate apartment, he stewed in pessimism. He planted himself in his old living room chair surrounded by little light and, for the moment, little sound. As a result of the wild emotional gamut he had experienced in the previous hours, he resorted to doing nothing. He just shut down.

To his surprise, he found the longer he sat, the more composed he became. No longer concentrating on the fatalism invading his thoughts, a door gradually opened allowing his steadfast companion to reenter. Relieved that the darkness hadn't forsaken him, the man unwittingly began the process of viewing his day through a more positive, albeit myopic, lens.

At some point, he resolved he stood a much better chance of achieving his goals if he did as the shadows suggested. This led him to review his actions, in turn conjuring the image of a yellow blanket. This was just one example of how he went beyond the basic requirements of the darkness. His idea, the blanket represented respect for the dead, a concept he had learned as a small child.

The notion to use the blanket came to him after he dispatched the first boy into the darkness of the quarry. He realized he had missed something important. Though he knew nothing about the boy in life, they would forever be linked in death. To remedy this with his last two boys, he not only covered the bodies, but also placed them where they wouldn't remain alone for long. The contrasting nature of his actions went unnoticed by his resurgent mind.

Somewhat more positive now that he had reconnected with the soothing shadows, he stuffed most of the day's events into a box, which he taped up and set off to be forgotten. Only the information about the little boy from Steelton remained available for review. The news of the child interested him. Though almost certain he had nothing to do with the killing, he thought it might provide information to help on his journey.

Focused on his own curiosity, he glossed over the secondary interest of his friend, the darkness. Had he been aware, he would have understood it cared little about knowledge. A simple, but dangerous, entity with a jealous nature, the story of the boy had caught its attention merely because it hated competition.

At that moment, hungry for information, the man noticed the black screen of his television. He had access to the basic cable package, but knew little about the local news stations. Other than the occasional reality show, which held a certain voyeuristic excitement, he failed to see the attraction. To him, television programming paled in comparison to the spectacles he watched in his mind.

Tonight, though, was different. Drawn to the television, he wanted it for what it might provide. He turned on the secondhand twenty-seven inch tube set, only to learn that the local Fox station broadcast the earliest news at 10:00 p.m., two hours away. With nothing better to do until then, he fell back to his routine. He heated a can of condensed chicken noodle soup and tuned the television to some mindless, but mildly entertaining, show in which people paid to terrify their friends.

Time passed slowly as he flicked between channels catching segments of sporting events and a comedy marathon. Occasionally, an argument brewing at his neighbors' caught his attention. A more realistic brand of drama than the television, their squabbles came through his walls in stereo sound at least twice a week. Unfortunately, tonight's row only lasted a few minutes before someone stormed out the door leaving the other to smolder in silence.

Finally, just before the 10:00 o'clock hour, he turned to the news. A primly sexy, brunette anchor greeted her viewers and immediately launched into the lead story. As she spoke, her producers played the same grainy, long distant video he had seen earlier in the day. Then another image gradually appeared showing a yellow piece of plastic covering, what looked like, a small body.

As he watched and listened, he couldn't help but feel anger as he thought, "No. That's not right. That's just not right." The plastic appeared old and spent. He would never use such a thing.

The anchor, particularly serious tonight, conveyed a tale of a husband and stepfather who had angrily kicked his stepson, resulting in the boy's death. He paid particular attention as she related, "The police affidavit, signed by Detective Nick Benson of the Steelton Bureau of Police, reflects that Carl Spence wrapped his stepson's body in a yellow plastic blanket and drove it to its resting place.

128

While police are not speculating, it seems Spence intended to stage the scene in a manner reminiscent of the killer who still terrifies an entire community."

The anchor droned on but said nothing more of consequence. Eventually, she moved to other topics, and he lost interest all together, drifting off into a light sleep filled with memories from his distant past. Transported back to the beginning, the man saw himself as a child. More specifically, he saw himself as an innocent boy about to come face to face with the wolf of his youth and the darkness for the very first time.

At four years old, same as the little boy from Steelton, he lived in a small town in Texas called Crystal City, situated southwest of San Antonio. Born there to a mother who had fled her home and an abusive relationship in Mexico, he enjoyed full U.S citizenship. Though he knew the story, passed to him in later years, actual memories from this place and time had left the shallowest of marks. But that was soon to change.

Just prior to his fifth birthday, his mother, Juanita, announced her intent to bring home a father for her son. She judged every boy needed a father, someone to learn from and look up to. Unfortunately, she settled for the first man to come along and in doing so unwittingly let a wolf into her house. From that day forward his memories began to cleave sharp and everlasting imprints on his impressionable brain.

His new "Poppy," a poor gringo, had been born and raised in Crystal City. A lazy man, he had little interest in working and even less interest in becoming a father. He moved into their house within a week of his mother's proclamation, bringing nothing except a bad attitude, a penchant for drinking cheap whiskey, and an old red truck.

The first month passed slowly, like a walk across a thinly iced pond in the springtime. Though young, the man, then a boy, instinctively knew to tread lightly and remain on the periphery of adult activities. He soon learned the meaning of "underfoot" and "boot up the ass," terms he heard regularly after his mother departed for her menial second shift job.

Then one evening, after he had fallen into a deep slumber in the security of his bed, his door opened, and the blinding light poured in from the hallway. Disoriented from sleep and forgotten dreams, he quietly sat up rubbing his eyes. As his hands came away from his face, they were violently twisted behind his back, a move that flipped him over onto his belly.

The rest he tried to block from his memory, the fetid alcoholic breath, the slaps, and the punches. Amongst the garbled curses, he learned of Poppy's attachment to the television remote, which the boy had moved. Taught his first lesson, he had no idea of the number to follow.

Over that next three years, Poppy visited him regularly, always at night and always filled with liquor and rage. Sometimes it would start as he slept. Mostly it happened while he lay awake because sleep no longer came easily. Slumbering or alert, whimpering or crying, it never made a difference. No one came to help.

From the start, Poppy had taken a perverse pleasure in choking him to near unconsciousness during their sessions. Though he usually closed his eyes, on those occasions when he didn't, his swooning little mind would register the expectant look on his stepfather's face. He wandered what the depraved man saw.

Moments later, winded, yet somehow relieved, Poppy would simply stop. He recalled the silhouette as the light from the doorway surrounded the exiting figure. He remembered the stretched shadow on his bedroom floor moving its long, canine finger to its mouth, making a shushing noise, and slurring, "Ya deserve it, ya lil' leach. Keep quiet. Kill ya next time."

Once, he had nearly gotten up the courage to tell his mother, but she ignored him. Though he persisted, she angrily brushed him away. He never brought up the subject again. He lived with his fear. He lived with the pain.

At that moment, he found himself again seated in front of the television. The same news coverage continued, but now a middle-aged man with a bad comb-over talked about the unusually warm weather for January. The weatherman fought with the clicker controlling the map, while he explained about a cold front dropping in from Canada.

Not interested in the cold or the effect of a warm tract rising from the south, the man's thoughts returned to the lead story. He wondered if the little boy from Steelton had felt lost like he had at that age. Though sorry for the boy in his own dysfunctional way, he also envied him. The boy's stepfather had ended the pain.

He, at least, was at peace.

Chapter 18 (Tuesday)

A New Day Dawns

The next morning Thomas woke beneath the warmth of his covers. As usual, his first thoughts remained tangled in the fading dreams of the previous night, rendering him nostalgic for his wife's sleepy morning scent and the sound of her light breathing. Yet as his body and mind slowly revitalized, the sadness drifted away without lasting impact.

More rested than his fitful nights generally allowed, he rose and began his morning. In the kitchen, he poured a cup of black coffee from the automatic coffee machine and drank slowly. In short time, nature's miracle bean whisked the remaining cobwebs from his brain. Energized, he returned to the bedroom with the intent of dressing for a morning run.

From the pile on the closet floor, he hastily grabbed components of winter running gear. Black pants, green shirt, and blue jacket stood proof he had inherited the dominant male fashion-flaw gene. He topped off his ensemble with a pair of clammy lime green and black running shoes from the cold garage.

Fully clothed after lacing up the frigid footwear, Thomas opened the back door to his suburban two-story home. To his surprise, the sun's warm embrace softened the bite of the near freezing temperatures. Silently, he gave thanks for the welcome change from the previous day's cold and damp weather.

He made his way to the street, checked his watch, and began a slow jog. As his body loosened, he lengthened his stride, gradually building to a six-minute pace. Soon in the zone, muscles forgotten, his mind wandered back to the events of the previous day.

Mouse Spence had been taken to the Steelton Bureau of Police after waking from his involuntary nap and receiving treatment at the local emergency room. Thomas hadn't been surprised in the least when Robbie dropped the great boxer with one well-timed elbow. Both he and Thomas trained regularly and instructed in the mixed martial arts, a fact Mouse Spence may have been interested in prior to his ill-advised flight from justice.

For the remainder of the evening, the task force members had completed reports and discussed the case with the other officers from Steelton and Harrisburg. The possibility of charging Jennifer Spence, in addition to her husband, had been debated, but the decision makers thought it unwise to subject the young, abused mother to the criminal justice system on top of the loss of her only child.

As the evening came to a close, Captain Malino had pulled Thomas aside. Encouraged by the professional work of the task force, he swallowed his last bite of their pizza dinner and confided, "I'll let you in on a little secret. Had this been the same killer, it would've muddied the waters. No one outside HPD knows this, but we've been watching a possible suspect for the past twenty-four hours. He's a wannabe. Works as a security guard."

Malino went on to explain that a city council member who lived near the second victim recalled seeing a blue pick-up truck cruising the neighborhood around the time the boy went missing. The truck bore the clear markings of a private security company located in Middletown. After some discreet inquiries, investigators focused on one particular guard, who the company's owner considered strange.

"It's weak, but it's all we have right now," admitted Malino. "In any event, we had a loose surveillance going last night and knew our guy was nowhere near Steelton for the Englehart thing. Since the cases aren't related, our suspect, shitty as he may be, is still in play."

At this point in his reflections, Thomas noticed he had nearly completed his five-mile course with his house looming in the distance. Still fresh, he sprinted past his driveway, gradually slowed to a walk, and then stretched for a few minutes. Tranquil and loose, he returned to his house where he spent five minutes looking for his newspaper, which he eventually located in the bushes. Though his paper person changed regularly, his or her terrible aim remained consistent.

Inside the house he tossed the paper on the table and turned on the kitchen television. Now the top of the hour, the local ABC affiliate started its news coverage with the Steelton homicide or, more specifically, its differences from the two in the city. Disenchanted with the spin, Thomas turned the TV off in favor of the paper.

He glanced at the headline as he poured a bowl of Special K. In big bold letters, it proclaimed "Latest Homicide Not the Work of CK." Once again Thomas marveled at the slant taken by the media. He pushed the paper aside, refusing to start the day on a sour note.

He busied himself cutting and adding strawberries and then the milk to the cereal. A fleeting smile crossed his face when the liquid caused the flakes to spill onto the counter. His wife used to refer to his morning mess as the splash zone.

Unfortunately, the thought brought with it associated sad memories. So, rather than descend into the pit of his own musings, he concentrated on eating and work. Finished, he cleaned up the devastation he had wrought on the countertop and headed upstairs to shower, shave, and brush his teeth. Half-hour later, ready for the day's challenges, he grabbed his briefcase and headed to the office.

Traffic was heavy and fifteen minutes passed before he eased into his assigned parking space on North Street. He entered the capitol complex through the North Office Building and weaved his way through the clogged post-holiday hallways. Just before 8:00

a.m., he entered the office under the watchful eye of Maggie Bennett.

"New outfit?" he solicited.

"Why yes, and thank you for noticing," she replied. She stood and smoothed her grey skirt and white button down blouse. "It was a Christmas present from the kids."

"Well, it looks very nice. They have great taste."

A smile still lighting her face, Maggie changed the subject and informed, "Two things for this morning. First, Stan will be a little late. He stopped at the HPD to pick up reports. It seems they feel the need for timelier disclosure after the show you put on yesterday. Second," she added, handing over a desk memo, "I hate to start your day like this, but Mr. Murphy called about fifteen minutes ago. He'd like you to call him ASAP."

At the sound of Murphy's name, Thomas frowned but quickly regained his rhythm and stated humorously, "Can we lose the memo?"

"We should," she responded, "since he blamed us for yesterday's meeting fiasco. But, it wouldn't do any good. He knows where we live."

With a laugh, Thomas turned into the main bay and made his way toward his office. As he passed the members' cubicles, he received unusually cheerful greetings from Bill, Doc, and Ronnie. He nearly stopped after noting a few furtive glances, but chose instead to continue on his way.

He shook off his misgivings to concentrate on his pending call to Murphy. He hoped today's conversation would go smoother than yesterday's. In any event, he didn't intend to let the vile little man get under his skin again. Still, his mind flashed back to Bill Murray waking time after time to the same 1960's melody in the movie *Groundhog Day.*

Unbeknownst to Thomas, his reservations while passing through cubicle city had been well-founded. As he sat in his office with the door partially closed and the blinds angled to the side, Robby Franklin made his way into the office. He pushed an overloaded stainless steel dolly that clipped the door and banged into walls. As he struggled, the remaining task force members sat slack-jawed in their seats.

"A little help?" he glowered at his sedentary co-workers.

"Sorry, I only deal with adolescent behavior at home," observed Maggie dryly from behind her desk.

"Come on you weasels." Robby implore the others. "Half hour ago you thought this was hilarious."

He referred to an earlier discussion about the new office equipment, which took an ugly turn when Maggie informed them Stan's chair had broken already. After a reference to the man's great bulk, Bill had commented, "He needs one of those concrete benches from outside." One thing led to another, the gauntlet dropped to the ground, and the members challenged Robby to replace Stan's old chair with the new.

Annoyed by his comrades' change of heart, Robby resorted to questioning their manhood and in Ronnie's case, her womanhood. Sufficiently scolded, the others scampered from their cubicles to help unload and reassemble the seat. They laughed as they built. Finished, they stood back to survey their handiwork.

The first to speak, Ronnie observed, "Guys, that really seems...big."

"Yeah, it looked smaller outside," snickered Robby.

The merriment continued until interrupted by the door buzzer, which indicated someone had tried, but failed, to enter the office. The sound caused everyone to scurry for their seats. The room became remarkably quiet other than the occasional irrepressible giggle.

As Maggie rose to answer the door, she looked back at four sets of pleading eyes. She turned without comment, skirt swirling, and walked to the door. After a quick glance back, she opened the heavy metal slab. Stan stood on the other side, holding a cardboard box.

Without mention of the shenanigans occurring behind her, Maggie said, "If those are more reports, put 'em next to the scanner."

"Thank you, Maggie," responded Stan, after which he made his way into the office.

The tension built as he neared his cubicle and then subsided as he passed by. At the scanner he dropped the box on the floor. His return trip took him back to Maggie's desk for further discussion and another ebb and flow of the emotional waters. Unfortunately for the pranksters, the tide made another complete cycle as Stan passed his cubicle once more on his way to the conference room.

Oblivious to the sighs and groans from behind the partitions, he took his time filling a cup with coffee, stirring in creamer, and stretching his legs. Finally ready to continue his day, Stan sauntered to his cubicle. Wordlessly, he sat. For a moment he appeared ready to speak. Then without comment, he effortlessly centered the enormous chair on his computer screen and began to type.

Unaware of the drama transpiring outside his door, Thomas waited on hold for Deputy Secretary Murphy. Murphy eventually picked up and stated, "Agent Payne, thank you for returning my call."

"As if I have a choice," thought Thomas, but instead replied, "Yes, sir. I just got your message. What can I do for you?"

"Well, I just wanted to congratulate you on helping to clear up yesterday's homicide. I don't have to tell you how ugly things could have gotten if that had turned out to be our third."

The comment caused Thomas to sigh as he finally conceded that the life and death of Jeffrey Englehart had officially become a footnote in the unfolding story of a serial killer. With no attempt to hide his frustration, he responded, "Unfortunately, Jeff Englehart's mother doesn't share that sense of relief. But I understand what you mean."

"In any event," Murphy said dismissively, "I just wanted you to know I talked with the mayor of Steelton. He said the crime wouldn't have been solved so quickly if not for your help."

"I appreciate the kind words, but as usual, it took a team effort."

"One thing I wanted to discuss was the media coverage," said Murphy, again glossing over Thomas' words. "I noticed there was very little mention, if any, of the task force's involvement."

"I can assure you it wasn't by design," responded Thomas. "Chief Smith was very clear during the news conference that the HPD and the Major Crimes Task Force had been involved. Those comments must have ended up on the editing room floor."

"Well, it was a lost opportunity to highlight the good work of your task force," pointed out Murphy.

Though Thomas, cutting through the double-speak, heard, "You lost a chance to point out the good work of the governor's task force," a thought to which he, once again, didn't give voice.

Murphy kept his remaining comments short. As always, he left Thomas' head spinning and his stomach queasy. Payne thought back to Robby's comment yesterday about the difficulty trying to get inside the head of their killer. At that moment, he thought that process easy in comparison to trying to figure out Mark Murphy.

Still, as he rose from his desk, he smiled. At least today he had received a compliment along with his criticism. He continued to smile as he walked into the open bay housing the cubicles. Noting an odd quiet, occasionally broken by the shuffling of papers, he posed, "Ready to get together in the conference room?"

Wordlessly, Robby, Bill, Doc, and Ronnie jumped from their chairs. With heads down, they quickly shuffled into the conference room. To Thomas' surprise, only Stan remained seated.

It took seconds for him to connect the sight of Stan sitting on a concrete bench with noises he had heard while on the phone. Now he understood the members' earlier mysterious expressions. Certain he would hear the explanation soon enough, he simply said, "Nice chair, big man."

As he rose slowly, like a leviathan from the sea, Stan responded with a voice from the same depths, "Thanks, Boss. It's a little stiff, but I think it'll break in nicely." On that note, they walked together into the conference room without further comment.

Strangely, as they entered the room, no one would look at them. In an attempt to gain the members' attention, Thomas cleared his throat causing everyone to look up, except Robby. For his part, Robby remained resolute in his examination of the tabletop until the sounds of laughter broke his feigned contemplation.

He finally glanced up to see that his subjects had deserted him. "That's just not right," he remarked in response to the fingers pointed at him.

Thomas took pleasure in the resulting laughter. He allowed the bonding moment to end naturally after Robby finished describing the lengths to which he had gone to get the chair into the building.

Only when he felt he could laugh no more, due to the stitch in his side, did Payne call the room to order.

Once settled, the group discussed the previous day's investigation in Steelton. While they took pride in the accomplishment, both positive and negative lessons were identified. The process took nearly forty-five minutes and ended with Thomas saying, "Now let's get back to the city's homicides. No need to rehash what's already been said, so I'll open the floor. Ultimately, I'd like to dish out assignments for this afternoon."

The first to speak today, Robby Franklin offered, "One thing we didn't touch on yesterday was the fact that both bodies were found on Tuesday morning. The coroner's report indicates the first victim, Jesus Rodriguez, was most likely killed sometime after lunch on the previous day." He leafed through some papers before finding the one he wanted and paraphrased, "It says rigor was present and the stomach contained green vegetable matter and, most likely, chicken. That's consistent with what Jesus had for lunch at school on Monday."

"The time frame was narrowed if I recall," interjected Bill Travis. "Jesus is reported to have gotten off the bus after school on Monday and then played with friends. One of the boys indicated he last saw Jesus walking toward his house at about 6:00 p.m."

Robby agreed and then continued, "Along with bruising to the head and upper torso, the coroner's report mentions the presence of petechial hemorrhaging in both eyes and damage to the hyoid bone consistent with manual strangulation."

He paused and shifted to the second victim. He added thoughtfully "Though I couldn't find a completed coroner's report for Jamal Wilson, the investigator's report indicates the presence of rigor, petechial hemorrhage, and bruising to the neck. The investigator also documented the coroner's preliminary call at the scene which indicated death as a result of manual strangulation." Focused now on victim number two, Robbie went on, "Jamal left a friend's house to walk home at 5:45 Monday evening. His mother says he's pretty good about being home for dinner at 6:00. As for Jesus, there wasn't always a specific dinner time, but he was generally home by 7:00."

Thomas broke in, "The point being that it appears both boys met our killer at roughly the same time on a Monday evening, two weeks apart."

He looked at Stan and stated, "You've been quiet so far."

"Well, let me drop back for a minute," began Stan. "When I stopped at the HPD this morning, Captain Malino told me about the security guard. In fact we discussed their findings and suppositions at length." Aware Thomas hadn't had time to pass along the information, Stan looked at the remaining members and related, "Two days ago, the city received information which led to a possible suspect." He provided further specifics, but stopped short by saying, "I could provide more details, but to be honest, I think they're looking at the wrong guy. Other than someone seeing a security truck in the area, they have nothing. The company can't even say for sure it was the suspect's truck. They have people working contracts all over that section of the city."

Stan waited then provided another tidbit, "Also, I looked at the background information they've compiled on the guy. Though he's new to the area, which fits the bill, nothing else fits with the typical profile."

"Didn't you say we should expect some differences?" Thomas interrupted.

"Some," replied Stan, "but not this many. This guy's from a stable home, did well in school, and appears to be an extrovert. His only odd behavior is his obsession with becoming a policeman, even though he's failed the physical portion of just about every entrance exam in the area."

"Suggestions?" queried Thomas.

Pensive, Stan finally offered, "I think the captain shares my concerns, but he's getting pressured by the mayor and chief to follow-up on the councilman's information. Luckily, they haven't put all their eggs into that one basket. They're continuing to process evidence and conduct interviews elsewhere. Now, as far as we're concerned, I think we go back to the start. HPD's established a timeline for each victim, and we've developed a decent offender profile. Using both, let's return to those closest to the victims to get a fresh perspective."

"I like the idea of starting anew," responded Thomas. "We need to be on the inside looking out, rather than outside looking in. Reading reports just doesn't cut it."

"If that's the decision," Stan offered, "I have a few more observations. Assuming the profile and initial suppositions are accurate, our actor, most likely, finds himself in that area at that time on Monday evenings."

"So you think Monday is his day?" asked Doc.

"This type offender looks for opportunities. In this case, he's found them on Monday at about the same time which, you've probably noted, is after dark. Most disorganized offenders operate when they're comfortable, and that means their actions need to be hidden. Darkness provides cover."

Stan allowed the others time to digest the information, then warned, "Just because he's found opportunities on Mondays, doesn't mean he isn't in the area other nights. With that said, should he see a chance on another night, I don't think he'd hesitate to strike. A second caution, there may not be significance to the two-week intermission. As of today we're one day over two weeks since he last struck. Still," he finished, "we know *what* this guy's doing and *how* he's doing it through physical evidence. Yesterday we identified the *where*, Allison Hill, and today we identified the *when*, after dark. That's a good start in my book."

The exchange continued and the group debated relevant points for the next few hours. At noon, certain they had a good understanding of the circumstances surrounding both murders, Thomas began to wind down. By 12:15 p.m., with the time for discussion at an end and the time for action at hand, Payne handed out initial assignments.

He hoped they would soon learn the *who* and *why*.

Chapter 19

Big Brother Stan

Assignment in hand, Ronnie and Stan departed for the Allison Hill section of the city. As they walked to the car, they engaged in companionable conversation, leading Ronnie to realize how much at ease she felt around her new partner. He listened intently and provided good advice. This combined with his confident, yet self-deprecating, style and size imparted a sense of support and strength.

As the discussion turned to the events of the previous day, she recognized it had been his presence that tempered the self-doubt which gripped her upon entering the Spence house. Influenced by the insight, she inquired, "Stan, can I ask you something?"

"Only if you expect an honest answer."

Now at the car, she waited until they were inside before asking, "Do you ever get sick of this?"

True to his nature, Stan took a moment to consider her oblique inquiry before responding, "If you mean this line of work, no, not really." He noted the troubled look that dawned on her face. "Don't get me wrong," he clarified, "there are times it gets me down, but for the most part, I love what I do."

Mute for a few seconds, Ronnie rejoined, "I worked abuse cases for a long time before taking the undercover gig. I had to get away. I was suffocating."

She went on to explain how continuously dealing with dysfunctional relationships and the psychological damage associated with abuse had taken its toll. She had begun to internalize the victims' pain. Like mercury, it had slowly seeped into her system, increasing in concentration until it made her sick.

She waited, as did Stan, before she continued, "I took the undercover job because I was running away."

"Why the sudden need to explain?" Stan probed.

Thoughtfully, Ronnie replied, "I guess I needed to hear myself say it to someone else, someone who might understand."

She reflected further as she started the car. Spontaneously, she confessed, "Everyone makes a big deal of me working undercover. But I feel like a phony. I only took the job because there was nowhere else to go." Embarrassed by the admission and losing steam, she finished, "To be honest, I only took *this* job because it didn't focus on abuse."

While Ronnie shifted the car into gear, Stan carefully considered her words. Finally ready to respond, he offered, "Ronnie, I appreciate your trust. So, let me start with an observation. People normally talk about the past because of some effect in the present."

Surprised he had cut through the bull so quickly, Ronnie acknowledged, "You're right. Yesterday, when I interviewed Jennifer Spence, I was scared. I don't mean of her. I was scared I might get that same burned-out feeling from before."

"Did you?"

"I guess at first," she responded. "But it went away. In fact, once I got started, I felt pretty good, like I was in control."

"So why take this job if you didn't think you could cut it? You had to know you might have to interview abuse victims."

He waited patiently as she put her thoughts in order. Momentarily, she responded, "My undercover cases and trials were coming to an end. Since the media plastered my picture in the paper and on the television, I figured I was out of the business for a while. So, when Thomas offered me a job, it forced me to consider my future. My first reaction was to say no, but then I realized I had to do something. Not wanting to go back to just domestic violence cases, this seemed like a better option."

Contemplative, she waited and then added sadly, "Like before, I had nowhere else to go."

An introspective man, Stan took time to pick through the information presented. Relating Ronnie's information to situations from his own past, he submitted, "People aren't always happy with their jobs or their lives for that matter. Everyone has good and bad days. That's life. Some people dwell on the bad. They flounder in it. Most are easy to pick out because they bitch and complain and are basically worthless. Others," he emphasized with a glance, "are harder to spot. They soldier on, internalizing their feelings. In either case, the trick is to get them to see the positives. For instance, I don't believe anyone could have done a better, more professional job than you yesterday. In the end you helped a lot of people. That's something you can be both proud and happy about."

In the intervening silence, he decided to inject some levity into the counseling session. "As I said, sometimes life's just crappy," he started. "Think of the job like a sewer worker. Most of the time they work above ground in the sunshine, but occasionally someone has to go down into that big dirty pipe to clean out the clogs. Now, the public would never think about going into the sewer, much less rooting out someone else's crap, but somebody has to do it. Imagine if no one were there to keep it working. The trick," he continued with a wink, "is to get in and back out without getting splattered with shit."

He smiled at his own choice of words and posed, "In other words don't let the bad stuff stick."

The analogy, though humorous, did make a warped kind of sense thought Ronnie. She had spent time in that pipe and had begun to drag her feet. She had let her work weigh her down. Yet more important than this insight, she realized that someone else actually understood. Just knowing someone could relate to her plight afforded needed consolation.

They continued to chat for the next five minutes until they reached their destination, a large red brick double on Crescent Street near Swatara Street. One tree among many in a formerly proud early twentieth century forest of homes, it had born witness to countless smiles and tears, and the laughter and fears of multiple households of first and second-generation immigrants. Now, simply habitable, its absentee landlord only made enough repairs to keep the city's codes officer off his back.

Ronnie parked the car along the street to the north of the structure. She took note of the heaved concrete sidewalk leading to the dilapidated wooden porch, the old, but solid, hardwood doors, and the black wooden cross hanging from the window of the right-hand unit. This had been the home of nine-year-old Jesus Rodriguez, the first victim, prior to his untimely death.

The reality of her task at hand, she unexpectedly sighed, "Well, here we are."

"Chin up, chica." Stan advised, noting the morose tone. "Control *it*; don't let *it* control you. Stay positive."

Surprised and embarrassed by her reaction, Ronnie apologized and put on her professional face. During the walk to the front door, she asked, "When you talked to Captain Malino this morning, was he aware we were going to speak to the victims' families?"

"Not then," he responded. "But Thomas called him right before we left. He liked the idea of someone going back for a fresh look."

At the front door, Ronnie stood to the side and knocked. It opened almost immediately at the hand of a small, grey-haired elderly Hispanic woman, who asked, "Está la policía?" (Are you the police?)

Ronnie replied, "Sí, le he llamado hace una hora." (Yes, I called you an hour ago.)

At this point, a younger woman carrying a squirming infant came through the dining room and interrupted their conversation. Short and heavy with long dark hair and dark eyes, she introduced herself as Clementina Rodriguez. She handed the baby to the older woman and spoke in rapid fire Spanish, resulting in the woman scurrying off to the back of the house.

After she inspected their identification, Clementina invited the agents in and closed the door. As they sat on the old, but clean, furniture in her living room, she directed a comment to Ronnie, "Like I told you on the phone, I'm not sure what else I can tell you that I haven't already told the other police."

"Well," Ronnie responded, "we just want to clarify some statements we've seen in reports, plus give you an opportunity to ask questions."

"Questions?"

"Sure," said Ronnie, moving closer, "you must have thought of some questions in the past month."

Clementina considered the offer and, seeming pleased, responded, "Thank you, nobody's offered that before."

On this positive note, Ronnie and Stan walked through the biographical data and details of Jesus Rodriguez' last days. Of note, his mother indicated her son had last been seen by a friend, Antonio

Martin, who lived down the block. The boys had played until about 6:00 o'clock when Antonio went home.

When Ronnie asked where the boys typically played, Clementina replied, "All over the neighborhood. I tell the children to stay off the street, but they don't always listen."

"How many children live with you?"

Clementina hesitated and then answered, "I have two other children."

Ronnie breathed deeply and avowed, "Look, Clementina, we're not from Immigration. We're not concerned about status right now."

Clementina looked at the ground, obviously wrestling with her thoughts. "Sometimes my sister's kids are here too. That's four more," she mumbled.

Ronnie moved quickly away from the sensitive, but extraneous topic. In the next few minutes, she asked numerous relevant questions, including the address for Antonio Martin. Finished with her portion of the interview, she offered, "Well, that's all I need for now. Can I answer any questions before we leave?"

After a pause, Clementina inquired, "Are the rest of my kids safe?"

Ronnie debated how much to tell the young mother. She glanced at Stan and then responded, "We're doing our best to find the criminal who took your son away. I promise you that."

"With that said," she admitted, "I'd keep my children close until we do."

With nothing further to gain at the Rodriguez residence, Stan and Ronnie bid the grieving mother goodbye. As they stepped off the porch, Stan stretched his long, meaty arms and observed, "The air always seems so clean on a bright, cold day in the winter. It never fails to lift my spirits."

He winked at Ronnie, which caused her to impart, "I think I'm over it for now. No need to tiptoe around."

"I don't usually get accused of tiptoeing," he professed. "By the way, for not feeling on your game, you did good work back there. The rest we can work on. As they say, Rome wasn't built in a day."

"Great, now I'm a work in progress."

"Aren't we all," returned Stan. "Aren't we all?" He laughed before adding, "But enough philosophy. Now," he said with a flourish of his hand, "let's get to our next interview."

Ronnie thought for a moment and then stated, "I don't think Antonio will be home for about an hour. He's still in school."

"That's okay," said Stan cryptically. "We have one other interview before his."

Chapter 20

Of Love and Anger

Headed out the door, Robby posed, "Wanna grab a quick bite before we start the interviews? I didn't get breakfast this morning."

"Whose problem is that?" questioned Thomas.

"Come on, man," he pleaded. "I'm getting weak."

"And whiny," Thomas finished, but relented. "Okay, what's close?"

"How about O'Malley's? I've never been there, but I hear it's good."

With a nod, Thomas turned left toward North Third Street. A well-known capital eatery since the early 1960s, O'Malley's sat directly across from the capitol. It drew most of its breakfast and lunch crowd from the capitol complex. As such, its walls and booths had witnessed and provided cover for more than fifty years of deal making between the state's movers and shakers.

Before he even entered, Thomas could smell the delicious aroma of cooked meats, soups, and desserts. He hadn't thought himself hungry, but his growling stomached told him otherwise. Once inside, the agents threaded through the masses to two open spots at the silver-fronted counter. Along the way, they passed numerous legislators and lobbyists, who went about the business of spinning facts and massaging massive egos.

No sooner had they sat on the round stools when a young woman inquired if anyone had waited on them. Dressed in skinny fit jeans and a buttoned-down, long-sleeve white shirt, she didn't look like the other waitresses. Of above average height with a lean, lithe body, the woman wore her raven hair cut boyishly short. Her bright brown eyes and white teeth reflected the room's light. Not beautiful in the classical sense, she, no doubt, would still turn heads in a room crowded with women.

When Thomas asked to see a menu, she smiled and pointed behind the counter to a large board containing the menu items for the day.

Equally guilty of overlooking the five-foot by eight-foot rectangular sign, Robby, nevertheless, chided Thomas, "So much for all that time and money spent training you to observe and detect."

Sheepish, Thomas stammered, "Sorry, we just started working across the street recently. This is our first time."

Laughter lighting her face, the woman responded, "I'm just playing with you. I can get real menus if you'd like."

Unexpectedly, Thomas found himself feeling awkward, even nervous. Normally poised, his composure seemed to crumble beneath the glare of her optimistic energy. Not only beautiful, she seemed so alive.

"Let's start over," she said, noting his discomfort. "My name is Breanne, Breanne O'Malley." She waited, but no response followed. "And now gentlemen, it's customary for you to introduce yourselves."

Like two grammar school boys caught misbehaving, Thomas and Robby did as requested.

Not ready to let them off the hook, Breanne queried, "And what might you boys do across the street?"

First to speak, Robby related they worked for the state's Bureau of Criminal Apprehension. This seemed to pique her interest, which led to a brief discussion about crime in the city and ultimately to the "Cradle Killer." When she sensed neither Thomas nor Robby wanted to discuss the murders in depth, Breanne turned the conversation back to lunch, asking, "Well, I don't want to keep you from your work. Have you decided what you'd like?"

Caught up in the conversation, Thomas hadn't had time to look at the menu. Standard fare at most lunch spots, he responded, "Could I have a turkey sandwich on whole wheat with a side of fruit and water." In the same awkward position, Robbie seconded the choice.

Breanne efficiently took the order and glided away to provide it to the staff. Over her shoulder, she commented, "It's good to see you're eating healthy. Most of our customers like what's bad for them." Her face lit up when she added, "I guess that's why our legislators always seem unhappy. They're probably all constipated."

Both agents burst into laughter as she disappeared into the kitchen. Once calmed, Robby looked at Thomas and rebuked, "Smooth Romeo."

Embarrassed, Thomas replied, "What?"

"She was hitting on you."

"You're crazy," claimed Thomas. "She probably thinks I have a brain injury and feels sorry for me."

"We'll see," Robby responded. "We'll see."

For the remainder of lunch, they quietly discussed the afternoon's activities, starting with their interview of the second victim's mother. Twenty minutes later, conversation and meal finished, they prepared to leave. As a tall, thin blond waitress passed by, Thomas casually asked for the bill.

"Brea said no bill," she replied.

Taken aback, Thomas waited for the waitress to return and asked to speak with the manager. In reply, the waitress informed, "That would be Brea. You could argue with her, but she left for the warehouse."

Unable to wait, Thomas thanked the woman and laid a twenty on the counter. On the way out the door, he complained to Robby, "I hate it when people comp the cop. I can pay my way."

"My friend, that had nothing to do with either of us being cops. Twenty years off the market has dulled your radar."

Stubborn, but not stupid, Thomas recognized the truth in the comment. He sighed, "I didn't really know what to do. I've been married for such a long time."

"Thomas," Robby stated soberly, "you haven't been married for five years now. You know how much I loved Lynn, but she's gone. And knowing her the way I did, she wouldn't want you to spend the rest of your life alone. So, maybe it's time to open a new chapter."

"I don't know if I can," responded Thomas honestly.

Robbie remained quiet for most of the walk to the car. When they neared the parking spot on North Street, he hazarded a comment, "I know women have shown interest in you over the past few years, but you never reciprocate. This was different. You can't tell me you're not attracted to this woman."

Too quickly, Thomas responded, "I'm not."

Now at the car, Robby snickered, shook his head, and repeated for the third time, "We'll see."

In an effort to short-circuit Robby's romantic observations, Thomas quickly changed the subject. "I was just thinking about something that caught my attention yesterday. Did you happen to notice any change in Ronnie's demeanor when I assigned her to interview Spence's wife?"

"Not really, why?"

"Well," thought Thomas out loud, "she seemed out of sorts at first. It was almost like she hadn't expected it or was disappointed."

"I didn't see any change," Robby responded thoughtfully. "And Stan couldn't have been more impressed with her interviewing skills. That's like Ted Williams saying you're a great hitter."

"Maybe I'm reading too much into it," conceded Thomas. "Even so, how about keeping an eye on her to make sure she's all right?"

"No problem, boss," answered Robby with a smile. "If you haven't noticed, which you probably haven't, she's not too hard to keep your eye on."

Before the subject returned to the opposite sex, and Breanne O'Malley in particular, Thomas said, "How about programming the GPS with the Wilson's address."

His comment had the desired effect, shifting Robby's focus to the task at hand. As he entered the information into the computer, Robby asked, "Who do you plan to interview?"

Grateful the discussion had turned away from his personal life, Thomas responded, "I spoke with Latisha Wilson, the second victim's mother, on the phone. She said she'd be home this afternoon. Let's start with her and see where it leads."

As they discussed strategy, the bodiless voice of the GPS interrupted. In the sultry voice of a waking movie starlet, it informed Thomas to turn right onto Fourteenth Street. Not one to argue with a lady, he did as directed. Eyes on the road, he asked, "How far?"

"Four or five blocks, near Hunter Street. Just listen to the babe in the box," Robby answered, before correcting, "Then again, if she's like most women, she'll be upset for some strange reason and send us to the wrong place on purpose."

"Speaking from personal experience?"

"Is there any other kind?" answered Robby with a mix of humor and philosophy. "By the way, I like her Aussie accent," he laughed.

"Yeah," responded Thomas, "I fired the British girl, one too many wrong addresses."

As if making formal introductions between people, Thomas mocked, "Robby, meet Claire. Claire, this is Robby. You'll find he's a little emotionally closed off, but he's good to have around for heavy lifting."

"Too bad you don't have an option for an Irish voice. We could call her Breanne."

Lost for words, Thomas was saved further embarrassment by the GPS, which interrupted, "Your destination is two tenths of a mile on the right."

He drove an additional block until the GPS declared, "You have reached your destination on the right."

In vain, Thomas searched the main street for a parking spot. Forced to continue past the location, he turned right at the first side street. Much less congested, he pulled the vehicle to the curb and parked approximately thirty feet from the corner and the sign indicating Hunter Street.

As the growl of the engine subsided, Robby observed, "Did you happen to notice the lack of cars parked along the street, except in front of the Wilson house?"

"Hard to miss."

They exited the car and walked toward Fourteenth Street. On the way Thomas inhaled the familiar winter scent of wet, decaying leaves wafting up from the thawing ground. He noticed the sidewalks and roadways had finally shed the past days' rain. In addition, as he turned the corner from Hunter to Fourteenth Street, he discerned a mix of well-kept and rundown residential structures. Probably built around the First World War, some remained brick while others exhibited aluminum siding, most likely, covering brick.

At the dirty white porch fronting the Wilson residence, Thomas asked, "Did you happen to notice the voices coming from inside the house?"

"Hard to miss," returned Robby. "How do you wanna play this?"

"Let's knock and see what happens."

In tandem, Thomas glided to the left of the door, Robby to the right. Robby had just reached out to knock when the door opened and a tall, heavy-set black man asked if he could help them. Robby introduced himself and Thomas, indicating they had called ahead to speak with Ms. Wilson. The man took time to examine the proffered identification and badges before he allowed them inside.

As the agents crossed the threshold, the spirited conversation occurring in the house ceased. Amidst the now deafening silence,

Thomas and Robby found themselves the objects of ten sets of dark staring eyes. Awkward and tense, Thomas broke the quiet by introducing himself and Robby to the crowd.

He quickly scanned the room, noticing four females, two of the correct age to be the mother of Jamal Wilson. "Would one of you be Ms. Wilson?" he inquired.

Hesitant, a tall young black woman stood and indicated, "I'm Latisha Wilson, Jamal's mother." Though she stood, she made no attempt to offer a hand or place the agents at ease.

As the room fell quiet again, Thomas bridged the distance, extended his hand, and stated, "Ms. Wilson, I'm very sorry for your loss. I apologize for interrupting your grief, but is there some place for us to speak privately?"

She lost her chance to speak when a large, broad-chested black man stood to her right and took over. Radiating distrust, he said, "I'm Shaun Wilson, Latisha's brother. I think whatever you got to say, the whole family should hear."

Thomas glanced at Robby, who discreetly added separation, thereby increasing the target area should the interview turn physical. "Okay, no problem," Thomas responded as he examined the room for potential threats. "But before we get started, how about we go around and make introductions?"

Shaun Wilson contemplated the request as the others looked to him. Reluctantly, he nodded and introductions began. Those present included Latisha's two brothers, sister, mother, grandfather, and grandmother. The three other large men in the room introduced themselves as cousins, which immediately set off the bullshit meter in Thomas' brain. Beyond size, they bore little family resemblance.

Finished with the preliminaries, the room once again fell into an uncomfortable silence. Thomas hid his disappointment that the mood hadn't changed. If anything, it seemed to have gotten worse. Regarding Latisha Wilson, he asked, "Are you comfortable speaking in front of everyone, or would you like us to come back?"

Again, the young woman hesitated, allowing her brother Shaun to angrily interrupt, "Look, agent-man, I said the whole family should hear, 'cause I think you up to somethin'. Jamal was killed two weeks ago and we ain't heard nothin' from the po-lice since then. Now, all of a sudden, more cops show up."

He paused for effect, "I think the news people're right. Some crazy dirty cop's killin' our kids and y'all are tryin' to hide it." He didn't waver before adding, "This some crazy shit, cops killin' kids. Now you're probably back here so y'all can pin it on the brothers."

Puzzled by the adversarial direction of the meeting, Thomas concluded, "Maybe it'd be better if we come back later."

Shaun Wilson moved closer. With a stab of his thick index finger, he pronounced, "If you plan on walkin' out'a here, you'd best tell us what's really goin' on right now, boy."

Not one to ignore a threat, but hoping to stop the situation from spiraling out of control, Thomas responded succinctly and without emotion, "Mr. Wilson, I recommend you calm yourself. We're here for one reason, and that's to help find the person that took your nephew."

Unfortunately, Shaun Wilson wore his distrust and anger on his sleeve. He responded loudly, spraying spit as he alleged, "Y'all no different than them motha fuckers from the city." A preacher from the pulpit, he looked around the room for support and continued, "It's time we show you sorry asses to the door."

With that, Shaun Wilson, who would never be called a smart man, moved aggressively toward Thomas. As he did, the room filled with the sounds of gasps and shuffling feet. In the midst of the growing commotion a scream loosed, and a metal folding chair overturned. It struck the wooden floor with the ring of a cymbal or, more appropriately, the bell of a prizefight.

And that's when things, as they say, went to hell in a handbasket.

Chapter 21

Billy the Kid Meets the Hitman

As matters degenerated on Fourteenth Street for Thomas and Robby, Maggie and Doc, plodded away in the task force office. Nearly finished scanning reports into the database, Maggie stated, "Doc, you're a genius. The hardest part of this process is taking the pages out of the binder."

Pleased with the compliment, Doc turned away from the three monitors on his desk and responded, "More important, the information is immediately available to Overlord."

Prepared to expound upon the virtues of his creation, Doc fell silent as Bill Travis hurried past. With a wave, Bill apologized, "Sorry, don't mind me. I'm late. I'll be at the HPD for most of the afternoon." For Maggie's benefit he added, "I'm on the board."

To his surprise, he found minimal foot traffic in the hallway and little vehicular traffic on the streets. With ten minutes to spare, he reached the police station and began his scan for a parking space.

Four complete circuits of the block later, it became exasperatingly apparent where all the traffic had gone.

Reluctant to walk into the meeting late, Bill used the hands-free cell link to inform Captain Malino of his plight. A familiar issue on the city's tight streets, Malino advised, "Parking around here sucks. If you can't find a spot, make one. Just put a placard in the window, and no one will bother you. I promise," he added cynically.

Bill followed the captain's suggestions and located a spot next to a dumpster in a side alley. He parked directly beneath a no parking sign and prayed for the best as he placed his police placard on the dash. At the front of the building, he showed his identification and received entry through a locked steel door. Escorted up one flight of concrete steps to the second floor, he made it into the conference room just as the afternoon briefing began.

Introduced after Captain Malino called the meeting to order, Bill chose a seat in the back of the room. Technically an outsider, he sat quietly and listened as, one after the other, investigators paraded to the podium providing frustration laced renditions of conducting numerous interviews with little to show. Last to speak, the head of the surveillance detail summed up the meeting by grumbling, "Cap, we're wasting our time on this security guard."

"Tommy," responded the captain, "we don't have a choice. Not only did the information come from *a* councilman, it came from *the* councilman who could very well be our next mayor. You all know how the game's played," he said, looking around the room.

"The councilman lives in the area, so he wants to show he's doing something. He happened to see a white guy cruising the neighborhood the night a boy went missing. If it happens to be the right guy, he's golden in the next election. If he's wrong, he's just a good citizen providing information."

"But Cap," pleaded the investigator, "this dude's done nothing but work, go to the bar, and go home for two days. He hasn't even gone near The Hill since we've been on him."

Malino recognized the truth in his subordinate's words. To appease the man, he offered, "Give it one more night. If we get nothing, we'll pull out."

Not completely satisfied, the investigator mumbled in reply, "If this guy did it, I'll drop my drawers in the square and let you spank me."

"What's that, Tommy?"

"Oh, nothing, Cap," came the reply among some laughter. "Just saying we can use our people better and you'll thank me."

Malino had serious doubts about the veracity of the answer. Nonetheless, he chose to move on by saying, "I got an interesting call from the coroner this morning. He talked to the funeral director who buried both boys. The director told him when he washed the bodies, they smelled of gasoline." He paused before adding, "The coroner said that made him think back to the autopsies. He says he smelled gasoline as well, but attributed it to workers renovating the hospital basement. Thinking he might have missed something, he called the lab to check on the body swabs." His own frustration now evident, Malino directed his next comments to one particular member of his audience. "Unfortunately, they're not finished with the lab work and won't provide any information until the testing is complete."

In response, the focus of his gaze and lead investigator for the Rodriguez homicide, Detective Terry Hassinger, proposed, "I'll contact the coroner and scientist as soon as we're finished here, Cap. See what I can do."

A throwback to the gumshoes of the 1950's, Terry Hassinger stood nearly six feet tall with a burly build and receding brown hair. Dressed today in a tailored suit and Italian loafers, Bill thought he resembled a mafia hitman. As if to validate the thought, Hassinger immediately turned his sights on Bill and commented, "Since the lab's part of the BCA, maybe Agent Travis can help light a fire."

Thankful he had, thus far, made it through the meeting without sticking his foot in his mouth, the comment caught Bill off-guard. Now in the spotlight, he responded self-consciously, "Uh, I'd be glad to do what I can."

With the agent's discomfort evident, Malino quickly redirected the discussion. "Okay, Terry, you get with Bill and follow-up on the gas smell. Tommy, one more day of surveillance and I'll find something else for your guys to do. Everyone else, see me for your assignments." With nothing more on the agenda, the captain signaled the meeting's end and added, "Anything earth-shattering happens, let me know right away."

Jon D. Kurtz

As the members filed to the front of the room, Detective Hassinger gathered his paperwork. A policeman for over twenty-five years and a detective for fifteen, he had worked with many local, state, and federal investigators, some good, some not so good. He wondered into which category Agent Travis would fall. Prepared to find out, he approached Bill and stated, "Let's get to it." Then, without missing a beat he added, "Did anyone ever tell you that you look like Harry Potter?"

Caught flat-footed once already, Travis reacted without hesitation, "No, but I once was mistaken for Dirty Harry."

Hassinger chewed on the comeback, before he snorted and held out his hand. "By the way, I'm Terry Hassinger. Glad to meet you."

Bill responded in kind as Terry led the way to his desk. They discussed the case for a few minutes, before Terry related, "I'd intended to work on the blanket angle this afternoon, but Cap wants this gas thing checked first."

"Maybe we can do both," Bill submitted after consideration. "If you don't mind passing the blanket off, that is. I think I know just the right person for that assignment."

After Bill explained and received the go-ahead, he used his cell phone to contact Doc Patel. He would have laughed hysterically had he seen Doc's reaction to the forgotten phone vibrating deep within his pocket. Eventually answered, Bill heard a sigh and, "What's up, Bill?"

171

"That's my line, dude," Bill countered, suffering a momentary bout of immaturity.

At a loss, Doc, the MIT graduate, did his alma mater proud by responding, "Huh?"

"What's up...Doc?" laughed Travis.

Familiar with the cartoon reference, Doc replied, "Simple pleasures for simple minds."

"That's not very nice," chided Bill. "But I'll let it pass since I need you to do something for me."

"Well, you may not be very funny, but you do have good timing. We just finished scanning the reports."

Doc listened to Bill's request, hiding his growing excitement. Eager to start, he pronounced, "Your wish is my command, Saheeb."

Cognizant that Doc's family had immigrated generations ago, Bill retorted, "You're truly a piece of work. If nothing else, hanging around you is interesting."

Like the nerd when a cool kid recognizes his presence, Doc beamed. Prepared to respond in a manner demonstrating he deserved the compliment, he found himself at a loss, answering, "Ah, thanks," which he reasoned sounded hip in a minimalist kind of way.

Satisfied he had provided clear instruction, Bill said goodbye and turned back to find Detective Hassinger on the phone with the coroner. Efficient with his questions, Terry verified the information relayed by Captain Malino regarding the gasoline smell. Ten minutes later upon hanging up, he advised, "The coroner corroborates what Cap passed on. Now let's see if you can work some magic with the lab."

With Terry's desk phone on speaker, Bill contacted the BCA forensic scientist responsible for the case. While willing to discuss the case in general terms and provide specifics about the processes involved, she hesitated to offer conclusions. After twenty minutes of unsuccessful cajoling, his patience waning, the ring of Bill's cell phone saved him from alienating a co-worker. Phone to his ear, he heard "Tag, you're it."

"Doc, I'm in the middle of a conference call," he whispered. "What do you need?"

"I think we can track the yellow blankets to an owner."

"How can you do that?" Bill questioned, looking at the clock. "I only asked you to start looking thirty minutes ago."

Proud of his success, Doc provided the details, "Knowing your fondness for summaries, I'll make it short. First, Overlord noticed a discrepancy in the size of the blankets in evidence when compared to those offered for sale by the manufacturer, a company named Trilo Coverings and Mylar Products. After hanging from a few branches of the company's phone tree, I found the reason. They only made two runs of one-thousand in that particular size. Apparently, it wasn't a big seller. They sold the items to a wholesaler in Atlanta, who then sold them locally to the Big Box Discount chain."

"How many locations in the chain?" interrupted Bill.

"I'm getting to that," returned Doc. "They have six stores in Pennsylvania and Maryland. The closest are Middletown, Mechanicsburg, and Gettysburg."

Though Doc had done well with his summary to this point, as Bill expected, he eventually began to prattle. With increasing detail, he explained how cooperation had dissolved as his inquiry moved further out from the manufacturer. Eventually, getting to the point, he stated, "The owner of the Big Box Discount chain won't give up anything without a court order."

Bill, who had waited patiently for Doc to finish aggrandizing his accomplishments, smiled to himself and responded curtly, "Listen Poindexter, you've been working for the task force for what, a whole week?"

He let the question hang in the air, and then, softening his tone, he added, "And I have to admit, that's some damn good police work." He could almost see Doc's face change as he baited him with his comments. "Give me the information, and I'll put together a search warrant to serve this afternoon. While I do that, get back to the people at the outlet to see if they can compile the information so it's ready when I arrive."

"I have a better idea," returned Doc. "The owner seemed less than enthusiastic about helping out. So write the search warrant to include not only written reports of the data but also access to their electronic sales record files. Pick me up on the way. I'll bring a laptop loaded with Overlord. If he won't cooperate, I should be able to access the data, import it into the program, and search it on my own."

Bill agreed with the plan and took the information Doc had obtained for inclusion in the search warrant. He spoke to someone in the background prior to indicating, "Listen Doc, I have to get back to this other call. They're nearly finished." Just before he hung up, he added, "I'll be over to get you in a little bit."

Returned to the lab discussion, Bill was in time to hear a woman's voice state, "Look Detective, it's against protocol to provide any information before all testing is complete. However, I promise to rush the work. If all goes well, it should be done tomorrow. That's the best I can do."

Not happy, but acceptant, Terry breathed mightily before assenting, "Okay. Whatever you can do will be helpful."

He hung up, looked at Bull, and declared, "Well, that was worthless." After which, he softened and said, "Ah, I'm sorry about that. I shouldn't take it out on you. I appreciate you setting up the call."

Undaunted by the complaint, Bill offered, "You might appreciate this even more."

Bill explained Doc's discovery. Concentration soon replaced the look of pessimism that had invaded Terry's face. Deliberations now complete, the older investigator announced, "You know the blanket angle's a long-shot."

"Better than no shot."

As the truth of the words hit home, Terry slowly smiled. He declared, "Okay then. Let's get to it, kid."

Bill smiled back at the detective's choice of words and his change in mood. He retorted, "After you, old timer."

"It shouldn't take more than an hour to get the warrant together," Terry said, overlooking the impertinent remark. "We can pick up your computer guy, go to the magistrate, and be at the Big Box Discount Outlet by about 4:00 o'clock. Give me the information, and I'll fill out the search warrant template."

Focused on the task before them, Terry surprised Bill when he deadpanned, "By the way, that *old timer* comment was hurtful."

Facilitated by good humor and Terry's unexpected speed and dexterity on the computer, the search warrant took only a half hour to complete. Finished ahead of schedule, Bill attempted to call Thomas to provide an update. Unsuccessful in two tries, he commented, "No one's answering. They're probably off having fun. Let's go get Doc."

As they walked toward the door, Bill asked, "My car or yours?"

"What's your ride like?"

"A relatively clean late model sedan with a full police package."

"What size engine?"

"A good-sized V-8," Bill said proudly.

"Let's take your car," Terry stated. And then he added, "Can I drive?"

The request made Bill laugh. Policemen loved big engines. Somewhat embarrassed, he replied, "Sorry, man. You have to be employed by the state. It's a self-insurance issue."

Undeterred, Terry reached for his wallet. He displayed the portrait of a beautiful young woman in a silky evening dress and offered, "I'll introduce you to my daughter."

Bill's judgment faltered as he studied the goddess from the wallet. After a time, with a dry mouth and high voice, he responded, "Ah man, I can't."

The obvious conflict caused Terry to laugh loudly. As they walked to the door, he confessed, "That's okay. That's not really my daughter. The picture came with the wallet."

Chapter 22

The Blanket

In bed immediately after the news, the man had spent the night seesawing between light sleep and wakefulness. When semi-alert, his mind continued to dredge up unwanted memories of his stepfather. During the rare periods of slumber, it siphoned energy from his failed lunch to paint incredible images of the mysterious storm.

Near morning, as the tempest of his mind whipped up a particularly threatening display of light and sound, he woke with a start to his alarm. Though it quickly faded, the dream left behind its imprint of impending doom. As typical, once roused in this fashion, he found himself feeling sick to his stomach or, depending on the theme of his dream, in a state of sexual arousal. Last night he had experienced both conditions, not once, but numerous times.

Well acquainted with insomnia and its best friend fatigue, the man had dragged himself from bed and prepared for work. He spent the morning mechanically answering calls and avoiding people.

Though he tried to concentrate, his mind wandered with the changing scenery. By mid-day, it strayed into dangerous territory.

Eight years old again, that night came flooding back. Properly inebriated, his stepfather had paid him a visit. Only this time, Poppy treated him with more contempt than usual. Though the boy, now a man, tried to be quiet, on that night he couldn't help but cry out in pain.

Eyes clasped shut as his stepfather loomed over him, he missed the shadow stealing across his doorway. Only after hearing the roar of rage did he chance a look through his tears. He watched in amazement as his mother swung a cast iron frying pan at her husband. Swung hard, but not true, it caught Poppy a glancing blow on the shoulder.

Possessed of an unusually volatile temper stoked by alcohol, his stepfather retaliated. He pushed the petite woman into the wall, denting the sheetrock and causing her to drop the frying pan. Up quickly, she yelled in angry, guttural Spanish. Unfazed, Poppy hit her in the mouth with a closed fist. As if in slow motion, he remembered seeing her head snap back and her mouth and nose erupt with blood, spit, snot, and teeth. He witnessed fear in his mother's eyes before they rolled back in her head.

Not satisfied with having knocked his wife witless, the loving husband wrapped his dirty fingers through and around her long hair and dragged her out of the house onto the front lawn. There he proceeded to kick his bride for the next few minutes. Finally, convinced he had taught the little bitch a much-deserved and unambiguous lesson, he lurched back inside and promptly passed out on his bed.

No one noticed or, at least, seemed to care as his mother received her punishment in the front yard of their old house where he had been raised. No one came to her aid. Not even him, he recalled with shame. He remained in bed with the covers pulled over his head.

In the end, his guilt gave him courage. She had tried to help him.

He snuck from his room and outside to where she lay on the grass-bare front lawn. At first glance, she seemed to be resting peacefully on her back. Upon closer examination, he experienced short-lived relief, thinking this couldn't be his mother. Then reality swept over him, allowing him to see through the bruises, blood, and swelled tissue. Though unfamiliar, this body belonged to the woman who had brought him into the world, raised him, and unknowingly let the wolf slink across their threshold.

Gently, he touched her shoulder. He looked expectantly at her battered face. He quickly determined that while her eyes remained open, they saw nothing. Though he had just heard her scream, he knew she had taken her last breath. Slowly he retreated into the shadows.

Forced to look away, he glimpsed a shiny object on the ground near the house. Next to a sneaker, which had recently resided on his mother's foot, he found her cherished silver lighter. Given to her by her grandfather, its brushed silver surface displayed an engraving on one side of ducks flying over water. Always fascinated by the sound of its top clicking open and its ability to bring forth fire, he took possession of his lone legacy.

Again, he sidled back into the darkness, where he stood frozen. His eyes locked onto the horror before him. Not until he heard the distant sirens did he begin to return from his shock-induced trance. Summoned by spineless, anonymous neighbors, reflections of flashing lights soon announced the arrival of the first police car. Now mesmerized by the explosion of sights and sounds, he shifted his eyes away from his mother's still form and returned from the brink of madness.

Stillness and quiet now gone, he witnessed a police officer check his mother for signs of life and begin CPR. This continued until the arrival of the paramedics, who took over. Moments later, they confirmed what he already knew. "She's gone," one stated.

With this, the policeman slowly backed away into the shadows. Moments later he returned carrying a shiny yellow blanket. The boy watched as he straightened the tangled and torn clothing. Next, he crossed the arms over its chest and straightened its legs. Satisfied with his work, the cop draped the blanket over the ruin that, an instant before, had accommodated his mother. Nothing exposed, the policeman denied the vultures and looky-loos their next meal. Only years later as a man would the boy understand the significance of this simple act of respect.

For the rest of the evening, he shuffled from one adult to the next. The police asked him questions. The social workers whispered conspiratorially to each other. In the end, the county children and youth caseworkers whisked him away to begin his ten-year odyssey moving from one unsatisfactory foster residence to another.

Two visual memories imprinted themselves on his youthful mind as he left behind the only home he had ever known. Stuffed in the back of a county owned sedan, he recalled the image of his bloodied stepfather being dragged from the house through the brown fiberboard door. He heard someone in the car say he must have resisted arrest. Second, he remembered the yellow synthetic blanket the policeman had placed over his mother's broken body.

Though he had many recollections of the wolf of his youth, his mother's final night was by far the most painful. For the most part, he had successfully avoided this particular memory. Yet tonight, he found it actually made him feeling better. While thoughts of his stepfather normally brought distress, this, the most poignant of all, brought with it clarity. Guided by the shadows, he realized the events of that night had shaped the person he had become. Once ordinary, he now traveled a solitary road on a vital quest. But for the wolf, he would be nothing.

Fueled by this revelation, his ever-changing outlook progressively improved. His sole remaining regret, he had wasted yesterday, a Monday, a hunting day. Not a pleasant thought since he would, most likely, have to place his desires on hold for another week. Interestingly, the probability of not receiving immediate gratification made him want it even more.

At this point, lost in his thoughts as he cruised near Italian Lake, his radio lit up with an assignment from dispatch. Pulled from his personal contemplations, he refocused on work, but not before he made a decision. Though the previous afternoon had been a shit storm, followed by a ball-busting night and an ass-crack of a morning, he needed to push aside his recurring doubt and complete his journey.

So, it seemed, the man, not long ago on the verge of falling apart, had regained some of his lost footing. Unfortunately, for the people of one Harrisburg neighborhood, his gain normally led to someone else's loss.

Chapter 23

The Warehouse

On the sidewalk outside the Rodriguez house, Stan noted the bemused look on Ronnie's face as he suggested an interview prior to Antonio Martin's. "See that?" he said, glancing toward a home located diagonally across the street.

"I saw curtains moving," she replied, still confused.

As they crossed the street, Stan explained, "Every neighborhood has a resident or two that sees all and knows all. Normally, it's an older retired person or couple." He pointed to the front bay window of the structure and said, "When we pulled up, I noticed an elderly woman watching from that window. When we left the Rodriguez', there she was again. I call that an invitation."

With that said, Stan led the way up the steps of the well-maintained two-story structure. Decked out in new beige vinyl siding and energy efficient windows, the house also boasted a small front porch recently built with darker synthetic lumber. A beige screen door protected the mahogany front door and its shiny brass knocker.

Stan bypassed the decorative doorknocker and poked a sausage-sized finger at the doorbell. An audible chime sounded within the house. After fifteen seconds and no response, he tried again. Rewarded with more silence, he looked at Ronnie and said, "I know she's in there."

Consequently, he pushed the button twice more before opening the screen door and using the knocker. Determined to make contact, he continued until he heard the sound of hard soles against a non-carpeted surface. The patter increased in speed and volume and then stopped on the opposite side of the entryway. Stan envisioned the woman peering through the peephole, prior to hearing the deadbolt slide back. As the door swung open, both he and Ronnie instinctively glided to the sides, allowing the screen door to close silently on its own.

As one door opened and the other closed, a small, thin black woman with curly white hair appeared. A formless cotton dress with buttons running up the front hung loosely on her shrunken frame. The pastel color matched her stockings and tan walking shoes.

Behind the thin Plexiglas window, she examined her visitors. Her gaze stopped as she locked eyes with the largest of the pair. Hands on her hips, she snuffed, "Stanley Brown, you likely broke my door with all that pounding. Let me look at my knocker to make sure you didn't destroy anything with those huge paws of yours."

Ronnie looked at Stan with amusement as she saw her earlier confusion transferred to his face. Wheels turning rapidly in his mind, the light bulb finally lit. He blurted, "Ms. Emily?"

The woman responded, "In the flesh or, at least, what passes for flesh these days. Now, would you mind explaining what's so damn important you needed to break down my door?"

"Yes, Ma'am. But only if you open that door and give me a hug."

The comment seemed to relax the old woman, who opened the screen door as she shook her crooked index finger and declared, "Now go easy on me. I'm little and old. If I remember, you never did know your own strength."

"Ms. Emily, it's awful good to see you," said Stan after a gentle hug. "It must be twenty years. You look great."

"Well," she retorted, "you're probably right about the twenty years but wrong about me looking good." She cackled and added, "But then again, I'm ninety-two years old. I'm not supposed to look good. I'll soon be traveling to meet the good Lord, and He wants me humble when I arrive."

In a more serious tone, Stan asked, "Ms. Emily, would it be all right if my partner and I come in to speak with you?"

The old woman pondered the question. After she gave Ronnie the once over, she acquiesced, "Since it's you. Come on in."

Neat and orderly, the inside of the residence displayed brightly polished hardwood floors and antique furniture. The predominant scent, pine cleaner and soap, reminded Stan of his muddy shoes, which he removed and placed on the rug. He glanced at Ronnie, who did the same.

Ms. Emily walked them to the kitchen where she invited them to sit at a large wooden table with benches on each side. Without debate, she put on a pot of water to boil and laid out a plate of cookies. She hummed as she worked and didn't stop until satisfied with her efforts.

Now seated at the table, she revealed, "Stanley, I know why you're here. You want to ask me about that boy that got himself killed."

"Yes, ma'am," admitted Stan. "But first, I'd like to introduce my partner, Ronnie Sanchez. We both work for the Bureau of Criminal Apprehension."

Ronnie and Ms. Emily exchanged pleasantries, which ended with Ms. Emily winking at Stan, and saying, "You two are like beauty and the beast." The statement caused Ronnie to blush and Stan to drop his head. In response, Ms. Emily laughed and added, "Boy, you'd better lighten up a little. I was just pulling your chain."

Stan tried to respond only to be interrupted by the whistle of boiling water. Wordlessly, Ms. Emily turned and began hustling around the kitchen. When she returned, she placed three steaming cups of tea on the table and disclosed, "It's my special tea. It's good for what ails you."

So, as they drank tea and ate cookies, Stan spoke to Ms. Emily about the neighborhood. She related she had lived there for the past thirty years or so, since retiring. She talked about the families coming and going over that time and the other houses falling into disrepair. Stan guided her to talk about the children from the neighborhood, to which she responded, "During the winter, I don't see too many of the neighbors, other than Bob and Audrey who live next door. In the summer, I spend a lot of time on my front porch watching the children play."

"How about the Rodriguez children?" asked Stan.

"Well, they mostly stayed on the other side of the street."

The discussion remained on the children for the next few minutes, but little of consequence came to light. As the conversation wound down, and Ms. Emily began clearing the table, she nonchalantly inquired, "Did you check at the foot of the hill?"

"What do you mean?" queried Stan.

"Stanley Brown," she said with a disappointed tone, "don't you remember being a kid?" Noting his blank look, she offered, "Cameron Street?"

"You mean the children play down on Cameron Street?" he speculated.

"Stanley," she stated, "when you were their age, wouldn't you have been drawn to the noise of the traffic? Include the weeds, trees, and trash and you have a perfect playground for young boys. More important," she added, again shaking her finger, "the building at the bottom of the hill is vacant. I bet a dollar their parents don't know it, but in the summer they play around that old building all the time."

Stan considered the statement and questioned, "Do they go there in the winter?"

"I'm not really sure," she responded. "As I get older, which I didn't think was possible, I not only look but also act more like a bear. I spend most of the winter inside."

Stan and Ronnie spent the next twenty minutes obtaining further details from Ms. Emily. Finally, with no more information to be gained, they prepared to leave. As they walked to the front door and slipped on their dirty shoes, Stan inquired, "Ms. Emily, did you tell any of this to the local police when they came by?"

Embarrassed, she mumbled, "Well, some police did come to the door, but I didn't answer it. I probably wouldn't have answered this time, but it was you, and you always were so damned headstrong."

Disappointed, he understood many women of Ms. Emily's race and age still distrusted authority. Without hesitation, he produced a business card to which he added his home and cell phone numbers. He handed it to the old woman saying, "Ms. Emily, it sure was nice talking to you. If you think of anything else, or if you ever need anything, please call me."

Before they walked out the door, Ms. Emily hugged not only Stan, but also Ronnie. In a whisper, she told the younger woman, "I always knew he'd be a good man." Prior to letting go, she added, "Be careful, you two."

Now seated in the car, Stan noted the expectant look on Ronnie's face. "She was my teacher in high school," he offered.

"She'd retired, but was always in the building substituting or volunteering. She used to call me her 'diamond in the rough.'"

As the car went silent, Ronnie took the opportunity to note, "I get the feeling she sees you more as a finished gemstone now. Plus," she added with exuberance, "once a teacher, always a teacher. She schooled us about the kids playing down on Cameron Street."

Stan nodded his head as he continued to reminisce. A few seconds later, he stated, "I wanted to focus on Jesus' case first because he's the first victim we're aware of. If our perpetrator follows a normal progression, he'll have made more mistakes in his earliest crimes."

"You mentioned before that these crimes probably weren't his first. Why wouldn't we know about any others?"

"They may have occurred somewhere else. His actions are still very disorganized, but evolving," he explained. "I don't think he's committed a large number of murders in the past, but maybe a few. And on that note," he added after a thoughtful pause, "we need to enter the case information into ViCAP. If similar crimes have occurred around the country, we can connect with the investigating agency." He referenced the FBI's Violent Criminal Apprehension Program.

"Speaking of databases," responded Ronnie, "I noticed the HPD already checked the Megan's Law database for sex offenders in the area. So that avenue's covered."

"Okay," Stan said, "then our next move should be to speak with Jesus' friend Antonio. He should be home from school by now. Then we'll look at this building on Cameron Street."

Priorities identified, Ronnie pulled away from the curb. Focused ahead, neither agent noticed the movement of the curtain in Ms. Emily's living room. As if a breeze had passed through the white lace fabric, a single panel drifted away from the window frame. Oblivious to the surveillance, they continued down the block for approximately three hundred feet before stopping in front of another two-story brick double in need of repairs.

As Ronnie shut down the vehicle and opened her door, Stan turned to her and probed, "You still okay?"

"Good t'go," she responded, smiling at his concern.

After two knocks, the door opened at the hand of a young Hispanic woman. Of medium height and weight with the usual dark hair and eyes, Ronnie thought her pretty in a tired sort of way. With an inscrutable stare, she examined the two agents before asking, "Can I help you?"

"Mrs. Martin," responded Ronnie with a smile, "I'm Agent Ronnie Sanchez, and this is Agent Stan Brown. We work for the Bureau of Criminal Apprehension. We've been asked to help with the recent homicides that have occurred in the area. Would it be possible for us to come in and speak with you?"

The young woman sighed in annoyance, but turned and acquiesced, "Come on in."

She led them into a large living room populated with the same inexpensive, but sturdy, furniture they had observed in the Rodriguez home. In addition, what Ronnie could see of the house impressed her as extremely clean and orderly. As standard procedure, Ronnie showed her identification to Mrs. Martin and said, "You didn't ask, but to put you at ease, here's my badge and ID with picture."

"I knew who you were as soon as you came to the door," the woman replied with only a casual glance at the items. "You look like cops. Plus, the car gives it away."

Stan smiled and nodded for Ronnie to continue. She explained, "We'd like to speak with you and your son about the death of the Rodriguez boy."

"I know why you're here," the woman responded, irritation evident once more. "Do you have to talk to Ant again? He took it so hard. He and Jesus are best friends." She hesitated and then quietly corrected herself, "At least they were."

"I'm afraid so," Ronnie apologized. "Antonio may be able to help us clear up some important points."

Silence and staring ensued, but eventually Mrs. Martin conceded, "His bus should get here any time."

While they waited, the conversation focused in general terms on the Martin family and the dynamics of the neighborhood. Mrs. Martin, who asked to be called Reya, related that she, her husband, and Antonio had lived in their rented home for almost three years. She explained the adults in the neighborhood didn't interact much, but the children all played together. This exchange continued until the big yellow bus roared past.

Moments later, the wooden porch steps squeaked, suggesting the man of the hour had arrived. After a few unsuccessful attempts, the caller eventually conquered the lock and entered. Backlit against the outside light, the small form of Antonio Martin came into view. Less than five feet tall, well under a hundred pounds, and constrained by his bulky outerwear and heavy backpack, he labored to close the heavy wooden door.

Ronnie and Stan witnessed the struggle and stood in greeting as Antonio dropped the backpack to the floor. He shrugged out of his coat, which ended up on top of the pack, prior to realizing he had an audience. He first saw Ronnie and smiled. Then he spotted the man-mountain to her right. His eyes opened wider the further his head went back. Stan sat back down.

First order of business, Reya chastised her son to clean up his mess. Next, she introduced him to both agents. Warily, he crossed the floor and sat next to his mother. As he relaxed, Ronnie promised, "Antonio, we won't stay very long. We just want to talk about your friend Jesus."

The boy remained silent, his view alternating from the floor to his mother. Politely, Ronnie asked "Is it all right if I call you Antonio, or would you like to be called by another name?"

He looked at his mom and then offered, "Ant."

"Everyone calls him Ant because it's short for Antonio," explained his mother.

This seemed to offend him as he corrected, "They call me Ant 'cause I'm so small, but that's okay. I don't really mind."

Ronnie grinned and suggested, "You have plenty of time to grow. Plus," she added with a wink, "the other boys may be taller, but I'm sure they're not as handsome."

The comment seemed to please both Antonio and his mother.

Ice now broken, both Ronnie and Stan began their inquiry. First they asked general questions about the neighborhood children and then specifically about Antonio's friendship with Jesus Rodriguez. The night of Jesus' disappearance, they saved for last.

"Ant, can you tell us about the vacant building you guys play around on Cameron Street?" asked Ronnie, fishing for a reaction.

The question had the desired result. Antonio's eyes went wide, his breathing became rapid, and he shifted nervously in his seat. Ants in his pants, he looked at the wall and declared, "I'm not allowed to play there."

"We know you boys were playing there the night Jesus disappeared," she lied.

Caught, he looked up quickly and asked, "Who told?"

His comment had the effect of angering his mother. Ronnie feared they might get thrown out. But she needn't have worried as Reya Martin began to vent on her son, "I told you to stay away from there. You never told the other police about that building."

In an effort to calm the escalating emotions, Stan interposed, "It's okay, Momma. No problem. We just need to hear the truth now. Ant could help us catch a very bad man."

Still angry, she, nonetheless, allowed Antonio to continue. He went on to explain he and his friends not only played around, but also inside the old building. The admission further infuriated his mother, but he carried on, "Jesus and I were playing Army that night. But we left way before it got dark."

As the conversation progressed, Antonio indicated after playing in the building, they hung out on the bank until his mother called him for dinner. He said goodbye to Jesus, and they both started toward their own houses. He added in an attempt to minimize his lie, "I told the police all that. I just left out the part about the building."

"Ant, did you see Jesus go inside his house?" probed Stan.

Antonio thought for a moment and then responded, "I don't think so. The other police asked the same thing. I think he was just walking in that direction."

Stan inquired further, "Can you think of any reason for Jesus to go back to the building?"

Antonio's head dropped, and he seemed to be wrestling with his conscience. He looked up and answered, "Yeah."

"Go on, Ant," prodded Stan.

"We were on the bank looking for Jesus' gun."

"Gun!" gasped his mother.

Quickly, Antonio clarified, "It was just a branch shaped like a rifle, long and straight with a wishbone on the end. Jesus left it lay somewhere. He wanted to go back to the building to check, but it was already dark. I told him we could do it tomorrow."

Antonio continued to scoot around in his seat, showing his discomfort. This led Stan to offer, "Ant, we're almost done."

He allowed the boy a moment to compose himself. Once settled, he asked "How did you and Jesus get into the building?"

"There's a loose board on the window next to the side door."

"Was it dark inside?"

"Not so much during the day," answered Antonio. "The windows by the ceiling let in some light."

Their discussion continued for another five minutes until Antonio seemed to have given up all the information left out of his earlier interview with police. The agents thanked both mother and son and made for the front door. At the threshold, Ronnie handed Reya a business card. "Ant's going to need to speak with someone, a counselor. If you want recommendations or just need to talk, call me."

The young mother looked at the card for a long moment. She considered her words before saying, "Thank you for caring." Tears welled up in her eyes.

Ronnie gave her a quick hug and turned to lead the way back to the car.

Once safely ensconced behind the doors of thick Detroit steel, Stan commented, "You did a good thing back there. And," he added, changing tact, "as for young Mr. Martin, I can say for certain the boy isn't in trouble with the law."

He stopped and then finished his thought, "But if I read Mom correctly, Ant may have a hard time sitting tonight."

Chapter 24

The Buzz Saw

While the investigation continued to move smoothly for most of the task force members, Thomas and Robby had run into a little snag. What started as a simple interview had turned into an old-fashioned brouhaha. Emotion swelled to action, chairs and shouts flew, and combatants and civilians separated.

Shaun Wilson reached to grab Thomas' coat. He had just touched fabric when he suddenly and unexpectedly found himself on his knees, examining the floor with his right arm locked out behind him and torqued above his head. With their leader in a bad way, the second Wilson brother and the three cousins moved in. They had no idea they had entered the mill and run directly into the buzz saw.

As Shaun's brother shifted his weight to begin a football rush, Thomas looked for the inevitable opening. Unaware and untrained, the large man charged forward. His reward, a thrust kick to the groin, sent him crashing to the floor. He writhed in agony as Thomas continued to crank on Shaun's wrist.

At the same time, Robby drove a heal kick into the left thigh of cousin number one, sending him to the floor. Off balance, cousin number two fell over his downed comrade. Now alone, the remaining cousin raised his hands and slowly backed away to the door.

In a span of three seconds, the melee concluded. Eyes upon him, Thomas asked calmly, "Are you done being stupid?"

Between clenched teeth, Shaun Wilson responded, "Yesss."

As Thomas released his grip, the defeated man sat and then stood. He looked Thomas up and down and then granted, "Time to go to jail."

Thomas contemplated Shaun's words. He turned to his audience and offered, "This family's been through enough. Start acting like adults, and we'll consider this a learning experience."

As heads nodded, Thomas continued, "We don't have any hidden agenda, and we don't have time for bullshit. We're just trying to help."

He let the comment hang in the air until the grandfather broke the silence by stating, "I think it's time for everyone to go home." He looked at Thomas and added, "You can talk to Latisha, but I want to be here."

Reluctant to reject an ally, Thomas responded, "No problem, Mr. Wilson. Where can we talk?"

"Here's fine. Everybody's leaving."

Still wary, Thomas and Robby waited for the room to clear before beginning the interview. They smiled as the youngest Wilson brother limped across the threshold. Holding his crotch, he whined, "Ain't no fair kickin' a brother in the testicles, man. If I can't have me no kids, I might sue."

Embarrassed and angered by his grandson's parting words, Mr. Wilson yelled, "Get the hell outta here." Then he added for good measure, "Best if you didn't have kids anyways."

He turned back to the agents and apologized, "I'm sorry. The boys have a notion the police are involved in Jamal's death. The news people have the whole neighborhood wondering." He paused for a breath and then added, "They've been in trouble before, but have jobs now and are tryin' real hard."

"Mr. Wilson," offered Robby, "we're here for one thing, and it's not to mess with your grandsons."

Wilson acknowledged, "Seems you could've put a whoopin' on 'em if you'd had a mind to, so I'll trust you for now." He added, "Let's get on with it, before I change my mind."

With a precarious truce in place, Thomas immediately set out building the foundation of Jamal Wilson's victimology. While most information had already been covered by the HPD, one important point received clarification. Asked to explain the relationship between her son and victim number one, Jesus Rodriquez, Latisha Wilson answered, "The boys probably went to the same elementary school, but I don't remember Jamal mentioning the name. He mostly played with kids from around here and his cousins."

When they showed her a map of Allison Hill indicating her address and that of Jesus Rodriguez, she declared, "That's six blocks and some busy streets. Jamal wasn't allowed to go that far by himself." A distant look filled her eyes as she added, "He didn't always listen, but he was a good boy."

At this point, tears began to form, and the discussion came to an uneasy end. Thomas sensed further questions would be futile and inappropriate. He thanked the young woman and her grandfather. As the agents prepared to leave, Latisha Wilson inquired, "When can we get Jamal's things?"

Reluctant to lead her on, Thomas disclosed, "That's up to HPD, but normally they keep anything needed for lab testing or the trial. Is there anything in particular you're interested in?"

She thought and then replied, "I gave him a wristband he always wore. It's one of those yellow rubber ones with the letters WWJD. They stood for 'What Would Jesus Do?' I swear, he'd a worn that thing 'til it rotted off his arm," she reflected.

In answer, Thomas offered, "We can check with the investigating officer if you like."

"I'd appreciate that," she said.

As they moved for the door, Latisha Wilson fell silent. She pulled back into herself. Her large frame seemed to dissolve into the cushions of the chair. As he passed over the threshold, Thomas took a final look back to confirm she hadn't disappeared, absorbed by her own sorrow.

One of the few parts of his job he disliked, intruding upon the grief and heartache of others, exemplified, what he considered, the cop's Catch Twenty-two. If he spoke with a victim's family, he brought them distress. If he didn't, he could never provide them with a resolution.

At the front porch, Thomas stopped and again thanked Mr. Wilson. Somber look etched into his weathered face, the older man imparted, "It's just not right for a momma to have to bury her baby. Catch the man that done this. Make sure no other mother suffers." Mentally and physically exhausted, he turned and slowly walked back into the house.

Left in his wake, Robby asked, "You okay?"

"Yeah," answered Thomas. "They were...predictable."

"Yep. Hardly worth the trouble," stated Robby.

"Let's just keep plodding," countered Thomas, trying to remain upbeat.

In his heart though, he sensed slow and sure might not win this race. The situation seemed to be moving faster, like the proverbial snowball rolling downhill. He just hoped they could get ahead of it before the killer struck again.

Chapter 25

A Trip to the Outlet

Doc stood along North Street with his computer bag draped over his shoulder as the unmarked police vehicle ground to a stop inches away. In response to Bill's urgent gestures, he hurried to the curb. As he reached for the door handle, the car leapt forward.

Initially surprised, Doc's expression changed to displeasure at the sound of Bill's laughter. Now accustomed to the agent's occasional childish taunts, Doc collected himself and walked coolly to the car. For the second time he stretched for the door handle only to have it wrenched from his grip as the car rocketed forward. Anger and embarrassment showed on his face. He was left, quite literally, standing alone, holding his bag.

His change in demeanor didn't go unnoticed. "All right, I'm sorry," Bill shouted out the automatic passenger side window. "I'm just messing with you. Be a sport, we have to get going."

His plea fell on deaf ears.

Suddenly concerned he may have gone too far, Bill turned to Terry Hassinger, who was in the front passenger seat, and acknowledged, "I'd better go make up. We need him."

As he exited the car, he never heard Terry mutter, "When will these kids ever learn?"

On his way to catch his infuriated coworker, Bill threw out apologies and more pleas. Not until he reached the door of the building did Doc turn to face him. Prepared for the worst, Bill watched with relief as the frown on Doc's face slowly changed to a smile.

Bill assumed he had been forgiven, when suddenly he heard tires squealing behind him. Drawn to the sound, he turned in time to see smoke rising from where his car had been parked. He watched in disbelief as his grey state-owned ride fishtailed around the corner and disappeared from sight. Behind the wheel sat Terry Hassinger, a wide grin plastered across his face.

"Lose something?" inquired Doc innocently.

Stunned, Bill ignored the question and Doc's growing laughter and growled, "Son-of-a bitch."

Approximately two minutes later, Bill's commandeered police car slid around another corner with tires barking, tore up the block, and came to rest at the curb. Bill smelled burnt rubber and heard the exhaust tick as it rocked to a stop. With the window still down, Terry called out, "Hey sailors, need a lift?"

He laughed as he exited the car and extended a hand to Doc. Introductions made, Terry returned to the passenger seat and Doc jumped into the back. Left alone on the sidewalk, Bill stood speechless until Terry asked, "Ready to go…sport?"

Humbled, Bill lowered his head and returned to the now vacant driver's position. He intended to remain silent in protest, but Terry broke the ice by deadpanning, "You guys're a lot of fun. We'll have to do this more often."

The comment made Bill recognize how comical the whole scene must have looked to someone watching. Anger flushed away, he joined in the laughter. The three hooted and talked as they made the fifteen-minute sojourn to the magistrate's office in Middletown. Once in the parking lot, Terry put on a serious face and imparted, "Okay fellas, time to get professional."

Half hour later, Bill signed on the line, attested "I do," and took possession of the warrant to search the records stored at the Big Box Discount Outlets' headquarters. The judge bid them good luck indicating, "Gentlemen. I wish you Godspeed in finding this man."

They wasted no time in returning to the car. In the driver's seat again, Bill maneuvered to the edge of the highway and asked, "Which way to the outlet?"

"Go back into town and down the main street," answered Terry. "It's about two miles from here."

Five minute later, they reached the outlet complex and parked in front of a newer two-story section signed "Corporate Office." Inside the brightly lit foyer, a pretty blond haired girl of about twenty inquired from behind a sliding glass window, "Are you here to see Mr. Branton?"

"Yes, ma'am, we are," Bill answered with his most disarming smile. "Could you tell him Agent Travis from the Bureau of Criminal Apprehension is here?"

Taken in by Bill's flirtatious manner, the young woman giggled as she moved from the window and let them in a side door to her left. "You're quick," Bill complimented once inside. "We never even made it to the window."

She laughed and pointed to a bank of monitors on the wall, "Mr. Branton said to expect you. I saw your car pull up."

Alerted to their presence, a man, presumably Mr. Branton, came down a metal staircase from the second floor. He made no attempt to hide his study of the three men before him. As he closed, he introduced himself as Marc Branton, CEO and owner of the Big Box Discount chain. Of medium to tall height, he appeared trim and displayed a mostly bald pate. To Doc, he queried, "Can I assume you're Officer Patel?"

"Yes, sir," responded Doc, "but it's just Mr. Patel or Raj if you prefer."

Doc introduced Bill and Terry before saying, "Mr. Branton, we don't want to take up too much of your time, so I've come prepared to search your database myself."

Anger seeped from behind the calm façade. "You never said anything about *you* searching the customer records," forced Branton. "You only mentioned *us* providing information."

In an effort to defuse the situation, Bill placated, "Mr. Branton, we're only looking for data regarding the sale of one specific product. Doc thought it'd be easiest if he conducted the search."

Bill could immediately tell his comments hadn't pacified, but angered Branton. The man's head and ears glowed red. "No one ever said anything about *you* searching through my database," huffed Branton again, confirming Bill's observations. "We're very protective of our customers' information. Plus, the system's old, and the girls and our accountant are the only ones familiar enough to get what you want. It'll still probably take hours."

Patience gone thin, Terry Hassinger unexpectedly put his arm around Branton's shoulder and guided him to a back corner of the office. Doc and Bill watched as he spoke in a hushed tone to the business owner. Thirty seconds later they returned, and a more submissive Branton said without emotion, "Follow me upstairs."

A minute and no further conversation later, they stood at the desk of a small man, whom Branton identified as his accountant, Carl. At this point, Bill felt it appropriate to provide the owner with his copy of the search warrant. He explained the document in detail as Doc took the opportunity to speak with the accountant. Finished and ready to get down to business, he interrupted Doc's conversation and asked, "You ready?"

Doc nodded and spoke with the accountant for another thirty seconds in a computer language only they understood. He then sat at the man's desk, lit up the keyboard, and plugged in his laptop. A few keystrokes and another minute later he looked at Bill and reported, "Done."

He turned to Branton and added, "If it eases your mind, sir, I extracted the applicable material without any trouble and without compromising any non-related data. In other words, the only information we'll be seizing is that specific to our investigation."

Flabbergasted, Branton responded, "You're kidding?"

In response, Doc spun the laptop around, exposing a detailed spreadsheet of all blankets sold since the original purchase. He explained, "All the data is included on this worksheet for future search and review."

"That's amazing. It'd take the girls hours to compile that information."

Branton continued to stare at the laptop, now with more interest than anger. While the others remained intent on the wonders of the computer world, Bill pulled Terry aside. In a whisper he probed, "What did you say to him that changed his tune so fast?"

With a shrewd smile, Terry answered, "I made him an offer he couldn't refuse. I said if he didn't let Doc do the search, I'd do it myself. I also told him I know just enough about computers to fuck up his entire system."

"Would you have really done it?" Bill asked.

"Damn right, I would have."

Back with the group, Bill interrupted Doc's sermon, "Doc, we need to boogie. Please give Mr. Branton a receipt for the information seized, and we'll be on our way."

The paperwork took minutes. Document in hand and database intact, Branton shifted uncomfortably from foot to foot. He looked like a little boy who had mistreated a playmate. "Well, I guess that wasn't as bad as I'd thought," he admitted.

Embarrassment on display, the three investigators did nothing to lessen the man's discomfort. Eventually, he broke down and offered, "I jumped to a few conclusions. I'm sorry. I should've given you more of a chance to explain before I reacted."

"No problem, Mr. Branton," allowed Bill. "We got what we needed; that's what matters. Now it's time for us to run." Then, he added pointedly, "We can't be wasting time. Someone's killing children."

As they enjoyed the sheepish look on Branton's face, the investigators collected their belongings and headed for the steps leading back downstairs. On the descent, Bill remained quiet while Branton quizzed Doc further about computers. For his part Terry contented himself by watching and listening.

In the main office again, he noted Bill Travis throw a look and what might have been a wink to the pretty receptionist. From behind, he heard Branton whisper to Doc, "The state probably doesn't pay very well. Ever consider going into private work?"

With a smile, he realized, "My life has just gotten a lot more interesting."

Chapter 26

An Unexpected Opportunity

When he reached the Shipoke neighborhood in the south end of Harrisburg, the man realized he had neglected to mark down the address for the call. Reluctantly, he re-contacted his dispatcher, who acted annoyed but repeated the name and address. Never in a good mood, she seemed to look down upon everyone, or, at least, she looked down on him.

He briefly considered making her a side trip on his journey but quickly set the idea aside. In a physical sense, she did look down on him. A big girl, she towered above him and outweighed him by a hundred pounds. She also possessed an unpredictable temper and had hands the size of ham hocks.

He feared a confrontation with the Amazonian would most likely result in her knocking him to the ground after which she would take great pleasure in repeatedly kicking him in the nuts. To make matters worse, he pictured her accomplishing this while gorging on a giant, greasy, barbequed turkey leg that she would use, in the end, to knock him unconscious. Involuntarily, he shivered and shifted his weight in the seat.

Now on Showers Street, his thoughts returned to the matter at hand. He gazed at the yardless row homes packed along the narrow roadway. "More of an alley," he thought as he edged down the block. Eventually he stopped in front of a familiar turn of the century three-story brick structure.

To his chagrin, the homeowner, Ms. Henrietta Bower, stood expectantly in the doorway, awaiting his arrival. An elderly lady who craved conversation, she regularly called with "emergencies." His coach had warned him about the lonely old woman, joking, "She'll talk your ear off and reattach it so she can talk some more."

With a cringe, he parked and notified the dispatcher of his arrival. Reluctantly, he took his clipboard from the passenger seat and trudged to the front porch, where he endured ten minutes of mind-numbing dialogue about children, grandchildren, and great grandchildren. Overjoyed when the family history lesson concluded, he found himself in a deeper hell when she smoothly transitioned into a scintillating discussion of the weather. Eyes glazed and head spinning, he terminated his business prematurely and scurried back to the safety of his vehicle.

Once inside, he threw his clipboard onto the seat. He ignored the woman's dejected look as she stood on her porch peering through the vehicle's closed passenger side window. Given the chance, she would have jabbered for hours. Conversely, he limited his interaction with adults to a minimum, only the facts and only that necessary to complete his work. Though he masked it well, his formative years had left him emotionally stunted and anxious around anyone but children.

With undisguised haste, he fled the scene. He had just reached the end of the street, when his mobile radio came to life, broadcasting the voice of the witch from dispatch. She repeated his vehicle number and inquired, "Bart wants to know if you'll be able to finish all your calls for today."

Though her tone remained even, he interpreted it with a nasty edge. Her manner alluded to his inherent laziness. His blood boiled. His hand shook as he checked the log for the rest of the day. After a quick perusal, he estimated he had four hours of work to accomplish in the final two hours of his shift. He stewed in the recognition that he would have to validate the thoughts he attributed to her.

Though angry, he picked up the black microphone and responded calmly. Rewarded with silence from the radio and laughter in his mind, attributed to the woman from Amazonia, he continued to simmer. Five minutes later she returned and stated, "Bart says to finish what you can and plan to work later tomorrow to catch up."

Initially exasperated by the contempt he perceived in her words, his resentment quickly dissipated. As the words sunk in, he realized he would be working tomorrow until after suppertime. At this time of year, that meant darkness, and darkness provided opportunities.

The longer he reflected on the change, the more excited he became. An event of this magnitude didn't happen by pure chance or dumb luck. Someone or something must have an interest in him or his experiments. Maybe the darkness had more power than even he suspected.

He felt a resurgence of energy as he pondered possibilities. His thoughts seemed to clarify. Outwardly more lucid than moments before, he decided he had been letting his mind wander too much lately. The examination of recent explorations had become a distraction. Providence had just provided a wake-up call.

He needed to move forward to create new memories and experiences. While the past provided comfort, it hadn't and wouldn't offer the explanations for which he yearned. He had killed three times, yes. But he still had no answers. Even though he had fresh memories, they ultimately only punctuated his failure and, as he had learned the previous day, with failure came conflict and confusion.

Now, invigorated by the prospect, he felt something close to joy. Not true joy he knew, but it would do. Once again, the singular thought had focused his muddled mind. He could feel the familiar and welcome energy building in his brain, building in his arms and abdomen, and, especially, building…down there.

With renewed vigor, he believed his answers lay as close as tomorrow. Additionally, the reminder that he no longer toiled in solitude provided balm to his wounded psyche. Though he had felt the darkness within and around him during the past six months, he had remained ignorant to the true extent of its power.

At that moment, as he ran *from* Mrs. Henrietta Bower, he also ran *toward* his destiny. He smiled for the first time since yesterday's aborted lunch. Just as he had on two special Mondays in the past, tomorrow he would manipulate the schedule to ensure his presence on The Hill after dark. Given an unexpected present from the shadows, he didn't intend to look that particular gift horse in the mouth.

It never dawned on him that, as the proverb indicated, his gift would be another man's, or in this case, boy's curse.

Chapter 27

Evidence Bonanza

Stan and Ronnie pulled onto Crescent Street, leaving Antonio Martin and his mother inside their residence to discuss certain punishment. "Make a right on Berryhill and go down to Cameron," Stan directed.

As they neared the intersection of Berryhill and Cameron, he noted, "Look to the right. You can see the hill from Crescent slope down to the backs of these buildings. All the kids have to do is walk through their backyards."

Ronnie drove slowly as she turned onto Cameron, inspecting the fronts of the first few buildings on the east side of the roadway. Situated close together, the initial two housed active businesses. The third building fit the description provided by both Ms. Emily and Antonio. Positioned close to the roadway, it sat apart from the buildings on either side. Its deteriorating concrete block exterior had once been white, but years of neglect and traffic grime had transformed it to a dull grey. Boards covered the front door and display windows, serving to keep out trespassers and provide advertising for the realtor selling the building.

Ronnie turned right into a well-worn macadam lot on the left or north side of the building. She parked directly in front of a side entrance. Like the front of the building, plywood sheathed each door and window at ground level. Only the upper windows remained uncovered, resulting in significant breakage, most likely the result of the prevalence of loose asphalt chunks and children in the neighborhood.

"Let's walk the perimeter," suggested Stan.

Without comment, they strolled together around the outside of the building. To the rear or east, they observed a metal door and a loading dock with four ten-foot garage doors at dock level. A fifth garage door, which apparently provided vehicular access into the structure, stood alone on the far end at ground level.

Next, they walked along the south side where they found another boarded door and several more boarded ground level windows. As on the opposite side, the second level windows or, in some cases the surviving frames, remained uncovered, other than with years of accumulated dust and dirt.

Once again at the front of the building, Ronnie indicated, "I'd like to look inside."

"Yeah, me too," responded Stan. "But we need consent. We don't want any legal headaches, plus I'd rather not enter through the same opening as the boys and risk destroying evidence."

Ronnie contacted the real estate company using the number from the sign on the door. Twenty minutes later, a black luxury SUV pulled into the parking lot. The woman driver examined the investigators before cracking her window and asking for identification. Satisfied with their credentials, she turned off her vehicle and got out.

An attractive woman in her fifties, Mary Zimmerman wasted no time in introducing herself. Well-dressed and coiffed, she wore a dark pants suit and low-heeled shoes. In her hand, she carried a large ring of keys.

"We have to go around back," she indicated, leading the way.

At the closest back corner, she hiked up the four steps of a small stoop. "Just a minute, while I try to find the right key," she said.

On the fourth try, the mechanism disengaged, prompting her to explain, "The building's been vacant for about five years. The owner died leaving his third wife and children battling over his proceeds. Finally, this past summer, there was a resolution allowing us to list the property."

Discourse completed, she reached for the handle of the now unlocked door. As she pulled it open, Stan cautioned, "Ms. Zimmerman, it might be better if I go first. I don't think anyone's inside, but you never know."

Tactical flashlight in hand, Stan led the way with Ronnie following. Once inside, he called to the realtor, who brought up the rear, "Ms. Zimmerman, are there any dangers in the building we should be aware of?"

"No more than any old building. There's no electricity, and there's outdated equipment strewn about, but the building itself is solid."

Now in semi-darkness, Stan let his eyes adjust. He found himself in a sprawling warehouse space. Open from floor to ceiling, twenty feet above his head, it took up approximately two thirds of the building. The remaining third hid behind a distant block wall inset with two doors at floor level and a large window near the top.

"On the other side of the wall is the showroom," the realtor offered. "The offices are above."

"Okay," pronounced Stan, finally turning on his flashlight. "Let's take the tour."

Unhurried, Stan made his way up the middle of the large room. He swung his flashlight right and then left. Ronnie followed suit, panning her light to the left and then right. They spoke little as they progressed, occasionally working around the hulk of an old machine or parts of scavenged equipment.

Near the center of the warehouse, Stan passed his beam by an exit door to his right. He realized they had parked outside this door in the north side parking lot. More important, he knew the boys had entered the building through a window on this side of the structure. Carefully, he played the beam of his flashlight around the area. Seconds later, his beam passed over and then returned to an object on the floor to the left of the door under a window. He considered the object and then he whispered, "Shit."

In the quiet of the large room, Ronnie picked up on the tone, if not the exact comment. She also noted Stan's profile and position change as he moved to the right. When she started to follow, he held out a hand and cautioned, "Hold up."

The two women watched as Stan carefully walked toward the door. Now within five feet, he stopped and played his flashlight on the ground. With deliberate motion, he swung the light back and forth. Its beam stopped on occasion. Finally, he called back, "Ronnie, let's get Ms. Zimmerman to sign a formal waiver for the entry."

He paused and then began to work his way back to the women. As he reached them, he instructed, "Let's make our way back out on the same line we used to come in."

"What did you find?" Ronnie solicited as she turned to lead the way out.

"Our crime scene."

They cryptically discussed his findings on the way to the back door, where Stan instructed, "Ronnie, I'll get the waiver. Let the boss know what's going on."

Moments later Ronnie made contact with Thomas. Back in the office following the encounter with the Wilson family, he answered, "I was just about to give you a call."

"Thought I'd save you the trouble," she replied good-naturedly. Then, turning serious, she added, "Stan and I are at a vacant building on Cameron Street below Allison Hill. We think we've located the site where Jesus Rodriguez was grabbed and probably killed."

She went on to summarize the interviews with Jesus' mother, Ms. Emily, and Antonio Martin, and the brief search of the vacant building. Finally, she advised, "We need the crime scene techs."

Thomas contemplated the situation for a few seconds before responding, "I'll have our people saddle up, but it's still an HPD investigation. Call Captain Malino and advise him what's going on. He'll want to send his forensic team as well."

He thought for another moment, then added, "See if the captain can get one of his investigators to manage the crime scene. I'd like you two and him back here to discuss today's findings. Also, any work at that scene needs to be kept low keyed. I don't want the media or the perpetrator to know we're there. Make sure you pass that along."

They discussed the matter for a few more minutes before Thomas begged off to order up a BCA forensics team. He caught the unit supervisor, Bob Reynolds, heading out the door for the day. As Thomas explained the job, he spotted Bill Travis, Doc Patel, and another man entering the office. Before he hung up, he added, "Bob, stealth is the word on this one. Also, it might not hurt to have somebody clandestinely video the area to see if we draw anyone's attention. We're working on the premise the killer's familiar to the area."

Instructions complete, Thomas left his office to greet the new arrivals, who had gravitated to the conference room. He said hello to Bill and Doc, then introduced himself to Terry Hassinger, who already had a hot mug in hand and made himself comfortable at the table. They all sat as Bill explained the afternoon's activities.

Close to 6:00 o'clock, the front door opened and in walked Stan, Ronnie, and Captain Jack Malino. Without hesitation, each strode directly to the conference room and the coffee pot. While they filled cups, they talked excitedly about the warehouse. Finally, Thomas said, "Okay, okay, listen up everyone. Get a drink, go to the bathroom, make any necessary quick phone calls, and then we'll go over today's events."

No one moved.

"Or," he granted. "We could just start now." With a smile, he began, "Robby and I had an interesting time at the Wilson's, but we didn't find the proverbial smoking gun."

Without going into detail, he explained the disruption caused by Jamal's uncles and friends. This elicited a snort from Terry, who interjected, "That whole family's nuts. Believe me, it didn't hurt you put some manners on them. Maybe they'll think twice the next time they decide to go to war with the man."

Not one to embellish, Thomas turned to Bill and guided, "Moving on. Bill, you're up."

"Doc should explain the search warrant and the information we obtained about the blankets," asserted Bill with a look toward his partner, who was typing away on his computer. "He did most of the work."

Bill waited, but when Doc failed to grab the baton, he added, "The store owner wasn't as cooperative as I would've liked. If we'd had time, I would've asked Doc to give the prick a computer virus."

While a few laughs erupted, Doc remained unaware and continued to type. With no other recourse, Bill cleared his throat and shouted, "Doc!"

Interrupted in the depths of his concentration, Doc resurfaced with a flinch. All eyes riveted on him, he smiled nervously and slowly closed the laptop. Once more making his alma mater proud, he asked warily, "Huh?"

"My God, Doc. Explain what you found today," directed an exasperated Bill, ignoring the resultant giggles.

Thrown off by the disruption, an uncomfortable Doc started slowly. Gradually he gained momentum and his explanation quickly transitioned to include agonizing detail. Acquainted with Doc's penchant to ramble, Bill rolled his head and implored, "Doc, can we get to the point?"

A wounded look on his face, Doc keyed his computer and huffed, "Before someone started yelling, I was able to determine that the outlet purchased two thousand blankets from the wholesaler. It appears one thousand stayed at the facility in Middletown while two hundred were distributed to each of the remaining five stores. Reviewing the sales information," he said as he continued to stroke keys, "I've put together a prioritized list of possibilities."

Typing complete, he spun the laptop and related, "Focusing on the sales at the Middletown outlet, which is the closest to the crime scenes, I noted the biggest buyer of the blankets has been Harrisburg City."

"Well, that's just *swell*," moaned Jack Malino. "The media's got everyone thinking the killer's a cop or someone connected to the ER community. Now you're telling me the city owns most of the blankets. Just shoot me," he complained.

"Jack, do you know of anyone with access to those blankets you might suspect?" asked Thomas.

"I didn't even know we had the blankets, but to answer your question, no. The only suspect we've had is this security guard, and between you and me, he isn't guilty of anything except providing fodder for the politicos." As further explanation, he said, "The councilman that supplied the tip is a strong contender to replace the current mayor. The current mayor is running for the state Senate and is backing the councilman. They have it all figured out. If the guard's the killer, they both look like heroes."

"Painful or not," advised Stan, "We do have to consider some link to city government. Any idea what departments or bureaus would use the blankets?"

Jack Malino breathed deeply before responding, "We'll have to check with procurement to see how the items were bought and distributed." He eyed Terry Hassinger and directed, "Terry, that's job number one for tomorrow. And stay under the radar. I don't want this leaking to the media."

"Shouldn't be a problem," assured Terry. "Bo Hawkins is the director. I've known him for years. I'll deal directly with him."

Ready to move on, Thomas turned to Doc and inquired, "Anything more?"

"Well," started Doc, "there is one other large buyer and numerous individuals. Most can be tracked because they use cards. Cash purchases can't be, but there's only a handful. I had Overlord look at the individuals. Accessing public and private files, I think we can eliminate all but ten as potential suspects. These ten can't be excluded because they possess a criminal record. Unfortunately," he breathed, "none have a record of child abuse or crimes against persons, and none show any connection to the target area around Allison Hill."

As Doc paused, Jack Malino asked, "Without sounding stupid, what the hell's an *Overlord*?"

The question caused Doc to perk up immediately, but before he could expound upon the virtues of his creation, Bill Travis interrupted, "The short version, it's a computer program created by Doc that searches files. Now, continue with your summary, Doc," Bill commanded. "With the emphasis on summary."

Disappointment evident, Doc reluctantly replied, "Uh, I guess that's about it."

As Doc glanced in his direction, Bill inserted, "He's like an unsanded block of wood, but I'll keep working with him."

This prompted a few snickers around the table and caused Doc to blush. Thomas laughed as well, and then offered, "Doc, real nice work."

Left with Stan and Ronnie, Payne turned in their direction. Ronnie began with a summary of the interviews leading to the vacant building. Then she tapped Stan, who discussed their walk through the building.

At the point in which he had gone alone to the side door, Stan indicated, "My flashlight caught something on the floor by the window. As I got closer, I could see it was a tree branch. It looked just like the stick Antonio said Jesus had used as his rifle. Looking around, I noticed the dust had been disturbed in the area, more so than in the surrounding areas. Finally," he breathed, "I could see dark droplets that looked like dried blood in the dust and on the concrete. The drops are consistent with the type injuries noted to Jesus' face, particularly his nose and mouth."

Finished, Stan fell silent. Noting the clock on the wall indicated 7:30 p.m., Thomas queried, "Is that it?"

"For now," responded Stan.

"Okay, anyone have anything else new?" asked Thomas.

Silence followed, prompting him to say, "I'd normally call it for the night, but the investigative momentum is on our side right now. Also, after our discussions the past two days, I'm concerned our perpetrator may strike sooner rather than later. If anyone needs to get out of here, I understand. Those who can stay, I'm willing to buy pizza and soda. I wanna make plans for tomorrow before we break."

For the second time, no one moved.

"You'll be out of here by 9:00," promised Thomas with a smile.

Never one to allow a moment to remain solemn for long, Robby asked innocently, "Now, just so I'm clear. You did say you were buying, right?"

An hour later, Thomas wiped the pizza sauce from his fingers for the second evening in a row. Other than the occasional sound of chewing or drinking, the room fell silent as he called everyone to their seats. He directed his first comments to Captain Malino. "Jack, I hope I'm not overstepping my bounds, but in light of today's evidence bonanza, I see three major objectives for tomorrow." Waved on by the captain, he continued, "First, I want everyone to catch up on their reporting in the morning." He turned to Malino again, "Jack, if possible, could you have someone deliver the rest of your reports in the morning, so we can scan and enter them into the system?"

"No problem," answered Malino. "After seeing its capabilities, I'll make sure you get more regular deliveries from now on."

To Doc, Thomas directed, "I'd like you and Maggie to get everything into the computer. Use your judgment as to the search parameters, but see if Overlord can put any more puzzle pieces together. Also, I'd like you to be available to provide data support for the teams in the field."

"My second point," Thomas continued after glancing at his notes, "there's a lot of work to be done in and around the vacant building. The scene needs to be completely processed to everyone's satisfaction, and we need to canvass the businesses in the area."

Malino nodded and interjected, "That brings something else to mind. Over the years, we've had some burglaries in that area. I know a few of the businesses have security cameras. We need to get to their footage before it gets erased or deleted."

"Good idea," acknowledged Thomas. "On that same note, I'd like to set up our own physical surveillance and remote monitoring of the building and the area around it. That way, we can record what goes on there and react if necessary."

Malino went thoughtful and then offered, "I can put together a surveillance detail if you can get your tech unit to install the cameras. How long would we want to keep it in place?"

As Thomas considered the question, Stan cut in, "I think we should plan to physically and/or remotely monitor the area for at least two weeks, and it should be 24/7. That takes us through the next two Mondays."

With a look at Thomas, Malino commented, "I can schedule for a few days just using my personnel, but, beyond that, I'll need help. If my math is correct, fourteen days at three shifts per day is fifty-two shifts."

Without hesitation, Thomas responded, "Go ahead and schedule as many days as you can. Let me know what you need, and I'll try to get BCA personnel to fill in."

Gone pensive, Thomas finally asked, "Has anyone checked the other businesses on Cameron Street going south from the Allison Hill area to the body dumpsites?"

The room turned silent as those around the table considered the question. Momentarily, Captain Malino spoke up, "That was assigned last week. Most of the businesses have been covered, but a few remain."

"Okay," said Thomas. "If you get me a list of the businesses missed, Robby and I can hit those tomorrow. Which takes me to the third objective," he said with a look toward Bill Travis. "I'd like you and Terry to follow up on the information regarding the blankets. Start with Terry's friend in procurement. If you find any interesting leads, follow the threads. If not, start working through Doc's list of potentials."

In acknowledgment, Bill Travis turned to Terry and held out his fist. Either not familiar with the fist bump or not ready for that level of intimacy, Terry reacted as if Travis had a foot growing from his forehead. Obviously embarrassed, Bill faltered and dropped his hand. He whined, "Hey man, you can't leave me hanging like that. It's just not right."

A smirk for the crowd, Terry pronounced, "An unsanded block, but I'll work with him."

At this point, Thomas noted the 9:00 o'clock hour had arrived. A good note to end on, he invited, "Any further questions, concerns, or observations?"

The remark caused Jack Malino to push his chair back and stand. The others turned in his direction. He started, "First, a comment. I want to thank you all for the great detective work I've seen the past few days. Yesterday in Steelton and today working on our homicides has been an extremely positive experience. Second, I just wanted to thank you for the lovely dinner. I'd expected candles and wine, or at least a beer, but I understand how it is on a government salary."

Group self-control and discipline now gone, Thomas saw the comments and their effect as an appropriate climax to the meeting. Amidst the growing laughter and loud conversation that ensued, he tossed his papers on the table in mock frustration, and shouted, "See you all in the a.m."

Chapter 28

A Walk in the Night

Thomas departed the capitol a little after 9:00 p.m. He intended to make a few calls on his drive home, but the crisp clear evening air enticed him to conduct his business as he meandered west on North Street. First on the list, he contacted the supervisor of the BCA Tech Unit to discuss installation of surveillance cameras at the vacant building. Next, he called Director Greene to provide him with the latest information.

He had just finished his summary of the day's events when the director cut in. In an almost fatherly tone, he said, "Thomas, I discussed the case in Steelton with their chief. He more or less said you saved the day. I just wanted to say, for the record, you and your unit are doing a great job. I'm not normally a fan of task forces, but I may have been wrong about yours."

He paused, then added, "Keep up the good work, and I'll try to keep that asshole Murphy out of your business In fact, I'll call him tonight to save you the agony."

After he clipped his phone on his belt, Thomas took stock. To his surprise, it appeared the director shared his opinion of the deputy secretary. More important, he had saved Thomas the pain of contacting the man with an update.

Buoyed by the candid conversation, Thomas found to his surprise he had walked to the corner of North and Third Streets. Prepared to turn and head back to his car, he noticed a light coming from a building across Third Street. While its neighbors sat idle and dark, an interior light shone from O'Malley's.

He had mostly forgotten about his lunch that afternoon and his unusual discomfort upon meeting the gregarious restaurateur. He contemplated the light. Its glow beckoned to him.

Unable to resist its pull, he found himself peering through the eatery's large front window. A single fluorescent strip glimmered behind the counter. "A light to deter burglars," he thought. Satisfied that nothing untoward had occurred, he turned and walked away.

He had just reached the streetlight at the corner when a bell jingled behind him. Its sound caused him to stop.

Mouth suddenly dry, he turned to see a figure in the doorway. As it moved into the light and clarified, Breanne O'Malley greeted, "Well, Agent Thomas Payne, what a pleasant surprise." Her smile seemed to take the chill from the night.

Freeing his tongue from his pallet, Thomas reacted awkwardly, "Uh, I was just passing by and saw the light." Embarrassed by the unintended cliché, he tried to recover by clarifying, "I saw the light and thought it was unusual at this time of night."

"Well, I appreciate you watching over my business," she returned coyly.

They stood in silence for an uncomfortable moment before Thomas cleared his throat and proclaimed, "Well, I should go."

Too quickly she asked, "Would you like to come in for a cup of something hot?"

Uncharacteristically, Thomas found himself answering back, "That'd be nice."

Minutes later, he found himself seated in a small, but tastefully decorated, office in the back of the restaurant. The clinking of glass or porcelain rose from the kitchen behind him. Momentarily alone, he examined his surroundings. The room contained a desk set, two chairs, and one filing cabinet. Framed family pictures hung from a side wall. In one, Breanne sat on a beach with a young child in her lap.

Interrupted by the sound of footsteps, Thomas stood and turned toward the door. Breanne entered, carrying two cups. He reached to help, but she kidded, "I can handle it. Remember, I'm a professional."

He smiled and sat as she set the coffee on the front of the desk for him. Moving around the desk, she set down her teacup and said, "I hope decaf is okay." She looked at the clock and announced, "It's 9:30, so I figured the caffeine might not be a good idea."

"Perfect," he responded.

"I have sweeteners, but for some reason, I thought you might take it black." She laughed and added, "Is that stereotyping?"

"At least you didn't bring a donut," he allowed.

Breanne smiled at the comment, causing a flutter in Thomas' chest. Distractedly he sipped at his coffee. The first step in a chain of unintended consequences, scalding liquid hit his lips, inflaming the pain receptors around his mouth. In less than a nanosecond, nerves, fine-tuned over millennia, efficiently dispatched a message to his brain. The result: a spasm of motion to include a startled look, a quick jerk of his arm away from the assaulted area, and a small, but hot, wave of liquid slopping into his lap.

It took all of Thomas' willpower not to jump from his seat. Burnt by the coffee on the outside and by his klutziness on the inside, he looked down in embarrassment. Breanne, however, felt no need to display such manly resolve. She immediately leapt from behind her desk asking with obvious concern, "Are you okay? Are you all right?" followed by "I'm so sorry."

Her apology took Thomas by surprise. "You're sorry?" he stuttered.

"I made the coffee too hot. It's cold out. I just wanted to make sure it was warm enough," she lamented.

Her explanation and willingness to take the blame caused Thomas to replay the scene. This time, he found himself chuckling. More relaxed, he said, "Maybe I should be the one to start over this time. I don't normally act like this, but for some reason I do around you."

She examined him closely before responding, "Well, I don't see any permanent damage."

"I guess I'm a little nervous," he admitted.

"I think it's sweet. But," she smiled, "let's not do this every time we see each other." With a look at his red lip and then his stained pants, she clarified, "Not only is it painful, but it could get expensive."

They both laughed as she moved to a chair next to Thomas in front of the desk. They faced each other with their knees nearly touching. Hands on her lap, she leaned forward to look into Thomas' green eyes. Serious again, she entreated "Are you sure you're all right?"

Without thought, Thomas found himself reaching for her hand. He replied, "I'm fine, really. Other than a little embarrassed."

The touch of her soft skin caused a tingle. Suddenly aware, he considered pulling his hand back when Breanne put her other hand on top of his. She smiled, and professed, "I'm glad. I thought I'd scarred you for life."

Ice broken, they sat and spoke comfortably for the next hour. She related that her dad had started the business, and she had grown up there. She had attended Penn State University and graduated with a degree in nutrition. Since then she helped manage and run the restaurant.

She inquired about his work and his length of service with the BCA. He explained that he had attended a small state-run college in northern Pennsylvania. On a whim, he took the BCA entrance exam and the next thing he knew, twenty years had flown past and his driver's license listed his age as forty.

"Boy, you're not kidding," she agreed. "The time since college really did go fast. Turning pensive, she added, "I've worked here since graduating. That was fifteen years ago."

She seemed to shift gears and offered, "We're only open for breakfast and lunch on weekdays, but it takes a lot of extra hours to run the business. More since mom and dad retired. Luckily, I had scheduling and bills to do. Otherwise, I wouldn't have been here tonight."

The comment caused Thomas to smile.

Without much thought, he pointed out, "I noticed the family pictures on your desk and around the office."

Breanne took a moment to respond. Focused on her mementoes, she related, "I married my college sweetheart, but things didn't work out. His career took him across the country. Mine kept me here. We've been divorced for ten years."

"I'm sorry if that seemed like I'm prying," Thomas apologized. "I didn't mean it that way."

"In the spirit of full disclosure," she added, "I should probably tell you I have a ten-year-old son as well. His name is Chase. He's with my mom and dad right now."

"Actually, I kind of figured that one out," said Thomas. He tilted his head toward the pictures on the wall, "Being an investigator can come in handy once in a while."

Taking on a more serious look, Breanne petitioned, "Now that you know all about me, what about you?"

At first, the question caught Thomas off guard. However, he soon found himself describing his life, particularly the last five years, in detail. He discussed his time with Lynn, her cancer, and, finally, her passing. He spoke of how he thought about her each day, and how it had been difficult for him to move on romantically. She listened intently, allowing him to continue until he seemed weary.

As his purge ended, Thomas happened to look at the clock on the wall. In disbelief, he stated, "Oh man, it's midnight. I didn't mean to keep you so long."

"It was worth it," responded Breanne with a look of sympathy and caring. "I enjoyed getting to know you."

As he stood, Thomas held out his hand to help her up from her seat. On contact, a surge of electricity charged their fingers, arms, and hearts. It caused their eyes to meet. Each searched for something to say. Not until their lips gently touched did either realize they had been slowly moving toward each other.

Suddenly unsure, Thomas blurted, "I'm sorry. I didn't mean to be so forward."

In response, Breanne slowly moved closer for another kiss. "That's all right," she whispered breathlessly. "Since I almost burned your lip off, the least I can do is make it all better."

Thomas would think about that first kiss until he fell into a deep slumber, alone in his bed at home. Wakened by the alarm the next morning, he realized that for the first time in five years, he had slept through an entire night.

Chapter 29

Moving On

While Thomas enjoyed the sleep of the righteous, the killer found himself sitting in his old overstuffed chair with the shades drawn. Except for the constant hum of the ancient refrigerator and the occasional drone of tires on the street, the quiet of the night enveloped him. He had tried to sleep, but sleep would not come. Though physically tired, his mind hungered to consider tomorrow's possibilities.

He had promised himself that very afternoon to focus only on the future. Nevertheless, his thoughts remained frenzied, ever shifting. Like the little silver sphere in a pinball machine, he found himself rolling and bouncing with wild abandon as the bumpers and flippers whimsically fired him from the present into the future and then off to the past.

On some level, he recognized the accelerated and uncontrollable shifting of his thoughts had begun to impair his ability to complete even normal functions, such as working, eating, sleeping, or even expelling bodily waste. A preprogrammed projector loaded with hundreds of film shorts, he had no choice but to sit back and watch until the entire reel unwound upon the tray. Unfortunately, at this point in his journey, he lacked the capacity to recognize his crazy swings in cognition and lack of restraint as signs of his worsening psychosis.

To demonstrate, at that moment, he savored thoughts of tomorrow. An extended day in the middle of the week didn't occur often. In fact, he couldn't recall it ever happening in his short time on the job. He took this as another sign that he remained on the proper course, one charted for him, if not by the darkness, then by some other powerful and unseen navigator.

True to form, the future became the present and, seconds later, the past. As if a trap door had opened, his thoughts involuntarily fell back to a time following the death of his mother. He remembered her burial in the dusty, barren ground of the Crystal City, Texas, pauper's field. He remembered each of the many foster homes he had lived in for the next ten years. He remembered the tiresome counseling sessions forced upon him.

Paused at this point in the past, he considered the countless visits made to a vast array of counselors, one no different than another. Vain and arrogant, most overestimated their own talents and underestimated him. Within the first few years, he had learned how to respond to their canned questions, how to play the system, and how to appear normal.

During this period, he remained vigilant, keeping the darkness and, as a result, everyone else away. Cognizant of the constant oversight by foster parents, social workers, teachers, and counselors, he dutifully built his barriers. He let no one know of his thoughts and his fight with the shadows.

But this all changed when he turned eighteen and, soon after, graduated from high school. As required by regulation, county officials helped him find employment. Then, legal mandates completed, the great societal machine flung him out of the suffocating cocoon which had served as his prison for the past decade.

As had become the norm of late, the trap door of his mind once again opened without warning, and he found himself in Texas City on that hot and sticky night. In his mind he stood on the edge of the precipice after feeding for the first time as the wolf. Initially energized by his actions, he now feared he wouldn't be allowed to live with the result.

That whole first night he expected to see the lights and hear the sirens of his youth. "They will come for the wolf," he thought with certainty. Only this time, the wolf had taken a different form. No longer an angry young gringo, the wolf now existed as an inquisitive young Hispanic man in search of answers.

Anxious, the next night he took a different path to work. Upon arrival, he overheard a foreman talking about a young boy inadvertently falling and breaking his neck in the old quarry up the road. Stunned and relieved, he learned through the nightly news the authorities had labeled the child's death accidental due to a fall. For better and for worse, the world, once again, remained indifferent to his presence.

Though the news lifted a burden, he no longer felt comfortable in Texas City. The event had scared him witless, but at the same time, exhilarated him. He had changed.

The time had arrived to leave his old shell behind. He needed to prove the child, once tortured by a sick man, no longer existed. No more the boy who watched his mother's vicious murder or the teenager shuffled by the system like a used car, he had grown. To remain anywhere in Texas would only serve to hold him back and remind him of who he used to be.

By the end of June, he had picked up stakes and taken a bus as far as his meager funds would allow. He arrived in Harrisburg two days later, carrying a small duffle, loaded with a few articles of clothing, some toiletries, and two items of incalculable value to him: his mother's silver lighter and a dead boy's love-worn stuffed bunny. Alone, but not lonely, surrounded by the shroud of his darkness, he felt the possibilities open before him. The great expedition had begun. Only the goal of his journey didn't lie in the finding of far off lands or fortune, his involved self-discovery.

For the first time in his life, the man, once a boy and, now, a killer, felt he had a purpose. He had come to this city to learn, not about reading, writing, or arithmetic but about himself. Simply put, he yearned to know the reason for which he had been born.

Paradoxically, he never thought the questions haunting him similarly haunted others. He merely internalized one of the great mysteries, the meaning of life. Exposed to an obscene and tragic childhood and a totally screwed up adolescence, he had failed to learn social convention. His early lessons had taught him to focus only on himself.

Now, six months and two additional bodies after leaving Texas, his mind returned to the present. Weary from his uncontrollable, manic considerations, he felt frustration and confusion once again threaten to crash his party. He had just started to examine his failures when his mind settled and went blank. As if someone had pushed the button on a remote control, his mental pictures changed from reruns and first-runs to...nothing.

No longer subjected to the constant assault of his thoughts, the man tried to make sense of the calm. Too far gone to correctly identify the change as simply another swing of the pendulum, he chose to interpret it as a sign. The darkness had once again come alive to show its power. It had sensed his pessimism and cast it out.

Though tired, his confidence built. The longer the silence lasted, the more his resolve fortified. In the end, he found the strength to brush aside any seed of doubt. He committed to redouble his efforts.

Once again a pragmatic man, he recognized this meant another life would end. Yet, balanced against his need, the price seemed more than fair.

Chapter 30 (Wednesday)

One Rough Morning

Wednesday, the third day of task force operations, dawned overcast and cloudy. The temperature had dropped into the twenties overnight with little to no prospect of reaching freezing during the day. Trees without leaves, sky without blue, a cutting wind without mercy, it heralded one of those grey, lifeless winter days that never end soon enough.

First to enter the office at 7:00 a.m., Maggie could tell by the look and smell that someone had worked late into the evening. Decomposing pizza, boxes, and soda bottles littered the conference room table. Not a big fan of cleaning up after adults, she, nevertheless, took a minute to shove the dinner remnants into a trash bag, which she tied and set outside the main office door for the janitor. Satisfied the area no longer resembled a fraternity house, she returned to her desk to organize her day's work.

She had been laboring away for about twenty minutes when the phone rang. "Major Crimes Task Force, Maggie speaking," she answered absentmindedly.

"Maggie, this is your mother," responded Joan Goodspeed.

Atypical for her mother to call at work, Maggie immediately focused her attention and questioned, "What's the matter?"

"I just wanted to let you know I'm taking your dad to the doctor's office this morning."

"Why?" Maggie asked, knowing her father hated going to the doctor.

"Well, he just hasn't been himself lately. He's having some balance problems."

Silent for a moment, Maggie reflected upon her grandfather on her dad's side of the family. Diagnosed with Parkinson's disease following his sixtieth birthday, he passed away soon after. Her father, Charlie Goodspeed, retired police sergeant, had reached that milestone two years ago. "Any idea what it might be?" she quizzed hesitantly.

"I'm sure it's nothing, but I'd rather not take any chances," her mother answered, apparently unwilling to voice a similar concern. "We have an appointment at 10:00. I'll give you a call, if there are any problems."

With little more to say, Maggie ended the conversation by insisting, "Give me a call, one way or the other." Then she added, "I love you guys."

"Love you too, dear."

Gaze locked on the wall, she removed the receiver from her ear and slowly set it in its cradle. Five minutes later, she barely noticed the door open as Thomas walked into the office. Had Maggie been more observant, she would have detected the additional spring in his step this morning.

Cheerily, Thomas greeted her, breaking her concentration and leading her to react distractedly, "Ah, good morning, Thomas."

Surprised with the unusual reception, Thomas looked more closely and noted her pretty, unlined face seemed troubled. "Wanna tell me about it?" he inquired.

"It's probably nothing," she said distractedly.

"Why don't you let me be the judge of that?"

Eyes now clear, Maggie explained her conversation with her mother. For his part, Thomas listened attentively until she finished, then responded, "Well, first, he hasn't been diagnosed with anything yet. Second, Parkinson's isn't as much of a mystery now as it was twenty years ago. And last," he added with a smile, "Charlie's way too tough to let something like Parkinson's interfere with his life."

Maggie considered the words. She had used Thomas as her sounding board many times in the past, and he always provided clarity to her concerns. This time was no different. Gradually her frown faded. Replaced by a smile, she responded, "You're right. I guess I'm worrying about something that might not ever happen." She stood and with a hug said, "Thank you...again."

"Just paying back the favor," he indicated, gently kissing her forehead.

As she sat back in her seat, the door clicked and slowly opened revealing Bill Travis and Doc Patel. Like vampires dragging themselves across the threshold, they squinted against the bright office lighting. Both appeared under the weather, particularly Patel whose brown skin seemed oddly pasty.

Familiar with the look of someone who had tipped back too many adult beverages the night before, Thomas questioned in a loud voice, "Hey fellas, ready to get to work?"

With a noticeable cringe, each moaned a barely audible response and trudged to his desk. For his part, Bill settled delicately into his seat. With minimal motion, he placed his forehead on the hard cool surface of his desk. As for Doc, he flopped down and immediately grabbed for his trashcan.

Thomas watched as the wave passed and Doc finally sat back. The can remained between his legs. "What happened to you two?" he asked with a grin.

After a few seconds, Bill Travis gently turned his head and uttered, "That damn Hassinger. That's what happened to us."

"Did the old guy teach you a lesson last night?"

Bill answered, but not before gently sitting back in his chair. "He took us to his favorite watering-hole for a drink. One thing led to another, and we started playing cards with some of the HPD guys. Terry went home around 10:30. Doc and I stayed until closing."

"Did you win or lose?" questioned Thomas.

"I thought we were winners," replied Bill. "I'm not so sure this morning."

By this time, Ronnie Sanchez had come into the office. As she walked through the bay toward her desk, she noted Bill's obvious distress and probed, "Bill, are you all right?"

His response included another moan as he gingerly dropped his head to the desk once more. Curious, Ronnie looked to Doc for an answer. Noting his similar condition, she surmised the problem and offered, "I think I can help."

She went directly to her cubicle, where she rummaged around in the overhead cabinet. Then she walked into the conference room. Five minutes later she returned with two large cups of strong black coffee and four acetaminophen tablets.

She set a coffee and two pills on each desk and ordered, "Take the pills with the coffee. It's not hot, so drink it all at once. In forty minutes you'll be right as rain." With a wink to Thomas, she returned to her desk.

Enough said on the subject of hangovers, Thomas instructed. "Okay, reports, and then out on the streets by 10:00." Mischievous grin in place, he smacked the desk for emphasis, smiling wider at the resultant whimpers.

As he walked by Ronnie, he whispered, "Will it work?"

"Absolutely, but it's like lifting weights: no pain, no gain."

She observed his curious look and explained, "The caffeine and medicine will make their heads feel better, but there's one tiny side effect. The concoction has a tendency to unsettle an already unsettled stomach."

246

She paused for effect, "Let's just say I wouldn't want to be in the bathroom in the next few minutes."

To punctuate her point, an odor, reminiscent of a broken garbage bag left in the hot sun, wafted through the area. At the same time, both Bill and Doc rushed past. Ronnie would later describe their movements as a choppy speed walk.

Thomas laughed until the smell overwhelmed him. Nose and mouth covered in the crook of his arm, he exclaimed, "Holy shit!"

Ronnie retorted, "Ugh, there's nothing holy about that!"

"Get a decontamination team in here," Thomas yelled over his shoulder as he fled for the safety of his office.

Now alone in her cubicle, surrounded by the invisible cloud, Ronnie realized her joke had backfired in more ways than one.

Twenty minutes later, Bill Travis returned. Though he didn't feel great, the caffeine had begun to kick in, and the apocalypse no longer seemed imminent. He thought back on the past few minutes and reminded himself of the pact he and Doc had made: neither would ever speak about the scene in the lower level bathroom. Hot and cold sweats, diarrhea, and vomit weren't a good legacy.

He slinked past Ronnie's cubicle only to have her say, "You might wanna get that thing checked out."

Embarrassed, Bill grabbed his coat and, without his normal flourish, stole from the office. At three quarter speed he made his way to his car and set about cleaning the frost from the windows. While he lethargically scraped away, he noticed Terry Hassinger walking down the sidewalk toward him. Terry waved and, as he got closer, announced, "I hear you guys got sent home in a taxi last night."

Surprised by Terry's appearance and unwilling to perpetuate further verbal abuse, Bill ignored the comment and asked, "Wasn't I supposed to come to you?"

"My contact in procurement won't be in until after lunch, so I thought we could hit some of the others on the list," responded Terry, overlooking the snub.

With a final scrape, Bill said, "Okay, hop in. I'll look at Doc's list."

Once in the driver's seat, Bill shuddered, "It's freezing out there."

By feel, he reached into the backseat and grabbed the computer-generated list of blanket purchases. With minimal head movement, he scanned the pages and indicated, "Doc highlighted the ten individuals with criminal records, but let's check this other business first. It's a company down in Middletown. After the city, they're the largest buyer."

"Sounds good to me," Terry replied quietly. Then after a quick sideways glance to affirm Bill's continued discomfort, he laughed loudly, backhanded the suffering man's arm, and shouted, "Lead the way, Sherlock."

The physical and audible assault caused Bill's breath to catch. It took a few seconds, but, eventually, he found the will to shift the car into gear. Near his abuse limit for the day, he thanked God when Terry initiated discussion of the previous day's findings and their objectives for today. They spoke for the twenty minutes it took to drive south on Route 283 to Middletown Energy Solutions.

Located by GPS at the end of Susquehanna Street, the facility consisted of two huge white aboveground storage tanks, a depot area big enough for two tanker trucks, and a grand old two-story brownstone building with a large eight-bay garage. Back from the road, a ten-foot high chain link fence topped with razor wire surrounded the entire operation.

They entered through an open gate and passed by a large sign indicating Middletown Energy Solution (MES) – Home Heating Oil Division. Bill sidled up to the curb in front of the main building and shut off the engine. With the list of buyers in his hand, he rechecked the address and confirmed, "Well, this is the right address, but apparently this isn't the main location. I hope we aren't wasting our time."

"We're here now," noted Terry, "so let's poke around. Before we go inside," he added, looking toward the garage, "I'd like to look at one of those rigs." He pointed at two trucks with white cabs and silver tanks emblazon with the company logo.

Before they exited the car, they bundled themselves against the cold. A breeze had begun to kick up, causing the wind chill to drop into the teens. Near the larger of the two vehicles, Terry observed, "This is a pretty good size delivery truck. I'd say over five thousand gallons."

He hopped onto the step side and peered into the cab. He noted the contents and moved on to the second vehicle. Before he reached the door, someone called out, "Can I help you guys?"

A tall, skinny man of about forty appeared from around the side of the garage. He wore stained coveralls and a heavy parka. In his hand, he held a rag, which he used to wipe grease from his fingers. "I hope so," responded Bill, flipping out his badge and ID.

Upon witnessing the man's reaction, Bill asked Terry, "Something I said?"

Stopped dead in his tracks, the man appeared ready to run. In the end, he must have recalled the ten-foot high fence surrounding him, because he chose to remain. With a look at the ground, he confessed, "I know I'm behind on my payments."

"How far behind?" asked Terry.

"About two months. The magistrate fined me almost two thousand dollars. I still owe eight hundred."

"What's your name?" inquired Bill, playing along.

"Luke Johnson," the man responded hesitantly.

"Okay, Luke," Bill continued. "We're willing to let that slide, if you can help us out."

Luke considered the offer and evidently decided he had no option. He tendered, "Whatever you fellas need. I'm your guy."

"Just a little information," conferred Terry.

For the next twenty minutes, Luke, the mechanic, filled them in on who owned and operated the facility, as well as his personal daily routine. In response to questions about equipment, he related the company had recently purchased two new tanker trucks. The rest varied in age from one to ten years old, but each remained in good mechanical condition.

At one point, Terry queried, "Luke, what do you keep in the utility compartments of the vehicles?"

In answer, Luke walked to the bigger of the two trucks and opened the stainless steel compartment located behind the cab. He explained the uses for the various hoses, connectors and other items inside. One item he left out as unimportant: a pack of yellow synthetic emergency blankets pushed to one side.

In an attempt to appear disinterested, Bill inquired casually, "Why the blankets?"

"Sometimes the tank's plumbing or one of the lines springs a leak. It doesn't happen often, but when it does, the drivers can use the plastic blankets to keep the oil from spotting customers' driveways or sidewalks." He added, "They're also for accidents. The boss figures the drivers put a lot of miles on the vehicles, so they're as likely as anybody to see or be involved in a crash."

Not ready to tip their hand, Terry quickly guided the subject away from the blankets. "Luke, how're your drivers dispatched?" he inquired.

"Each driver gets a printout at the beginning of the shift. That's the schedule for the day. If something changes, we have a girl working in the office who doubles as a dispatcher. She can get them on the radio."

Sufficiently informed, both investigators seemed to understand they had drained Luke of germane information. After they had shaken hands and walked away, Bill stopped and turned back. He directed, "And Luke, make sure you stop at the magistrate's to set-up a new payment plan."

After his wave of acknowledgement, they turned and made their way to the main building. First to reach the door, Bill grasped the handle and opened it for Terry pronouncing, "Age before youth and intelligence. Oh yeah, and beauty," he added with a wink.

"Anything else?" asked Terry.

"No, that's it," responded Bill with a half-smile. "I'm not conceited."

Chapter 31

Candid Camera

By the time Stan arrived at work around 8:00 a.m., the ventilation system had scrubbed the air of the fog threatening to shut down the works for the day. It took him nearly two hours to complete his mandated reporting, but by 10:30 he and Ronnie set off for the vacant building on Cameron Street. As they drove, Stan inquired, "How're you feeling today?"

"Pretty good," Ronnie replied. She had expected the question at some point in light of yesterday's conversation. "What you said made sense. How'd you get to be such a smart man?"

"Let's just say you have to make a few mistakes before anyone claims you're smart."

"Well, next time I get whiny, just kick me."

"Count on it," Stan offered with a smile.

With the stage now set for the day and, perhaps, the term of their partnership, the two investigators found themselves passing the abandoned building. From the outside, neither noted any obvious changes as a result of the crime scene techs' work. Two buildings farther south, at Cameron and Berryhill Streets, Ronnie pulled into the parking lot.

She shut off the engine and imparted, "Let's check these businesses before we hit the target location. That way we can leave the car here, out of sight."

Stan nodded as they exited the car and walked to the front of the first commercial structure. "Used to be called Cameron Street Plumbing," he advised as they passed the Dauphin Plumbing Supply sign.

Upon entry, they identified themselves and located the manager. It took little time to determine the harried executive possessed little knowledge or time to assist them in their pursuit. Ready to depart, Stan remembered to inquire about video surveillance equipment. This caused the manager to perk up as he proudly indicated, "We've got alarms and cameras. The system was installed a little over a year ago after our second burglary in three months."

"How long do you keep each day's video?" asked Stan with growing interest.

"Well," the owner thought out loud, "it's on a hard drive, so I don't clean it off that often. Hmm, maybe once a month, when I remember."

Intrigued, Stan inquired further, "Do you review the video every day?"

"I used to," responded the owner sheepishly. "Not so much anymore. It was a waste of time."

Gone momentarily thoughtful, he grinned and offered, "We did get parkers in here once in a while." Stress now forgotten, he added in an animated fashion, "One night we recorded this really large couple in a small Japanese pickup. It was like a tsunami of fat."

On a roll until he noted the look of indifference on Ronnie's face, he coughed into his hand, looked away, and said, "Uh, like I said, I got tired of wasting my time. I figured I could look back if something happened."

"Do you still have the videos from December?" Stan queried.

Without pause, the owner answered, "I'm sure I do. The last time I remember clearing the disk was after Halloween. We had some kids soap our windows. I provided the video to the police then wiped it clean."

"Would it be possible for us to copy the hard drive containing the videos?" Stan questioned.

"I don't see why not," replied the owner. After a brief pause, he asked, "What makes you think you might find something on my video?"

Hesitant to discuss the crime scene two properties away, Stan dodged, "We're looking for any businesses in the area that might have video. Since there's little to go on otherwise, we're hoping to develop a lead."

The rest of the discussion led nowhere, so before leaving, they obtained a voluntary written waiver and copied the hard drive onto a one terabyte external drive. "Please don't delete the original files until we get back to you," directed Ronnie as they made for the door.

Near the exit, the owner pulled Stan aside and whispered, "If you watch the video and see the great white whales parking again, close your eyes. It's not a pretty sight." In response, Stan nodded and hurried out the door to catch up with Ronnie. No more interested now than before to hear about the parkers, she had wasted little time moving on to the next establishment.

Housed in a structure similar to the first, Innovations in Graphic Design sat directly to the south of the target warehouse. When asked about video cameras, the manager related they did have a security system, but no cameras. Overlooked in the last round of commercial burglaries, his biggest external concern seemed to be children playing around the vacant building next door.

Five minutes and no useful information later, Stan and Ronnie stood outside the graphics shop discussing their next move. They decided to touch base with Captain Malino since they hadn't heard from him this morning. Ronnie listened as Stan talked into his cell phone. "Jack, we're down on Cameron Street interviewing the owners of the businesses around the target building."

He smiled when the captain revealed, "Yeah, I'm watching you on my computer. Wave to your adoring public."

"I guess that means I'm already on candid camera," stated Stan.

Malino came back, "Yeah, maybe you should stop picking at the seat of your pants."

"My bad," responded the big man, who added, "anything new?"

"Well, our evidence teams finished up the inside of the warehouse at about 6:00 a.m. They started on the outside but were getting noticed, so I shut 'em down. We'll have to talk about that. Also, as you must have figured, your tech people installed cameras inside and out. They say we should be able to watch them on any computer or smart phone."

He paused before self-consciously adding, "Because of some contractual issues, I can't put up a physical surveillance until after midnight tonight. Right now I have a clerk on the cameras. We've been fighting with the union again," he explained apologetically. "It's a love-hate relationship."

Disappointed, Stan kept his thoughts to himself. He went on to describe their morning interviews, including the surveillance footage obtained at the plumbing shop. When he described their plan to take the hard drive back for Doc's review, Malino said, "Stop by the station before you head back. I have another box of reports. Maybe Underdog can put together some more leads."

Stan snickered, "You know if Doc hears you making fun of his baby, he may take his toys and go home."

"We don't want that," Jack yielded with a laugh.

They continued to talk until Stan's call waiting rang. "Gotta go, Jack," he said, looking at the display. "That's Thomas. We'll talk later."

He immediately hung up and took the second call. "Hey boss, what's up?"

"Just passed you," advised Thomas. "We're heading south to start interviews around the dumpsites. Anything new?"

Stan explained their progress, which led Thomas to instruct, "Okay, get the HPD reports and take them and the video back to the office. I'll give you a call if we find anything."

The conversation lasted another minute until Thomas found himself near the southern-most dumpsite. He begged off with Stan, and for the next hour, he and Robbie conducted interviews at several commercial establishments in the vicinity. Disappointingly, no one had seen anything and none of the businesses utilized security cameras.

Dejectedly, they returned to the car. Thomas had just unlocked the doors when Robby pointed up the hill to the east and inquired, "Is that a bank?"

Thomas followed the direction of the finger and observed a building on a side street running perpendicular into Cameron. "You mean that building on Sycamore with the three drive-through lanes, the ATM, and the sign that says South-central Credit Union?" he responded.

He paused and then added, "What gave it away?"

Robby chose to ignore the mockery. He asserted, "I know we were only going to hit businesses on Cameron, but I think we should stop there."

Forced to drop the sarcasm due to Robby's insistent tone, Thomas finally reasoned, "Cameras."

"Yeah," responded Robby, "you know there are cameras around that building."

Now headed up the hill, Thomas patted Robby on the back. Maintaining a serious air, he said, "Who knew you were more than just a pretty face?"

Once inside the credit union, they introduced themselves to a friendly customer service representative at the counter. Within a few minutes, they were seated in comfortable chairs in the office of the branch manager. Thomas estimated the woman's age at about 30.

After she reviewed their credentials, the woman indicated, "We have an extensive security and video surveillance system around this branch. We're a little off the beaten path which seems to draw robbers and crazies."

In response, Thomas queried, "Do you have any cameras pointed down toward Cameron Street?"

"We have a couple of cameras on the west side of the building. I think you can see Cameron in at least one."

At Thomas' request, she showed them the current view of the two cameras on that side of the facility. With growing excitement, the agents saw one of the cameras captured not only part of Cameron but also a small portion of the access road leading back to the electrical generation plant. This had been the dumpsite of Jesus Rodriguez's body in early December.

"How long do you keep the videos?" Thomas asked, trying to hide his enthusiasm.

She answered, "Two weeks and then our internal system overwrites the older data."

Crestfallen, Thomas turned to Robby and muttered, "We can't catch a break this morning."

"You didn't give me a chance to finish," interrupted the manager. "The older data is archived with our security subcontractor. Their policy is to store it for a minimum of three years."

Suddenly revitalized, Thomas inquired, "Would it be possible for you to contact the security company so we can view the video?"

"I can call, but I know our lawyers and theirs will require a court document to compel release."

As the manager made numerous phone calls, Thomas and Robby caught the gist of the conversations. During the last, the bank manager talked as she wrote, "Okay, so they'll need a search warrant, and it should be made out to whom?" She wrote furiously, then stopped and listened some more before saying goodbye.

As she hung up, the manager looked at them contritely and affirmed, "I guess you heard. No release without a search warrant."

"Well, nothing worthwhile is simple," responded Thomas.

"If it helps," she offered, "we've had other search warrants asking for archived records. The location for the warrant should indicate the security company in Susquehanna Township, just north of the city. Serve it here, and I'll fax a copy to our legal department and the security company."

She noted Thomas knit his brows, and as apology offered, "Look, I realize that means driving to the township to get the warrant, then driving back down here to serve it, and, once again, driving back to the township to obtain the records, but it's the fastest way to get what you want. I'll call the security company now and have them retrieve the data so it's ready by the time you get there."

An hour and a half and numerous miles later, they arrived at the offices of Sennheiser Security Solutions. Their heads spun as they entered the building and received immediate escort to the third floor office of the Vice President of Operations Jerry Grafton. A tall man of about 60, the VP came around his desk with his hand extended in greeting. Aware of the time sensitive nature of the agents' business, he said, "I'll get right to it. Pam at the bank faxed me the search warrant. It's been reviewed by their legal department and seems to be in order."

He picked a DVD off his desk and handed it to Thomas. "I had all the data for the past three years available, but the search warrant only compels the release of data from this past December first to present. That's what you'll find on the disk."

With a somber expression, Thomas responded, "If the camera from the bank picked up anything of use to our investigation, it'll be during that time frame."

After a reminder to maintain the original camera footage, they thanked the security administrator and hurried from his office. Once in the car, Thomas directed, "Let's get this DVD back to Doc. We need him to look at the tape of that access road on the night Jesus disappeared."

Lost in thought, they made the short drive back to the office. As they turned onto North Street to park, Thomas noticed Robby staring at him. Self-conscious, he stared back and asked, "What?"

"Do you realize you were just smiling and sighing?"

Caught off guard, Thomas sputtered, "Uh, just thinking about the videos."

As he lied to his best friend, he didn't feel at all deceitful. His mind had slipped back to the previous night with Breanne O'Malley. Though he knew he would eventually fill Robby in, he didn't want to place too quick a meaning on the burgeoning relationship.

He hid his smile as he thought of the way she felt and smelled in his arms. Feelings and desires long dormant bubbled to the surface. Today he felt different, more alive.

As he considered his mood, he thought back to a sociology class from college. The professor had discussed the interaction of men and women as a function of the desire or need to procreate. Older and wiser now, he thought that explanation too simple. As evidence, he reflected on other women he had met over the past few years. None had affected him like Breanne.

Though he thought the professor might be wrong on this first premise, he recalled a second idea the instructor had forwarded: that man is a hunter. Projecting the notion onto his present circumstance, he gave the professor his due on that insight. At this very moment, one very bad man hunted little boys. At the same time, he hunted the man.

As he walked into the building, one question formed in his mind: who would be the first to find his prey?

Chapter 32

The Scent of Lavender

Finished with the majority of the breakfast crowd, Breanne returned to her office to sort through the morning mail. She skirted her desk and spied the empty ceramic mugs on her blotter. Like Thomas, her thoughts returned to the previous evening, more specifically the heat of their parting kiss, which caused her to flush like a schoolgirl.

Her thoughts fell back to their first meeting in the afternoon. Though she normally helped the girls with the lunch crowd, yesterday she had felt strangely compelled to wait on the two unfamiliar men at the counter. Like a word stuck on the tip of her tongue, the reason eluded her.

In any event, she had waited on Thomas and his friend, only to discover herself drawn to him. His initial discomfort in her presence did little to weaken the attraction. In fact, it made him more endearing. Smiling to herself, she realized such thoughts had become foreign.

Since her divorce, she assumed romance, an elusive condition, had visited and gone on its way. She had loved her ex-husband, but more in a physical than emotional sense. Older and, hopefully, wiser, she now admitted to that fact, a truth she once vehemently denied.

As for her social life, she had dated, but, sadly, no suitor could make it past the first round. None possessed the depth for which she yearned. Continually disappointed, she eventually gave up dating and acquiesced to a life without a man's love...until now.

Mind afloat with long-abandoned possibilities, she suddenly recalled the thought that had escaped her earlier: the reason she felt obliged to wait on Thomas. The revelation seemed facilitated by a fleeting flowery fragrance. It was the same smell that caused her to turn and look at Thomas as he sat at the counter. While she couldn't place the origin or significance of the scent, either now or yesterday, in this instance, she recognized it as lavender.

Her reflections would have continued had she not heard the familiar sound of dishes and silverware clanking in a passing busboy's tub. Guilty others worked as she sat, she stood and walked into the main dining area, now less than half full. She found her assistant and inquired, "Carol, can I help you with anything before the lunch rush begins?"

"Not unless you can make my feet stop hurting," answered the tall blond woman. "I feel like I've been working since yesterday morning."

265

"At least you got out of here before dinner," countered Breanne. "I was here until midnight."

"Brea, honey, you have to do something other than work all the time," lamented Carol. She added with conviction, "We need to find you a man."

Suddenly self-conscious, Breanne reddened and looked away.

The change didn't go unnoticed. "What was that?" probed Carol.

"Nothing," lied Breanne.

"That wasn't *nothing*," disputed Carol. "Spill it."

Now both self-conscious and uncomfortable, Breanne finally admitted, "I had a drink with a guy last night."

"That's great," shouted Carol, unable to curb her enthusiasm. "Where'd you go?"

Initially bemused, Breanne amended, "Not that kind of drink. He had coffee, and I had tea. In fact, we did it in my office."

"You did it in your office!" responded Carol with a red face. "Wasn't that a little impetuous?"

Words misconstrued, Breanne corrected, "Not sex, you pervert, just drinks. You know me better than that."

"Yes I do," laughed Carol. "It was a joke. I almost wish you had been talking about sex. It's been a long time since somebody curled your toes."

Face now scarlet, Breanne found herself at a loss for words. This didn't stop her friend, who inquired, "Anyone I know?"

On the business end of the friendly interrogation, Breanne finally relented. As her color returned to normal, she sighed and divulged, "Remember the two guys that came in yesterday for lunch? I told you not to give them a bill?"

"Of course, I remember. Which one?" asked Carol. "Not that it matters. They were both good looking."

"His name is Thomas. He was the one with the dark hair and green eyes. He sat to our right."

Her thoughts on the previous day, Carol said, "He seemed uncomfortable not paying his bill. In fact, he left a twenty dollar tip."

Breanne considered the comment. Thomas had left more for a tip than the cost of both lunches. More and more, she thought him to be an unusual man. Lost in thought, she distractedly walked away toward her office. She never heard her friend calling her name.

Ignored, Carol stood dumbfounded as Breanne floated around the counter and disappeared into her office. Not accustomed to seeing her boss in this state, Carol found the situation humorous. She started to smile until reality hit home, and she thought out loud, "Well, this is either going to be really good…or really, really bad."

Chapter 33

Faulty Wiring

To say he hadn't slept well the night before would be an understatement. After he had celebrated the return of his pragmatism, the man's remaining hours proved a challenge. Ensconced in his well-worn piece of furniture, he switched feverishly between periods of fitful sleep and alertness.

More abbreviated than normal, his episodes of slumber continued to provide a complex and constantly shifting milieu. A careless mix of past and future, their nonsensical nature could have easily resulted from a hit of LSD. While he possessed little control over these dreams, he worried little about them, because, other than a hazy memory, he forgot them as soon as he woke.

Conversely, last night he had suffered a significant and disconcerting change to his waking dreams and visions. Generally, when awake, his revelations took the shape of familiar and very recent past events or considerations of the future and its possibilities. To some extent, he exerted control over their direction.

However, last night, his fantasies had evolved and become indiscernible from his sleeping dreams. As it sped faster and faster, the pinball of his thoughts encountered more and more trap doors in the waning hours of darkness. By morning he lacked the ability to influence them in any manner.

Most distressing, though, not only had his waking dreams turned into frenzied nightmares, but he still retained his ability to remember them. He couldn't escape those kaleidoscopic, 1080p images and sounds. As example, he recalled one particularly troublesome vision. The storm had come again. Like before, he witnessed the destructive power of its winds in the wake of each blinding flash of lightning, and he felt the rolling awesomeness of its thunder. Only, this time, he remembered everything.

After the vision of the storm, sleep teased him, yet remained aloof. Afraid to experience another rousing nightmare, he had made a pot of strong coffee and spent two hours consuming it. Somewhere into his third cup, he began to feel better. By the time he finished his sixth, he had found the power, at least temporarily, to push last night's dreams and visions aside.

Buoyed by the coffee, he had prepared for work and made the one-mile walk to the station. Now, an hour later, driving along I-283 in his blue, winter uniform and jacket, he finally struck upon a thought that breached the armor of his pessimism. In the fuss of the past days, no matter how often he screwed up, another opportunity came along. In his mind, he interpreted this to mean a higher authority must be watching over him, ensuring the inevitable success of his quest.

Suddenly pumped by more than caffeine, he once again pictured himself as the wraith. Cloaked in the darkness created by his patron and the expectations of others, he remained invisible to the masses. He cracked a crooked smile and enjoyed his first calm breath in hours. His reprieve lasted for nearly two minutes.

Out of the blue, he experienced an abrupt and gripping concern. What if, for some odd reason, he had no assignments on The Hill today? Preoccupied earlier, he had neglected to review the second and third pages of his schedule. Suddenly, he wanted, no, he needed to check the entire schedule.

Powerless, he surrendered to the unusual, neurotic impulse and pulled to the berm of the busy highway. He anxiously grabbed the clipboard to review his agenda. Even in the cold cab, his fingers left wet imprints on the paper. At the same time, he felt a prickly heat move up his torso, which caused him to unzip his heavy winter coat. His first experience with, what some called, a hot flash, he wondered if he might be getting sick.

To his relief, he noted numerous calls to the Allison Hill area on page three. This represented his afternoon and evening's work. Relief spread through his body. As he relaxed, he interpreted the perfection of the schedule as simply another sign. Respiration, heart rate, and blood pressure returned to normal, he pulled back onto the roadway.

Headed west, he reflected upon his sudden angst. He wondered if others lived with similar feelings. Denied a normal family, he had never really discussed his emotions with anyone. Once, he had nearly opened up to a foster mother. He pictured the woman whose image meshed with his memories of his mother. He had been fourteen when he went to her home.

A middle-aged Hispanic woman, she had taken the time to speak with him about his cultural heritage. One of the few times he had actually begun to feel a link with another human being, he never got the chance to explore the connection. Like every other foster home in which he had received placement, something happened requiring him to move on.

Typically, the county relocated him without explanation, but in this instance he learned through a caseworker that the police had arrested the woman's husband. No one identified the alleged offense, but he had his suspicions. He recognized the way the man looked at his children, especially the fifteen-year-old daughter.

Without conscious effort, his thoughts automatically moved to his next home placement. This one hadn't been so pleasant. The elderly couple seemed fine, albeit slightly controlling at first. As the days turned to weeks, the retired couple began to show their true colors. They became more domineering and physical.

One evening, he must have looked at the old man wrong. This resulted in receipt of an unexpected backhand strike to his face. The large, turquoise and silver ring the man wore on the middle finger of his right hand knocked out two of his teeth. Unable to afford proper repair, the noticeable gap in his smile provided a daily reminder of the abuse that had been part of his childhood.

Given the opportunity to study the man, now a killer, and his behavior, some would argue the traumatic events of his youth caused his depraved actions as an adult. Others would, no doubt, blame it on faulty DNA or some other genetic predisposition. In actuality, they would both be right...and wrong. A sociologist's dream, he personified both sides of the nature versus nurture debate. Normally an unlucky individual, he had hit the jackpot. Not only had he endured a screwed up childhood, but if mankind possessed the ability to complete a detailed schematic of the wondrous electrical system called the human brain, his would exhibit numerous areas of short circuiting and faulty grounding.

Suddenly, he found himself back in the present. Even with his numerous disadvantages, he recognized the exit for his first assignment. Involuntarily, he sighed and reminded himself of the need to focus for the rest of his workday. He didn't realize, but at that moment his thinking had come as close to normal as it would ever get. Like millions of American workers, he dreamt about what he would do at the end of the day.

Unlike those other workers, though, his deliberations had nothing to do with getting home to the family or meeting friends. He thought of the void, and he relished his desires. Focused for the moment on the future, he hoped to satiate what seemed to be his unquenchable thirst for information.

"Information," he thought, "which could only be found in the welcoming and protective shadows of the night."

Chapter 34

Blankets and Oil

Inside the lobby of the Home Heating Oil Division of Middletown Energy Solutions, Bill Travis sensed he had gone back in time. Set in a checkerboard pattern, the one-foot square beige and green linoleum tiles reminded him of grade school. Add to this the solid walls of shiny beige finished block with white plaster above, and he nervously searched the room for Mrs. Simpson, his second grade teacher, and her ruler.

Relieved when he failed to spot her bulky form nearby, Bill marched up to the sliding glass window. A perky woman in her mid-twenties greeted him. "Good morning," he offered, displaying his badge and ID. "I'm with the Bureau of Criminal Apprehension. Would it be possible to speak with the manager?" Still queasy, he lacked the energy for his normally flirtatious manner.

"I'll check to see if Mr. Severin is available. If you'd like, take a seat."

As the receptionist closed her window, Bill and Terry sat in two of the six hard plastic chairs provided for visitors. Quietly, they discussed the day's itinerary. "My friend in procurement has a doctor's appointment this morning," explained Terry. "He's the only one I trust to keep quiet."

"That's okay," responded Bill, settling into his chair. "We have plenty of buyers to interview."

Finished discussing strategy, both investigators fell silent. Each enjoyed the abundant heat pumping through the vestibule. Bill stretched out and languidly considered the cases in his mind. Twenty-five minutes later, he woke with a start as Terry elbowed him in the ribs and whispered, "Time to wake up, Sleeping Beauty. The prince will see us now."

Groggy, Bill shook his head and checked his watch. To his amazement, he had been magically transported into the future. "I guess the heat must've gotten to me," he yawned.

"Yeah, it probably had nothing to do with not sleeping last night and drinking too much," Terry responded dryly. Embarrassed, Bill silently demurred, which led Terry to add, "Don't worry. Only about ten customers came in while you were out. For the most part, they didn't even notice, except when you started snoring."

Now petrified, Bill lamented, "Ah man, why didn't you wake me?"

"Well, for one, I didn't have the heart," explained Terry as he stood for the now opened office door. "You looked so peaceful.

Then you started to twitch and moan. At that point, I was afraid to get too close."

He left his words hang in the air as the receptionist, who identified herself as Jill, appeared and indicated, "I can take you up now."

She led them through the main office and up a sturdy staircase. As they reached the top, she apologized, "I'm sorry it took so long. I didn't realize Mr. Severin ran to the bank."

On the second floor, she turned left and continued to a partially closed door at the far end of the long hallway. She knocked and stood aside allowing them to enter the large contemporary space, which ran the entire width of the building. Directly ahead, a small dark man in his mid-fifties sat behind an expansive cherry desk. Dressed in loose fitting jeans and a green checked flannel shirt, he stood as the investigators entered and casually offered, "I'm Ed Severin, the manager. What can I do for the police today?"

For the next few minutes, Bill and Terry took turns explaining their parts in the two homicide investigations. They discussed tracking the blankets from manufacturer to final purchasers. Groundwork laid, Terry asked, "Mr. Severin, can you verify you purchased the blankets from the Big Box Discount Outlet?"

In answer, Severin moved the mouse of his computer and clicked, then typed and clicked some more. Finally satisfied, he turned the screen to face Bill and Terry. It displayed an electronic invoice indicating his division had purchased 300 of the blankets three months ago. "It appears we bought the blankets from the outlet last October," he responded.

"Can I ask what purpose the blankets serve?" inquired Terry.

"The main reason is to prevent marring customers' property."

"Why not just use a roll of plastic?" asked Terry.

"Well, if I remember correctly," said Severin, "we got the blankets pretty cheap."

He scanned some entries on the computer and added, "Yeah, we can't buy rolls of plastic this cheap. Plus, these are thicker and already cut to a decent size."

Terry paused and then queried, "Where do you keep the blankets?"

Severin again tapped and scrolled before he related, "We have ten trucks, and each truck is supposed to have two packs or twelve blankets in the utility bin. They come in packets of six. That makes 120 blankets in the trucks. The rest should be in inventory. I can show you the packets in inventory," he offered, "but most of the trucks are out on service calls."

"Speaking of service calls," Terry broke in, "do you service the Allison Hill section of Harrisburg?"

"Sure. Most of those homes were converted from coal to oil in the sixties. We do a pretty good business there. In fact, I'm sure we have at least one truck making deliveries in that area today."

The discussion continued to focus on the blankets for the next few minutes before Bill requested a look at those in inventory. Escorted by the manager, they retraced their steps downstairs and entered the garage through a large metal door. "That's one serious door," declared Bill as they passed through.

"This building once belonged to the government. It supposedly housed a sanitarium during the first half of last century," expounded Severin. He emphasized, "It is a solid old structure."

Inside the cavernous garage, they turned right and entered a large room containing supplies. Lined with wall shelves and packed with freestanding racks, the space held a huge assortment of items. Unfortunately, organization didn't seem to be a central theme.

Disorder aside, Severin made his way directly to the back corner where they discovered the blankets, stuffed on a shelf on top of cleaning supplies. Clearly, he understood the method behind the perceived madness. After a quick count, he announced, "Thirty packs of six. That accounts for the one eighty in stock." With a smile, he added, "It may not look like a good system, but somehow it works."

Terry hid his skepticism, while asking, "Mr. Severin, do you keep track of the blankets in the trucks or who uses them?"

"Not really. They're considered a disposable item," he answered. "But, if it helps," he offered, "I can have someone check the vehicles."

"That might not be a bad idea," allowed Terry.

"That's no problem," replied the manager. "I'll be in late tonight anyway waiting for the overtime truck. I should have a count by no later than 8:00 p.m."

Appreciative of the cooperation, Terry stated, "That's great, Mr. Severin. We've got a few more interviews today, but I'll get back to you tomorrow morning."

Interview over, the three men returned to the warmth of the main building. As they walked toward the lobby, Mr. Severin shook hands with both investigators. Before they left, he passed a business card to Bill.

As he pocketed the card, a thought struck the young investigator. "Oh, Mr. Severin, one more thing, please," he said before the door to the lobby closed. "Do you by chance have any new workers on your payroll?"

Severin paused to think and then responded, "Actually, we have two. One started as a janitor but was recently moved up to driver. The other young guy is his replacement as janitor."

"Okay, thanks again," sidestepped Bill, noting a quizzical look dawn on the manager's face. To prevent any lingering questions, he headed out the door. Terry followed directly behind.

Quickly cutting through the icy breeze to the relative warmth of Bill's car, Terry professed, "We got a little behind in there. Let's grab an early lunch and head back to the procurement office. Bo should be back by then. There's a great Szechuan restaurant in town if you like it hot and spicy," he added mischievously.

Still not fully recovered from the prior evening, Bill, who loved hot food, responded dejectedly, "I'd better take a rain check. Maybe some dry toast or a bowl of soup."

With the wound thoroughly salted, Terry bit his tongue. No further comment necessary, he turned toward the window and hid his widening grin.

Chapter 35

Ups and Downs

As he had most days since starting this job, the man, now a killer, found a quiet spot along a side road to sit and eat his lunch. Today's fare, a premade sub purchased at a local convenience store, stood as testament to the painful memory of Monday's catastrophic lunch. No more dining in restaurants he told himself as he gnawed on the tasteless cardboard-like roll.

Down the street from a daycare center in the Oberlin section of Swatara Township, southeast of Harrisburg, he watched preschoolers amusing themselves on the fenced-in playground. Four women stood or walked about, assisting the children with the various endeavors that, at that moment, held their attention. Some swung smoothly on swings, others spun happily on a merry-go-round. Large clusters played games of tag, while sets of two or three engaged in animated conversation and role-playing.

Children of this age never excited him. In fact, he found their actions relaxing. Their world, like his, boiled down to the moment. They acted without thought or consideration of consequences. A simple comparison, he failed to identify the corresponding disparity that existed. While most children's actions represented innocence and purity of thought, his epitomized a narcissistic and malevolent nature.

His vigil continued until the cold convinced the lead caregiver that the time had arrived to shepherd the children inside. With the tact of a drill sergeant, she ordered her young troopers into a single file. Finally satisfied her fidgety charges had reached some modicum of organization, she opened the door and marched them into the warmth and onto their next great adventure.

No sooner had the door closed, and the man, once more, drifted off into the recesses of his mind. This time, he found himself in an unfamiliar setting. No older than four, he played in a small grassy area baked by the Texas sun. In spite of the heat, he laughed and ran through the cool spray of the hose held by a young version of his mother. She stood under a tree, smoking a cigarette, her smile a stark contrast to his last memory of her under the yellow blanket.

A slap to the face, the thought of his mother's final moments brought him back to the present with a shudder. Mouth gone dry, he regarded the half-eaten sub in his hand. Its partner half now churned in his stomach. Disgusted, he tossed it back into the brown paper bag and grabbed the nearby twenty-ounce iced tea. He downed the drink in two deep draughts, seeking relief within the plastic bottle.

He managed to quench his thirst only to discover it replaced by feelings of confusion. Hidden behind the mental debris of abuse and marginalization, he had glimpsed a light from his past. A long forgotten memory, the associated feeling of bliss contrasted with the person he had become.

The sudden shift from delight to death, and now this bewildering feeling, caused him to shut down. As before, he simply stared into space. Soothed by the silence, the swollen river of his mind slowly receded back into its banks, and the memory of the light diminished. Once reduced to an obscure notion, he found the strength to force shut the door to the room housing the comforting, but troublesome, recollection.

As his stomach settled, the man reviewed the ups and downs of the past few moments. Thoughts of his flagging self-control and his tedious mood swings caused anger to slowly replace fear and confusion. It built with each passing moment. Soon, he felt the return of his companion, the darkness. Bolstered by its presence and a shared rage, he returned and added a padlock to the door to the light.

Loath to experience more unexpected mental turbulence, he put the vehicle into gear and pulled onto the roadway. As he drove northwest toward the city, his ire built and his memories of his mother faded completely. Once more, the pendulum of his emotions had swung back into the shadows and his journey resumed. Now the juggernaut, he wore blinders as he considered his desires and the gratification that could only come on the heels of death.

By early afternoon, his anger had peaked and continued to percolate. Reinvigorated, he completed all his work off The Hill by

2:50 p.m. Add to this an overcast sky, which heralded an early and extended twilight, and things seemed to be falling into place.

Quite a turn-around from just a few hours before.

Now on the upward swing of another manic mood change, he forgot his earlier anxiety. He rode the wave. More relaxed and confident than he had been in days, he drove and he watched.

At Market Street he turned left, off North Cameron Street, and headed up The Hill to Thirteenth Street. After a right at Kittatinny Street and a left onto Evergreen, he arrived at his first stop in the area. An older wood framed structure, the house cried out for a fresh coat of paint and a good cleaning. He heard voices on a covered back porch as he made his way to the side of the structure.

Apparently aware of his presence, two children, a boy and a girl, poked their heads around the back corner of the house. The man estimated the girl's age at five, and the boy's at seven or eight. He noted the inquisitive looks in their dark brown eyes. Struck by their inherent innocence, he contrasted it with the burdens of life as one gets older.

Though reluctant to begin a dialogue with adults, the man had no such problem with young kids. He even smiled an unconcerned smile because children usually didn't care about his missing teeth. They often had missing teeth themselves. "Just the oil man," he offered with a wave.

The greeting caused the little girl to shy away, but the little boy couldn't hide his interest. He disappeared and then rematerialized on the old cement sidewalk running between the two houses. Before long, the little girl followed, hesitant but unwilling to miss an adventure.

With the artificial confidence of someone whose protector is nearby, the little girl spoke first and asked, "Whatcha doin'?"

"Well," responded the man, once a child, and now an oil deliveryman, "I'm filling your tank, so you can stay warm this winter."

"Not my house, but okay," she informed, turning toward her companion. "It's Perry's house. You're keepin' him warm."

The boy remained quiet as he studied the long hose and the nearby idling truck. His silence led the man to remove his leather work glove and extend his hand, saying, "Hey Perry, nice to meet you."

Trance broken, the young child eventually grasped the proffered hand in his own tiny paw. At the same time, he lifted his eyes to meet those of the young adult towering over him. Unease spread through the man. The boy seemed to look right through him. The sensation made him release the little hand as if it had somehow turned into a snake.

The disquiet remained, until Perry innocently asked, "That your truck?"

The man blinked and glanced at the big white and silver vehicle. "Ugh, yeah. Yeah, it's mine," he responded, finally able to set aside his apprehension "Maybe when you're older," he added, gaining traction, "you can go for a ride."

"I'm already plenty old enough," countered the boy.

Suddenly more interested, the man apologized and acknowledged, "Okay, okay, maybe you are old enough."

Happy with the recognition, Perry added, "Momma says I'm almost growed up."

Feeling a need to correct him, the little girl interrupted, "You're not growed enough to make your own supper. He comes to my house to eat supper 'cause his mamma don't get home 'til later," she explained further.

The man digested the harmless comment. At first, he thought the boy too small, but now he wondered. This child seemed different, special in some way. Had an opportunity just presented itself?

In the midst of this thought, the automatic sensor on the nozzle began to slow and eventually shut off, drawing his attention. He removed the handle, screwed the caps back on the pipe and vent, and wiped down the residual oil. Finished, he turned back around, only to find the two children had vanished.

Chapter 36

A Picture is Worth a Thousand Words

By that afternoon, Thomas sat in his office playing mental chess. He pondered his options and his opponent's possible errors, while absentmindedly watching Robby type and Maggie scan reports. Though he couldn't see Doc behind his wall of monitors, he occasionally heard his voice as he discussed the videos from the bank and the plumbing store. With Stan and Ronnie due back anytime, and Bill and Terry tracking the blankets, his game pieces appeared fully engaged.

With little else to do at that moment, Thomas dialed Jack Malino to provide an update. Five rings later, Malino fumbled with the phone and responded gruffly, "Captain Malino."

"Jack, this is Thomas Payne. Just checking in."

"Sorry," Malino apologized. "This phone's been ringing all day. I feel like a one-armed paper hanger."

"No problem, Jack," Thomas empathized, glossing over the terse greeting. "I just wanted to let you know we were able to get some video from a plumbing store near the target building and a bank down by the first dumpsite."

Embarrassed, Malino asked, "How'd my guys miss the video? They hit all the businesses close to that dumpsite."

In response, Thomas explained how they had checked the bank, located on a side street, at Robby's insistence. He then went on to detail the rest of the morning's efforts before inquiring, "Have your guys come up with anything new?"

"Well, my best guy's with you," Malino responded, referring to Terry Hassinger. "The others have been rearranging schedules to work the surveillance at the vacant building starting tonight at midnight. On another note," he transitioned, "the labs are back on the swabs from Jesus Rodriguez' neck. Remember the gas smell?" he asked rhetorically. "It wasn't gas. It's a distillate fuel oil, consistent with number two heating oil."

The term heating oil immediately struck a chord with Thomas, which he set aside to examine later as Malino rambled on, "In addition, the fibers containing the oil were determined to be leather, specifically cowhide."

Thomas offered, "The killer wore leather gloves when he strangled Jesus."

"My thoughts exactly," replied Malino, "but there's more. I spoke with the forensic scientist. She said the concentration and variation of the hydrocarbons in the leather fibers lead her to surmise the donor object had been in regular contact with oil over a period of time."

Both men reflected on the new information. Thomas had just begun to form a sentence, when a scene in the main office drew his attention, causing him to say, "Jack, let me call you back. I seem to have a fire burning."

He hadn't even stood before Doc broke from the group and rushed through the office door. The tech wiz talked in a rambling fashion and gestured wildly with both hands and an occasional foot. In an effort to end the clumsy ballet, Thomas put a hand out and soothed, "Doc, slow down."

"Sorry," breathed the tech man heavily. "But rather than explain, I can show you all."

In the conference room, the task force members took seats at the table, while Doc plugged his laptop into the console connected to the large screen projector. He explained as he worked, "I imported the videos from the bank and the plumbing store into our computer system. The challenge was coming up with an efficient method of review. Crossing that hurdle, I was able to analyze the bank's video in fairly quick order. I found something I want you to see."

A picture froze on the screen as he clarified, "Only the top right corner of the bank video captures the entry to the access road. I asked Overlord to cull out segments with movement in that area. What you're about to see is a compilation of those segments starting at dark on the evening the first victim, Jesus Rodrigues, went missing until his body was found the next morning."

Without further ado, Doc activated the video. The first few vehicles observed appeared to belong to the power company. At approximately 6:30 p.m., a patrol car or security company vehicle with roof mounted lights passed through. It departed within two minutes, leading Doc to point out, "Not to be a doomsayer, but this isn't the last time you'll see a similar vehicle on the video."

At about 7:30 p.m., a large tanker truck crept through the camera's field of view as it accessed and then egressed in a period of five minutes. Between 8:00 p.m. and midnight, the video captured three passenger cars and a pickup truck on the road. None of the cars returned before a half hour had passed. The pickup returned in less than a minute. Finally, two more patrol/security cars used the road around midnight and again around 4:00 a.m.

Finished with the video, Doc offered an observation, "Only the patrol vehicle repeats."

A thought stuck Thomas as he reconsidered scenes from the video. "Can you enhance the video?" he asked, overlooking Doc's observation.

Seemingly wounded by the question, the tech wiz responded by typing on his keyboard. Hesitant to interrupt, the others discussed the ramifications of what they had just seen. "This guy's most likely risk adverse," observed Stan. "So I don't see him staying around the body too long. Our focus should be on the vehicles with the shortest stays."

A few minutes into the discussion, Doc looked up and cleared his throat. "To answer your question," he related, noting everyone's attention, "Overlord does have the ability to augment video, which I'll demonstrate."

The video began another loop, this time with the enhancements. Missing pixels had been added, images magnified, and the resolution sharpened. Each of the vehicles was now identifiable by brand and color. "If I can draw your attention to the first scene showing the patrol car," said Doc, "you can probably guess by the color and markings it's from Harrisburg."

"That's good work, Doc," interrupted Thomas. "But can you go to the tanker?"

With a quizzical look, the tech wiz nodded and moved to the appropriate portion of the video. He tapped a key and a clear image of a white truck with silver tank filled the screen. Embossed on the side of the tank in unambiguous, big red letters, everyone could read, "MES – Home Heating Oil."

"Bingo," breathed Thomas.

As the puzzle piece fell into place, Thomas explained his interest. "I just spoke with Jack Malino. The labs came back indicating Jesus had heating oil on his neck, most likely from the killer's gloved hands. It didn't click until I saw the tanker on the video. Then I remembered the list. One of the big buyers of blankets was a company called Middletown Energy Solution. MES is their acronym."

He pointed at the screen and observed, "Whoever was driving that truck had access to the right blankets and probably uses gloves saturated in oil."

An excited discussion ensued as Thomas' theory was poked and prodded by the other investigators. As this occurred, Thomas noted Doc's faraway look as he retreated into the world of his computer. He hoped he hadn't hurt the man's feelings by disregarding his comments, but now wasn't the time for such considerations.

Returned to the debate, all soon agreed the pieces fit. After fifteen minutes, Stan summed up their thoughts, "Not exactly a smoking gun, but certainly a loaded one."

To everyone's surprise, Doc, whose concentration had been misinterpreted as sulking, interjected, "You want a smoking gun. You got it."

He manipulated his computer causing three still pictures to show on the white screen. The first portrayed the now familiar MES truck on the access road. The other two revealed a closer, but more obscure, image of a similar truck from another perspective.

"How did you get the head-on shots of the truck?" asked Thomas. "The bank camera doesn't have that angle."

"They're not from the bank," replied Doc. "I thought about what you said, so I used the same search method and image augmentation on the other video. Pictures two and three are from the plumbing store from the nights both kids went missing. Number three," said Doc, clicking on the image to start the linked video, "is your smoking gun."

As they watched, a figure exited the driver's side of the truck. It then climbed onto the passenger side running board and opened the door. Seconds later, the individual could be seen struggling under the shifting weight of a cradled bundle. Shortly thereafter, both the figure and its cargo disappeared around the back of the building.

"That," indicated the vindicated tech master, "is what could very well be our killer carrying Jamal to the same vacant building in which he attacked Jesus."

The members remained silent until Robby Franklin whispered, "Holy shit!"

Brought from his reverie, Thomas smiled, winked at Doc, and reached for his cell phone to make a call. On the receiving end, Bill Travis answered, "Hey, Thomas. What's up?"

"Where are you?" Thomas asked, ignoring the question.

"In Harrisburg at the procurement office."

"I thought you did that this morning?" stated Thomas in surprise.

"Actually," Bill replied, "we hit the energy company in Middletown first. Terry's contact had a doctor's appointment." As further explanation, he added, "We didn't get much there, but we're making out pretty well here."

Thomas started to explain Doc's discovery, but Bill continued undaunted, "The blankets purchased by the city went to the police and fire departments. Terry can't think of any obvious suspects, but he doesn't know many of the fire guys."

Thomas watched as the sand drained from his mental hourglass. Frustrated, he hollered, "Bill!" Amidst the resultant silence, he ordered, "Get back down to the oil company."

He explained the information from the lab report and Doc's smoking gun. "We need to know who was driving those trucks. Doc's sending still pictures to your phone as we speak. Show them to the people at the oil company. While you're doing that," he finished, "we'll be discussing our next moves on this end."

Urgency understood, Bill responded, "Heading out now, boss."

Phone back in his pocket, Bill turned to Terry and Bo Hawkins, the procurement director, and related, "Bo, we really appreciate your time, but we have to run."

Deep into a side discussion on golf, Terry seemed intent on staying until Bill grabbed his coat sleeve and guided him out of his chair. With a quick goodbye to his friend, Terry waited until the door closed behind him to state, "What the hell. Bo was explaining the fix for my slice."

As he hustled to the car, Bill enlightened Terry to the recent discoveries. Once inside, he pulled out his cell phone to review his emails. Doc had sent three pictures, each labeled and dated. Most interesting, the third included a shadowy figure carrying something near the truck.

With a low whistle, Terry conceded, "Okay, I guess this qualifies as more important than my golf game."

"I thought you'd agree," returned Bill, who added with a cheesy Cuban accent, "seems like someone's got some splainin to do, Lucy."

The return trip to Middletown took almost twenty-five minutes in the late-afternoon traffic. As they pulled into the lot, things appeared much the same as they had that morning. The only differences of note, the two trucks, which had been outside the garage, now sat next to the depot, and the day edged toward darkness.

The two investigators hurried up the steps and into the lobby. Behind the sliding glass, they noticed the receptionist, Jill, organizing papers on her desk. She glanced up and greeted, "Well, hello again. Forget something?"

"Actually, we did," responded Bill. "Would it be possible to speak with Mr. Severin again?"

She checked her desk clock whose luminous dial indicated 4:30. "We have an overtime truck out tonight, so he's probably still upstairs. If you want to have a seat, I'll check."

Before she could close the window, Terry interposed himself and stated, "We're in a little bit of a hurry this time, so if he's out, please let us know."

Offended by the comment, she slid the window closed and picked up her phone. Seconds later, she opened the door and stated coolly, "Mr. Severin asked that I send you up."

Immediately she resumed her end-of-the-day activities, seemingly oblivious to their existence. A chill in the air, Bill and Terry walked unescorted through the main office to the stairway. As they climbed the steps, Terry commented in a low voice, "I think I hurt her feelings."

"Her loss," responded Bill.

"What?"

"I can't ask her out now," Bill explained. "She's giving off a *Fatal Attraction* vibe."

Amazed by the comment and, in general, with the workings of Bill's mind, Terry remained silent until he knocked on Mr. Severin's open door. "You first, Romeo," he offered.

Still seated behind his desk, the manager stood and joked, "Two visits in one day. You either have more questions or just missed me." After a slight pause, he added, "Since it's probably not the latter, what else can I help with?"

In a more serious tone, Bill explained in further detail about the connection between the blankets and the recent murders in Harrisburg. He showed the digital images to Severin, who admitted, "Those certainly look like our vehicles. How're they related to your case?" he inquired.

Without too much specificity, Bill responded, "These pictures were taken at times and locations important to our investigation. The third appears to show someone carrying an object, the size of a child. These pictures, along with the blanket connection and some forensic evidence found at the scenes, lead us to believe someone in your employ may be involved."

Severin considered the implications. Finally, he breathed deeply and declared, "Well, boys, I'd say this puts us on a first name basis. How about you just call me Ed?" He paused for a contemplative moment and considered, "Ya know, I have four grandkids. Since this started last month, their parents have been on edge, and they don't even live in the city."

As if his words gave him strength, he suddenly sat straight in his seat. With a look at both officers, he concluded, "This might not be good for the company name, but what's right is right. Whatever I can do to help, I will. Ask away."

Chapter 37

Insight

Blind to the figurative noose tightening around his neck, the man worked steadily, whittling away at his list of deliveries. With one service call remaining, he found his attention drawn to a meandering community cemetery at the south end of The Hill. There, under the streetlights, a wondrous vista stretched before him. Amongst the grass and snow covered acres, he spotted a group of kids playing in the remains of a snow pile.

Parked nearby, he watched as the children happily built tunnels and threw snowballs. His anger blossomed anew as he flashed back on his own pathetic life. He had so few memories of such simple bliss. Even his earlier recollection of his mother holding the hose remained locked away as if it had never happened.

Unable to access positive memories, he gave himself no choice, but to reflect upon his stepfather, his mother's death, the numerous foster homes, counseling sessions, and most recent of all, his explorations. These memories formed the foundation for his journey. Joy and happiness had no place. They could only weaken the structure.

Now, six months into his quest, he had lost sight of the numerous defensive barriers and delusions he had created along the way. As a result, he failed to realize that without joy, he had been slowly drowning in a cesspool of his own creation. More important, hidden behind the veil of his fantasies, he failed to understand the extent of his mental illness.

Unfortunately, another of life's ironies, the sick mind doesn't recognize its own fault. Unable to differentiate between reflection, happening, or premonition, he required repair. Had he been a computer, a tech would simply wipe him clean and reinstall his operating system. But, incapable of comprehending the existence or depth of his disease, he continued to imagine and plot.

This led to another inaccuracy in his thinking. Simply put, he wasn't a planner. He mistook his world of illusion for one of preparation. In reality, he had evolved into a creature of opportunity. To punctuate this point, he need only review the drastic difference between the perfection of his fantasies and the reality of his actions.

None of these considerations, though, passed through his head as he winnowed through the herd, feeding his desire. He counted seven boys and, what looked like, a little girl. Only interested in the boys, two appeared the proper age. Either would do.

At this point, he recalled his final delivery a few blocks away. Now conflicted, he recognized the need to choose between remaining and returning. He spent the next few minutes debating the finer points. In the end, he acknowledged the benefits of completing his work first. Unencumbered for the rest of the evening, he would have the freedom to explore to his heart's content.

Resolute in his decision, he snatched a final glimpse of his prey, put the big truck into gear, and drove east. He quickly made his way down Argyle Street to the address on Catherine. His last delivery took less than ten minutes. Not that anyone noticed, but he arbitrarily stopped filling at fifty gallons. He had places to go.

Anxious to leave, he shut down the pump, forced the hose into the spindle, and removed his wheel chocks. He had just reached the silver utility box when a thought struck him. After he stowed the rubber wedges to the right, he reached to the left and grabbed one of the plastic blankets hiding in the shadows. He would have use for it in the near future.

Eagerly he hopped into the cab and retraced his path back to the cemetery. He arrived a few minutes before 6:00 p.m., brimming with anticipation. Stopped along the roadway, he gazed in wonder at an empty field. Doubting his own eyes, he searched through the lit portion of the cemetery into the darkness to the south. Nothing moved other than the vehicle lights on I-83. A similar picture greeted him to the west out to Thirteenth Street.

Near panic, he opted to drive north on Fourteenth Street. Within seconds, his disappointment flared. He saw no sign of the elusive creature he so desired to capture. He had failed again.

Suddenly exhausted, he pulled to the side and put his head on the cool plastic of the steering wheel. Only moments before, positive and focused on the future, he had felt strong and alive. Now his previously awesome wave had turned maverick, hammering him into despair. Though he had promised himself to remain upbeat, he couldn't help but fall back on the failures of his past.

With disappointment and misery whirling his thoughts into a frenzy, the man became cognizant of a now familiar sound. It started as a whisper and grew into a tempest that blocked his five senses. Reduced to the same glassy-eyed, drooling state he had found himself in at the restaurant, he failed to take note of the four young boys lazily making snow angels on the other side of a snow pile, not thirty feet away.

Eventually, the storm of doubt and frustration clouding his mind passed, replaced by a curious silence. Alone without the chaos to occupy his thoughts, he suddenly felt the need to move. Wearily he wrenched the shift lever into drive and sluggishly maneuvered into the roadway.

He drove without conscious thought. Robotically he turned left at Kittatinny Street and continued until he found himself back on Evergreen. He mindlessly drove down the block until he saw the familiar old wood-framed structure. Its sudden appearance caused his slide into depression to slow and then stop.

New prospects began to take shape in his mind. He recalled his conversation with the little boy and girl. All the while, he watched a light through a front room window. It summoned him like a moth to a flame.

Now parked with the diesel engine running, he slithered from his seat and out the door. Although definitely the same house on the same street, the night lent a different aura to the neighborhood. Under the shadows of the old bare maple trees lining the street on this cold winter's eve, even the man could sense the evil in the air. Only, he thought of it as the darkness, and he was the carrier.

Despair and negativity temporarily wiped away, he cautiously made his way across the street and onto the sidewalk. He stopped momentarily and listened for movement. Only the distant sounds of traffic reached his ears. Other senses working, he caught the odor of moist, composting vegetation mixed with the diesel exhaust of his idling truck.

Then it happened. Fate intervened again, but this time on his behalf. While working his way to the side of the house, the front door opened, and the little boy scampered out. Hidden within a cave of obscurity between the two buildings, the man watched intently as the boy locked the front door. He recalled the words of the little neighbor girl, "He comes to my house to eat supper 'cause his mamma don't get home 'til later."

As the man slinked farther away from the light, he noted the energy increasing throughout his system. The excitement had returned and along with it, clarity of purpose and strength of body. Once again, in touch with the darkness, he had become the wolf.

At the same time the man experienced a boost in vigor, the little boy noted an increase in anxiety. He didn't like the dark. In order to combat his trepidation, he had taken to skipping and humming as he made his nightly adventure across the fifty-foot chasm separating the homes. Fortunately, he had made the trip numerous times and had survived each experience.

Nervous, yet resolute, he once again made his way from the illuminated area cast by the lamps and porch lights of the houses into the intervening darkness. Focused on his tried and true routine, he failed to perceive the evil that had taken up residence in the normally vacant shadows. At the mid-point, a place nearly void of light, his error became apparent. The blackness came alive. Transformed into a wave, it enveloped him and pounded his tiny body. It savagely pulled him, dazed and bruised, from his world into another.

For his part, the man operated on instinct. Prize in hand, he dragged the limp figure to the passenger side of his vehicle. Though less than a hundred pounds, the body of the child proved a challenge to lift into the truck. He had forgotten the difficulties of moving deadweight. Finally, under the anonymity provided by the night and the trees, he secured the boy onto the large vinyl seat with the seat belt.

Now in the cab, he loomed over the small, immobile form. Unexpectedly, the desire to explore overwhelmed him. At that moment a vehicle passed slowly down the street. It broke his contemplation and reminded him of the need to move on.

Shaken from his dark thoughts, the man worked his way across the cramped compartment. In the driver's seat he listened for the sounds of shouting from curious neighbors or the police sirens of which he often dreamed. Relieved by the silence, he put the truck into gear and, as quickly as the big vehicle would allow, drove away with his treasure.

Though he breathed heavily from the exertion, he couldn't help but smile. His evening had turned to shit. Then, all of a sudden, this gift had fallen into his lap. Even with all the ups and downs, he and the darkness always found a way. Once more solidly on the path of discovery, nothing would stop him from uncovering the secrets that had for so long remained buried from his view.

Movement in the cab caused him to shift his eyes from the road. The boy stirred. Soon he would regain consciousness. Not about to let that happen until he reached his lair on Cameron Street, the man pulled over with the full intent of rendering the child unconscious one more time.

Unclasping his seat belt, he slid over just as the boy said in a weak voice, "I'm in the Oilman's truck." He repeated the comment as his attacker moved in.

The man loomed over the child. He pulled his right arm back and made a fist. On the verge of release, he stopped suddenly when the little boy blinked and asked, "Oilman, are you here to help me?"

Momentarily disarmed by the random question, the man found he couldn't swing his arm. As if someone had grabbed ahold of his wrist, he felt paralyzed. He examined his stubborn limb, but saw that nothing external prevented it from moving. Mystified, he pondered the problem. In time, the unresponsive appendage unlocked on its own and dropped to his side.

He remained above the boy, studying him. At first he saw nothing. Then, as if someone had placed a mirror in front of him, he distinguished the familiar reflection. He and the boy radiated sadness. Though they seemed, at first, to be nothing alike, other than their skin and eye color, this discovery gave him pause.

More awake, the boy stated, "You've come to help me. I can tell."

"What?" stammered the man.

Rather than answer, the boy stated, "We're alike, aren't we."

"What do you mean?" probed the man, now intrigued.

In answer, the little boy pulled up his coat and shirtsleeves. The man, once a boy himself, retreated upon glimpsing what appeared to be fresh cigarette burns. His mind flashed back to his own childhood. As his brain spun up and his intestines began to churn, the little boy's words, now a question, kept repeating in his head, "We're alike, aren't we?"

Chapter 38

Coincidence

Ed Severin examined the images on Bill's phone and professed, "I'm just not sure. The resolution isn't very good. Can we look at them on my computer monitor?"

Reticent to lose control of the pictures, Bill observed a subtle nod of Terry's head and conceded, "I'll email you the two photos which just show the trucks. I'll trust you to delete them."

Two minutes later, after viewing the images on the twenty-two inch, high-definition computer monitor, Ed shook his head and grumbled, "Still no good."

"Can anyone identify the trucks?" asked Terry.

"Maybe Luke," thought Ed out loud. He met Terry's gaze and offered, "Our mechanic goes home by 4:30, but lives in town. Let me give him a call. If he's able to identify the vehicles, I can check the schedule to see who they were assigned to."

With Terry's consent, Ed made contact with Luke Johnson at home. He asked the mechanic to return to the shop to help finish some administrative work regarding the trucks. Less than a minute later, he announced, "On his way."

Ed then slid back to his computer to continue perusing the company's records. As he worked, he explained the operation of the business to include scheduling. As a general rule, the drivers worked from 7:00 a.m. to 4:00 p.m. or 8:00 a.m. to 5:00 p.m. on Tuesday through Friday. Each took an hour unpaid lunch.

Mondays, during the winter, a few drivers worked extra hours to catch up from the weekend. Additionally, the company scheduled emergency deliveries on Saturdays if necessary. Occasionally a confluence of events caused a driver or two to work late another night of the week. Tonight happened to be one of those nights, due to the recent holidays.

By this time, they heard someone coming down the hallway. A few seconds later, Luke stuck his head in the open doorway. He hesitated upon noticing the investigators, but finally walked in.

"Relax, Luke," invited Bill, noting his discomfort. "I already told you, we're not here for you."

"Do you two know each other?" queried Ed with a perplexed look.

"Old friends," answered Bill as a smile crept across his face. "In a good way."

The comment caused Luke to relax. Nevertheless, he remained standing inside the door until Ed Severin invited him to look at the pictures on the computer. Without explanation, Ed inquired, "How well do you know our vehicles?"

The mechanic moved closer and studied the photos for nearly five minutes. He talked out loud and asked Ed to zoom in on certain areas. In the end, he summarized his thoughts by saying, "The long distance shot of the first truck's hard to tell, but if I had to pick, I'd say that's 401. It's older and has damage to the pump housing." He paused and pointed to the second photo noting, "This is definitely 403. I can tell by the body style and the dent here on the right fender."

"How sure are you?" asked Terry.

"Hundred percent on 403," asserted Luke, "maybe seventy-five on the other. The picture's just too far away."

With a glance at Ed, Bill submitted, "I don't wanna keep Luke from his supper. Anything else he might be able to help with?"

"Nope, he's already been a big help," responded Ed knowingly.

To facilitate Luke's departure, he stood and offered his hand, stating, "Thanks, Luke. I appreciate you coming over. That should do it for tonight."

"No problem, Mr. Severin," replied Luke, taking the cue. "Glad to help out."

Though curious, he never asked the importance of identifying the trucks. He simply turned and departed the way he came, running the possibilities through his head. In the end, he determined one of the trucks must have been involved in an accident, surely something that could have waited until the morning.

It wouldn't be until some hours later that he would discover just how important his ten minutes of time had been.

As Luke descended the stairway, Terry returned his gaze to the monitor on Ed Severin's desk. "Ed, the first picture is time stamped Monday, December fifth at 7:30 p.m., the other for Monday, December nineteenth at 7:13 p.m.," he observed. "Let's see who was operating the trucks at those times."

Without comment, Ed went to work on his computer. A few keystrokes later he said, "It looks like John Thompson had 401 on the fifth. That's a problem because he's one of our senior drivers."

He tapped more keys and eventually sighed, "I just cross checked the information with the timesheets. It looks like John went home at 4:30 that day." As explanation, he related, "The older drivers normally don't pull the extra hours unless they want to. So, Luke made a mistake, or someone working later came back and used 401 rather than refilling the truck they were assigned."

"Is there any way to figure what happened?" queried Terry.

"Not really," replied Ed. "The drivers never mark it down."

Frustrated, Bill cut in, "Check the vehicle from the second picture. Luke was sure of that one."

Ed returned to the computer and manipulated the keys and mouse. He reviewed several timesheets before he indicated, "Four-oh-three was assigned to Manny Gutierrez on the nineteenth. When I cross reference the timesheets, I see he worked until 8:00 that night. Going back to the timesheets for the fifth, Manny worked late that night as well."

"Tell me about Gutierrez," entreated Bill, mulling over the offender profile.

"Well," Ed began, "he's young, early twenties. Quiet, doesn't talk much. He started working here in the summer as a janitor. I remember when we hired him," he added, perusing the electronic personnel record. "He seemed capable, and he's Hispanic, which helped with our company's overall diversity. He did the janitor job for about four months. Maybe not the most reliable person, but you don't have to be in that position. Then one of our regular drivers hurt himself and went on disability."

He paused for a breath and then continued, "Winter being our busy season, we were desperate, looking for a replacement driver on short notice. As it turned out, Manny had worked for a petro company in Texas. He worked as a guard, but they required him to obtain a commercial driver's license. We gave him a shot at driving, and he's done a decent job ever since."

Ed turned the screen toward the investigators. Along with background information, they observed the photo of a young, light-skinned Hispanic male with close-cropped brown hair. With his unsmiling face and brown eyes devoid of humor, the picture appeared more like a mug shot than a company photo. The associated descriptive data indicated he stood five feet six inches tall and weighed one hundred and forty pounds.

"So he's what, twenty years old?" remarked Terry as he studied the file. "He leaves a decent job in Texas at the end of June to come to Pennsylvania and unemployment. He lucks into a job, which purely by chance leads to a higher paying job with more freedom, which he starts in November. In December we start having kids picked off our streets and killed." He eyed Bill and asked flippantly, "Coincidence? I think not."

After a nod of agreement, Bill posed one final question, "Ed, you said you had people working tonight. Is Gutierrez?"

"According to the logs for today, he's the only one working tonight."

Bill considered the ramifications and announced "I need to call the boss."

He reached Thomas immediately and explained their discovery. "If this is our guy," Thomas stated, "he's been presented with another opportunity. Knowing what we know, we can't leave him out there."

He paused as the pieces of a plan fell into place. "Finish compiling info on this guy," he resumed. "I'll fill in Jack Malino, and then Robby and I'll start looking for an MES truck on The Hill, while Stan and Ronnie set-up on the abandoned warehouse."

With a sense that time was running short, Thomas signed off quickly. This left Bill with a moment to think. As he listened to Terry and Ed Severin discuss Gutierrez, he struck upon an idea. "We should think about getting a search warrant for this guy's residence," he interrupted.

Further discussion ensued, leading Bill to ask, "Ed, do you provide lockers or storage for your drivers?"

"Each has a locker in the shower room off the garage."

"Let's include the locker on the warrant," decided Bill.

A curious looked crossed Ed's face. He cleared his throat and offered, "I don't want to overstep, but I don't think that's necessary."

With a few taps of the keyboard, he brought up a picture of a scanned document from Gutierrez' on-line personnel record. He read through the text quickly and explained, "See here. He signed a disclaimer indicating the locker's provided as a convenience, but remains the property of the company. According to our attorneys, I can look through the locker anytime I want. Though, it's never been done before," he added.

Both Bill and Terry remained silent as they mulled over the situation. Finally, Terry spoke up, "Would you mind us tagging along if you look?"

With a sly smile, Ed responded, "I'd be disappointed if you didn't."

Chapter 39

Wolf or Cat

Still stopped alongside the road, mulling over the boy's statement, the man previously known by many names, but now simply as Manny, felt his stomach lurch. As if the emotional roller coaster he occupied tonight had reached the apex of its journey, he found himself looking over the precipice, ready to take the steep plunge. Did he have some strange connection to this child? Could the boy provide some insight?

Slowly he turned to his passenger. He no longer felt in control. His breathing had become ragged, his heart raced, and his head started to pound. Yet the tiny figure next to him seemed at ease. The boy looked up with an expression of hope.

"HHow ddid that happen?" stuttered Manny, nodding at the marks on the little arm.

"You know," responded the child knowingly.

The modest answer caused a ripple of fear in Manny's chest because he, in fact, did know. He knew on multiple levels, including that which had become the most important: in his mind's eye. "Who is he?" he asked with acceptance.

"My mother's boyfriend."

Manny recognized the injuries as just the most recent remnants of a life lived in pain and fear. Though hesitant, he continued, "How long has he been doing that to you?"

The boy fell silent. Then, he turned toward the window as if looking into the past and validated Manny's thoughts. Barely audible, he whispered, "As long as I can remember."

With these words, the projectionist fired up the well-used equipment in Manny's mind and filled his head with moving images. His stepfather grabbed him. He choked him. Only this time, Manny had a different perspective, as if floating above his own body.

Then the scene changed. Like an early silent film, the frames transformed to black and white. The door to his bedroom opened quickly. The silhouette rushed in, and then the door abruptly closed. This sight repeated over and over: the light, then the dark as the door opened and closed; light and dark, opened and closed.

Unsure how much time had elapsed before the nightmare movie trailer ended, he woke and noticed that the little boy had unbuckled himself. Though he could have chosen to escape, he had moved closer and placed his hand on Manny's. His touch had brought Manny back from his mental ordeal.

"It'll be okay, Oilman," reassured the child. "Don't think about the bad stuff."

As he stared at the tiny hand, Manny couldn't stop from doing what he had felt like doing on so many other occasions; he wept. His mind began to wander again but not into the past or future. It remained in the present as he compared his life to that of the child beside him. Although their formative years had been similar, his small passenger had yet to let the yoke of injustice break him down.

The boy had experienced and endured hurt and shame at the hands of the adults tasked to care for and nurture him. What would have crushed the will of those same adults had only sharpened his resolve to survive. Most important of all, it hadn't taken away his ability to display compassion for others.

He examined the little boy beside him and felt the wall surrounding him and blocking his view slowly crumble into dust. In that moment he realized something very important. He realized he had a choice. He had always had a choice. However, like a losing game show contestant selecting the gift behind curtain number one, hoping to trade his meager winnings for a car, he had chosen poorly. His prize, it seemed, was a life of selfishness and discontent.

The insight caused him to pull his hand away from...Perry, he suddenly remembered. He hadn't reacted in revulsion, but in fear, and not fear for himself, but for his passenger. Manny knew his hands had performed unspeakable acts. In coordination with a damaged mind, they had painted a tableau of horror.

Reintroduced to the sentiment of sympathy for another human being, Manny realized that at some point, he had lost his way. His quest for answers had become an obscenity, a perversion of man's basic instinct for understanding. Blinders removed, forced to consider his past actions in a new light, his mind smoked and sputtered. In the midst of his emotional dogfight, he found himself saying, "Put on your seatbelt. We're going for a drive."

Thirty seconds later, Manny sat at the red light on Market and Cameron Streets, still wrestling with old and new emotions. In the left turn lane, his first reaction had been to continue on to the abandoned building. Yet as the light turned green, he found himself lumbering north across the through-lane to a symphony of horns. On some subconscious level, he knew what this boy had to tell him would never be understood in the darkness.

Ignorant to the cacophony behind him, he continued north on Cameron Street, passing under the deck of the State Street Bridge. Mind awhirl, he glossed over the beauty of its curved concrete arches and pylons. He searched for something that persisted in eluding him. Near Herr Street, he suddenly knew why he had come this way. One block off Cameron he spied the truck garage.

At the red light, he turned right and drove to the large commercial vehicle facility located off the roadway to his right. After a quick search, he found an appropriate spot and backed in the conspicuous tanker. Nestled between a box truck and a dump truck, his vehicle became one more pebble of sand on the nearly block-long beach. Alone with this boy, who seemed so much like the Manny of his youth, he turned off the lights and shut down the chattering engine.

For minutes, he sat quietly listening to the ticking exhaust as the heat dissipated into the cool air. Finally, he faced his young passenger, and inquired, "Why aren't you afraid of me?"

The child tilted his head in consideration. Then as if explaining to a child himself, he said, "You and I are like cats. We play and watch out for each other. We're not like the dogs that chase us or the wolves that try to eat us. Like mamma's boyfriends."

Astonished by the boy's reference to wolves, Manny blinked and took in a deep breath. How did he know about the wolves? Then the rest of the boy's comment registered. He had mentioned his mother's boyfriends, not singular, but plural. "Have other wolves hurt you?" he probed.

Maintaining eye contact, the little boy answered, "Most of them."

At that moment, Manny's twisted and rapidly deteriorating mind found it difficult to wrap itself around Perry's comments. Taken with the story of the child, he continued to pose questions, to learn. For the first time in his life, he allowed himself to see through the eyes of someone else, eyes more black and blue than his own.

As they talked, Manny marveled at the resiliency of the young boy. He had already seen the worst the world had to offer, but its evil seemed to have had little effect on him. Though bruised and scarred, he continued to have hope.

Manny agreed they were alike, but in one key respect they differed. Whereas Perry had yet to sour to his mortal existence,

Manny's apple had long ago fallen from the tree. Now bitter, pitted, and worm infested, his fruit had lost its innate purity.

He wondered if the boy would change as he got older and began to understand more of what had happened to him. But as he peered into the brown eyes that had once reminded him of his own, Manny felt certain this boy would never share his fate. Though he searched, he saw no sign of the wolf, no monster.

The realization brought with it a dilemma. He felt a connection with this child, but to leave unfinished what he had started left him vulnerable. His confusion and anxiety grew as his perspective rapidly switched between cat and wolf. Suddenly he felt claustrophobic. He needed to move. As a result, at 7:15 on Wednesday evening, Manny Gutierrez turned over the engine and left his hidey-hole.

He pulled back onto Herr Street and then turned left onto Cameron. Headed south, he now had a decision to make. What type of animal was he, a cat or a wolf?

Intent on this unexpected turn of events, he remained ignorant to the fine tendrils of the web being spun around him. More important, he failed to notice the hunter had become the hunted.

Chapter 40

The Pieces Fall into Place

As Manny struggled with the tatters of his rediscovered humanity, Thomas completed the first leg of his grid search of The Hill. Methodic in his movements, he turned left onto Hill Street, and left again onto Fourteenth Street for the journey back north. Heads on swivels, he and Robby had no idea they followed the same path traveled just minutes before by their quarry.

"Thought anymore about the chick from the restaurant?" inquired Robby out of the blue.

Caught off guard, Thomas initially remained silent, then hesitantly answered, "Actually, I ran into her last night."

"You dog," uttered Robbie as his smile widened. "I knew there was something there."

"Let's not make a big deal out of it."

"Thomas," said Robby, turning more serious, "it is a big deal. Your social life sucks. Except the time you spend with me, of course," he added.

Thomas recognized the dog-with-a-new-bone-look on his friend's face. With no other recourse, he related the story of his encounter with Breanne O'Malley. After he had passed along the particulars, he added, "It's like some invisible hand is nudging me in her direction."

"Why do you care?" responded Robbie. "You're drawn to her, and she returns the sentiment. Let it run its course."

A simple, but logical observation, Thomas nearly had to call Robby a wise man for the second time in two days. His reprieve came in the form of his ringing phone. He answered without consulting the display.

"Thomas," the garbled voice responded.

It took him a second to recognize the caller as Bill Travis. "Bill," he stated, "you're breaking up."

In return, he heard, "Going outside."

Ten seconds later he was rewarded with a loud and clear, "Can you hear me now?"

"Yeah, that's much better. Where were you?"

"In the locker room at MES," replied Bill. "The signal's crap inside. We checked Gutierrez' locker."

"What about a search warrant?" Thomas cut in.

"Unnecessary," answered Bill. "The lockers belong to the company. The workers all signed waivers." Undaunted, he persisted, "This guy's collecting souvenirs." He let the comment hang and then explained, "We found a box under some clothing. As soon as I opened it, I knew we had the right guy. Inside was a stuffed bunny wearing a yellow wristband stenciled with 'WWJD?' On the underside of the band were the initials 'JCW,' Jamal Cedric Wilson. I also found a small branch that resembles a handgun. It might be a stretch, but if Jesus had a stick rifle, he may have had a stick pistol as well."

As Thomas considered the new information, his call waiting began to beep. Jack Malino's name showed on the display. He asked Bill to hold while he said, "Robby, Captain Malino just tried to call. Call him back, so I can finish here."

Back on the line, he asked, "What about the bunny?"

Silent for a moment, Bill responded stoically, "Stan said there might be others."

As Thomas chewed on the words, he noticed Robby put his cell phone away. He asked Bill to hold again, while he filled Robby in on the discovery of the possible souvenirs. During the short conversation, he noticed a troubled look on his friend's face.

"What's the matter?" Thomas invited.

"That ties in with the Captain's call. Another little boy's missing over on Evergreen Street."

Temporarily speechless, Thomas finally exclaimed, "Shit!"

A moment later, he remembered Bill Travis remained on hold. "Get back here right away," he said after passing along the bad news. "You take the southern end of The Hill, and we'll stay up north. We need to find that truck. Also," he added just before hanging up, "get the biographical data to Doc for a work-up."

After the call, he set his phone in the console. He remained quiet for a second before he resolutely declared, "We can't let this happen again. Not on our watch."

With an equally unyielding expression, Robby Franklin responded, "I hear ya, brother."

A he sorted through the new information, Thomas realized he needed to fill in the rest of the team. He first contacted Stan and Ronnie and instructed, "Maintain your stakeout of the vacant building. Keep eyes on the property, but also watch Cameron Street since it's the main thoroughfare in the area."

Finally, he closed the loop by calling Jack Malino to discuss the quickly changing playing field. After he digested Thomas' new information about souvenirs, Malino indicated, "Damn-it, this thing's picking up speed. I was heading to Evergreen Street, but I'm turning around and coming to you. We need to locate that truck like yesterday. Give me a minute. I'm going to call for patrol assistance. If we saturate the area, we'll find this prick a lot faster."

Thomas waited on line as Malino talked on his police radio. He picked up the disappointing response. A traffic crash on Third Street and a possible fight at a school basketball game had all the patrols tied up.

Back on the phone Malino said, "Our patrols are on calls. I'll have units respond as they come available."

"That's okay," replied Thomas. "We've got the area covered. What about the information on the missing kid?"

"Hold on," answered Malino. He read from his notes, "His name's Perry Lomax. He's an eight-year-old Hispanic male, approximately four feet seven inches tall, weighing about seventy-five pounds. He was home alone. He was supposed to eat at a neighbor's house but never showed up. The neighbor had a key and went to check, but the boy was gone. Nothing in the house appears to have been disturbed. We're checking with neighbors now, but nobody saw anything unusual."

"Did anybody see an oil truck in the area?" interrupted Thomas.

Silent for a moment, Malino replied, "I doubt the officer knew to ask. I'll call him back right now to make sure that's covered."

Conversation over, Thomas dialed the number for Director Greene. Thankfully, his call went to voicemail after five rings. Though he wanted to update the agency head, he had little time for questions, so leaving a message more than sufficed. He had just finished with the voicemail when he observed a dark unmarked police sedan coming up the street toward them.

It pulled in next to their vehicle in a convenience store parking lot near Derry and Thirteenth Streets. Now side by side with the windows down, the cars' heaters fought to keep the cold, damp air at bay. Jack Malino started the conversation, "Our officer at the missing kid's house asked about the oil truck. The little girl from next door was with the boy today when a man matching Gutierrez' description made an oil delivery."

He paused to consult his notebook then continued, "The deliveryman left the invoice hanging from the mailbox attached to the house. One hundred and seventy-eight point four gallons of heating oil was delivered by M. Gutierrez at 3:15 p.m." Unable to stop himself, he added, "The oil company charged three dollars and ninety-one point nine cents for the oil. If we can't arrest this guy for kidnapping or murder, I say we arrest somebody for highway robbery."

"When was the boy last seen?" asked Thomas overlooking the police humor.

"According to the little girl, she and the boy played until dark, and then she went home. So let's say roughly 5:00 p.m."

"That means he could've had the boy for over two hours," thought Thomas out loud after checking the clock.

He ran the calculations in his head before stating, "He could be in Scranton by now. But I don't think so," he corrected himself. "That's not his MO. He's around here somewhere."

"Any chance we can get a helicopter?" chimed in Malino.

"Good thought," returned Thomas. "Let me contact the hanger."

On the phone for no more than two minutes, the tone of the conversation and the disappointed look on Thomas' face told the tale. "Clouds are too low, and a snow squall's moving in. They won't fly for at least an hour; then they can only say they'll reassess," he explained.

Sarcastically, Robby interrupted, "Amazing how often a five million dollar asset is unavailable. Good use of my tax dollars."

"Give 'em a break," maintained Thomas. "Their ride costs as much as a fleet of cars, and if they develop mechanical problems, they can't just pull to the side of the road."

Properly chastised, Robby grinned and granted, "Just venting, boss."

Back on task, Thomas noticed he had received Doc's information packet on Gutierrez via email. Along with a narrative biography, the document included a picture. "If I send you the bio on Gutierrez, can you forward it to your dispatch, so it's available to all your officers?" he asked Malino.

Jack nodded, allowing Thomas to continue, "That brings up one other major point. We need to establish communications between agencies. Right now all we have are our cell phones. We can use them on group talk, but that doesn't help us communicate with you."

After a moment, Malino offered, "Get in with me. You have the phone for contact with the task force, and I have the radio for communications with the HPD and other police."

A logical plan, Thomas gathered his belongings and hopped in the passenger side of the captain's vehicle. They had just pulled out to resume their sweep of the area when Thomas' phone went active on group talk. A few octaves higher than normal, Stan Brown stated, "Boss, a large tanker is moving south on Cameron Street."

In the background Ronnie's voice could be heard, "White cab, silver tank. It's slowing down."

During the extended silence that followed, the task force members sat frozen, literally, on the edge of their seats. A few pregnant seconds later, Stan's, now incredulous, voice broke through the hush as he declared, "The son of a bitch drove right by. He just kept going. He's heading south on Cameron." He added, "It *is* an M.E.S. truck."

Again, Ronnie could be heard in the background, "I saw a driver, but I couldn't see anyone else."

The implications of Ronnie's comment sent a chill down Thomas' spine. Had they found their target too late?

"What do you want us to do, boss?" Stan posed, interrupting his morbid thought.

Thomas quickly went to work considering the changing angles. "Anyone monitoring the cameras on the abandoned building?" he asked Malino.

"A clerk, but she's a sharp girl," responded Malino as he vectored toward Cameron Street.

Without further input, Thomas directed the troops, "Stan, follow the truck at a distance. Robby, head down to Cameron. We'll go to Cameron as well. Bill, you get back to The Hill in case he returns."

As he spoke, he continued to picture the pieces shifting on the chessboard. He considered possibilities, probabilities, and priorities. Experience told him they would soon have Gutierrez. It also made him wonder if they had arrived in time. Often the difference between life and death came down to two frustratingly simple points: luck and timing. With a little boy's life hanging in the balance, he prayed God would provide plenty of both.

Chapter 41

Thundering Hoof Beats

As Manny neared the abandoned building on Cameron Street, he felt the tug of his desires. A mental dogfight raged in his mind: cat or wolf. In the end, indecision saved the boy's life. Unable to resolve the conflict, Manny did what came easiest, nothing.

To his surprise after he passed the familiar structure, its appeal diminished with distance. His failure to act had in fact been a choice. He liked being a cat.

Satisfied with his non-decision, he turned left onto Berryhill Street, where the truck's transmission dropped down a gear as it struggled up the steep hill. With Stan and Ronnie unknowingly in tow, Manny continued for approximately three tenths of a mile before turning left onto Thirteen Street. Neither he nor his passenger spoke.

In their companionable silence, they lumbered along in the clumsy vehicle, passing drivers and passengers headed in the opposite direction, all unaware of the drama unfolding around them. As he drove, Manny occasionally glanced over to see his tiny passenger rubbing the back of his head where he had hit him. He now wished he hadn't struck the boy, but it had all happened prior to the "cat discussion." Had he known then what he knew now, he might have acted differently.

He turned onto Kittatinny Street and drove the length of the first block before slowing at Evergreen Street. Prepared to turn left, he saw a crowd milling around down the block. Like a trendy block party centered on the boy's home, it appeared the entire neighborhood had turned out. Curious, he almost turned onto the street when he caught sight of a marked police car in the midst of the bedlam.

Manny's mind failed to process the information provided by his eyes. On overload, his mental engine seized. Unable to act, he continued straight on Kittatinny. This time, his indecision probably saved his own life, not from the police, but from the public.

Questioned by the officers investigating Perry's disappearance, those in the crowd had learned firsthand or through the grapevine that an oil tanker factored into the equation in some unknown way. With two children already dead, the possibility of a third had amplified community sentiment to a fever pitch. Within their gauntlet, the massive, but slow moving, oil tanker would have made the perfect object on which to vent their rage.

Wits otherwise engaged, Manny continued to the end of Kittatinny and turned left onto Crescent Street. He remained oblivious as he rumbled past the aging residence on his right, which had been home to his first victim, Jesus Rodriguez. Fixated straight ahead, he never considered the mother who sat in the dark living room hidden behind the bricks and mortar of her grief.

Likewise, he didn't realize that directly over the hill stood the very building to which he had taken his victims. Unable to perform in-depth calculations or analysis, he considered only his most basic needs. At that moment, focused on safety, he contented himself with driving up and down streets he no longer recognized.

When he finally wrestled his thoughts into a coherent, yet still broiling mass, he found himself on I-83 heading south. Unsure how he had gotten here, he soon discovered that the open highway allowed him time to think. As he listened to the noise of the rubber on the concrete and asphalt, he began to relax. Better able to process external stimuli, he noted with surprise the young, seat belted passenger, humming with the sound of the tires. He had nearly forgotten him in all the turmoil.

Curious, he asked, "Wanna go home now?"

After a contemplative moment, Perry looked over and replied, "Can we just drive for a little bit, first?"

With a nod of his head, Manny continued rolling south. They crossed the Susquehanna River from the east shore to the west shore by way of the South Bridge. To the north Manny took in the lights of City Island.

They stayed on I-83 until the highway changed to Route 581. Enveloped in an easy silence, they traveled the full length of Route

581 westbound, which eventually wound its way north to I-81. Twenty minutes after he had fled from Evergreen Street, Manny merged onto the interstate headed north, back toward Harrisburg.

Unaware of the vehicles following him, Manny flinched when the roof lights of a marked police car lit directly behind him. Additionally, he now noticed two unmarked vehicles had snuck along his left side and activated their emergency lights. With so much new information to process, he never took note of the other vehicles behind as one and then another added their lights to the show.

What had always felt like a building hurricane in his head now strangely seemed more like the thundering hooves of a hundred horses closing on his position. Transformed, the noise in his head, nevertheless, remained consistent in one manner: it filled him with a sense of dread. Unable to see clearly or hear past the clamor of his thoughts, he did the only thing he knew to do. He struggled to keep the big vehicle between the lines and continued to drive.

Amongst the red and blue lights of his nightmares, Manny weaved through the construction on the North Bridge re-crossing the Susquehanna River. He drove in a daze past the Front Street exit for Harrisburg. He would have persisted until his fuel ran dry, but somewhere, deep within the closet of his mind, he detected a faraway voice.

Taking shape, the voice tugged at his right arm, waking him from his self-induced hallucination. Face clarified, Manny found Perry patting the sleeve of his coat. He pointed toward the large green, reflective road sign indicating Exit 67A, Cameron Street – Harrisburg. With the noise in his head reduced to a bearable timbre, but the engine of his mind still stuck in second gear, he followed the boy's direction toward the once comfortable environs of Cameron Street.

A large animal beset by fireflies, the white and silver tanker exited the highway. As the host shifted lanes or roadways, so did the insects. As it slowed, they slowed. Onlookers stared in wonder at the spectacle of their dance.

South on Cameron Street, the ballet continued until the group began to slow at the traffic light at Elmerton Avenue. Enthralled by the blazing torches involved in the low-speed chase, traffic had come to a halt. Undeterred, the tanker weaved around the stopped vehicles and through the red light. The premier danseur led his troupe onward.

"Are you scared?" asked Manny.

Now surrounded by police cars, Perry responded, "A little."

"Me too," disclosed Manny as if considering his future.

They remained quiet as the truck passed the Farm Show building and rambled through a green light at Maclay Street. Manny knew, even with his faltering brain, this couldn't go on forever. But unable to shift the transmission of his mind, he simply moved forward.

Though his attention should have lingered on the seriousness of his dilemma, he found himself pondering the one constant in his life: himself. He couldn't help but continue to compare himself to the little boy seated next to him. He and Perry shared a history of abuse and neglect, but not a common future. Their destinies, though intertwined, wouldn't be the same.

The events of his life had molded him into a stick of dynamite. Perry's, on the other hand, had cast him into a flare. Similar in appearance, they differed in purpose. One lit the night to warn of impending danger, the other destroyed without conscience or warning.

Manny thought back on how his fuse had been lit long ago by the actions and inactions of others. He recognized he had become the destroyer. Unable or unwilling to change his own fate, he had made choices, bad choices. And his fuse had burned on. Now it seemed to have run its course, leading to its inevitable conclusion.

He sighed, glanced toward his passenger, and said, "We are alike." Then he added, "But we're also different. You don't have to end up like me." He continued without waiting for response, "I have to go away soon. You need to tell the police everything your stepdad's done to you. Your momma probably wants to help but doesn't know what to do," he babbled, not realizing he had interposed his early life into Perry's.

As they passed through another green light at Herr Street, he finished in a small voice, "It's not your fault. You're only a baby."

Mind lost in the past, Manny barely noticed the pulsing lights or the occasional siren. He paid no attention as a marked state police car passed him on the left and took up a position in front of the tanker. Just past Mulberry Street his head again filled with a familiar sound. His ballet changed to a rave. Mind bent by the growing discord, near the edge of lunacy, he gazed ahead and glimpsed...escape.

With singular focus, he knew what he had to do. He spiked the brakes causing rubber to bite into asphalt. He ripped the steering wheel to the left. As he did, the big truck bucked and bounced and careened wildly, yawing and sliding across the northbound lane of traffic.

Manny took little notice of oncoming traffic or his newest dance partner, a dark unmarked police sedan. He was going home, back to his building. Fate had brought him here in the beginning, and fate had returned him in his time of need.

The difference: where once he had sought to explore and learn, now he sought only salvation.

Chapter 42

Pursuit

Thirty-five minutes before Providence returned Manny to the abandoned warehouse, Captain Malino and Thomas had joined Stan and Ronnie near Kittatinny Street, creating a two-car, surreptitious tail. They sat silently as the tanker slowed near Evergreen Street without use of brakes, then sped up continuing straight.

"What's he up to?" voiced Malino.

Five minutes later confusion turned to bewilderment when the tanker entered the interstate heading south, causing Thomas to conclude, "We need to stop the parade and get control."

"We could use a state police cruiser," responded Malino.

"Go ahead and see if one's available," agreed Thomas. He recognized the advantages to using a clearly marked police vehicle for a traffic stop, particularly on an interstate highway. "Also, it wouldn't hurt to have a SWAT team on standby in case we end up with a hostage situation."

As Malino made the arrangements via his police radio, Thomas returned to his discussion with his team. On group talk, he advised, "We're going to try to have the staties stop the truck. If it works, we'll need to have a plan in place to block and surround it."

As he paused, Robby cut in, "Boss, I'm in line right behind you, and Bill's coming up fast. So it looks like we'll have the captain's car, plus three."

"Okay," responded Thomas, "lay back until we get this coordinated. Assume the boy's in the vehicle."

As Thomas finished his comment, his phone began to ring with an incoming call. He glanced at the caller ID and saw the name "Murphy, Mark." At the same moment Malino's phone began to ring as well. Reluctant to tie-up his only line of communication with unnecessary traffic, Thomas let the call go to voicemail.

Malino, on the other hand, answered his phone. He addressed his caller as "mayor." Thomas listened as Malino said, "Yes, sir, that's correct. We're tailing a suspect." Another pause and then an exasperated reply, "No sir, we aren't sure if the boy's with him."

This went on for another thirty seconds before Malino said goodbye and threw his phone into the console. "The consummate politician," he uttered. "I could be giving somebody CPR, and he'd want help with his coat."

Thomas smiled at the comment just as his phone began to ring in his hand. He didn't have to look at the display to know the identity of the caller. After he took the phone off speaker, he answered curtly.

"Agent Payne, this is Deputy Secretary Mark Murphy," came the slow and deliberate greeting that validated his suspicion. "I understand from Mayor Jenkins that you have another child abduction." He mistook Thomas' incredulous and angry silence as an endorsement to continue and added, "And that you're chasing a possible suspect."

Barely able to contain his fury, Thomas articulated, "Mr. Murphy, I can verify everything you've said to this point. Now, I need to have the phone clear to communicate with my team. We're in the middle of a pursuit." He added quickly, "Thank you and goodbye."

With a deep breath, Thomas loosened his strangle hold on the phone and hit the end-call button. He looked at Malino and imparted, "Your guy would ask for help with his coat, my guy would want his shoes polished and a ride home."

He had just completed his sentence, when his phone rang once more. His anger flared anew as he looked at the caller ID. With a stab of his finger on the green button, he answered, "Look, you narcissistic asshole! Don't call me again! If you do, the next time I see you, I'll butter your phone and stick it right up your ass! I hope I've made myself clear," he added before he punched the red button and threw his phone next to Malino's in the console.

Silence ruled the car for the next few seconds until Malino burst into laughter, pronouncing, "Holy shit. That was great!"

Embarrassed, Thomas apologized, "Sorry you had to hear that."

"No way, man. That was classic. Now I can retire. I've seen it all."

Caught up in the moment, an angry Thomas and a laughing Jack Malino nearly forgot about the situation unfolding around them when Thomas' phone began to chirp. He had neglected to reactivate the speaker. When he did, he heard Robby saying, "We should probably start to leap frog."

With that, the drivers began to alter positions in an effort to remain inconspicuous as they continued north past the Route 11 exit. They appeared to be headed for I-81, when the dispatcher radioed to inform them a state police car would meet them at the intersection of I-81 and Route 581.

After signing off with the dispatcher, Malino found the appropriate radio channel and began a conversation with the state trooper. During the discussion, Malino and the trooper identified two safe locations to stop the tanker, one along I-81 northbound and one should it take I-81 southbound.

They continued to track the large vehicle as it took the right hand fork which joined I-81 northbound. Thomas breathed a sigh of relief when he saw the marked state police car approach from behind and then pass to his left. It moved into position some distance behind the tanker as they prepared to bring the cavalcade to a halt.

As he waited for the rooftop lights to ignite, Thomas considered priorities. They would need to accomplish multiple objectives in a matter of seconds. First, they had to stop the twenty-ton behemoth. Then they needed to box it in to keep its occupants from escaping. And last, they needed to swarm the truck in a rapid and safe manner to minimize danger.

As they neared the predetermined stop location, two miles west of the Marysville/Enola exit, the marked car closed on the tanker and activated its emergency lights and siren. Reflected off the silver tanker, the intensity of the red and blue lights increased exponentially. This, along with the glow of nearby lights blinking along the profile of radio and microwave towers, provided a mesmerizing backdrop.

For their part, Malino and Robby pulled their unmarked vehicles into the middle of the three lanes. Just to the left of the big truck, they activated their covert emergency lights, mounted on the grill, windshield, rear side windows, and back window. Behind the tanker, Stan and Bill followed suit.

Boxed in, the team members hoped Gutierrez would pull to the side with little fanfare. However, despite their planning and preparations for moments like these, the final results often proved unpredictable. From personal experience Thomas realized that, as Robert Burns opined, "The best laid plans of mice and men oft go awry."

With the sage words in mind, he announced, "Maintain a safe distance, and let's see what he does."

Temporarily reduced to spectators, they soon found themselves off the interstate, traveling south on Cameron Street.

With four contiguous lanes, two north and two south, Thomas and Jack Malino debated options to safely stabilize the situation. In the end, they discarded the popular PIT (Precision Immobilization Technique) in favor of a rolling roadblock. The size and contents of the pursued vehicle required finesse.

Molino radioed the trooper to take up position ahead of the target vehicle. As the state car passed the tanker, the trooper tentatively identified Gutierrez and verified a passenger. He eased in front and slowly began to brake.

"Jack, ease up on the left to let him see us," said Thomas. "Robby'll follow us, and Bill and Stan'll be behind. When we come to a stop, he'll be boxed in."

"Not to be pessimistic, but what if he decides he doesn't want to stop?" responded Malino.

He had just finished his sentence when Ronnie's voice came over the speaker, "Hey, the vacant building is just down the street, he might...."

But Thomas and Jack Malino never heard the rest of the sentence. At that moment the tanker suddenly veered left. In a senseless but natural act, Thomas threw up his hands to ward off the monstrous truck. At the same time he shouted a warning that failed to breach the sounds of screeching rubber, popping glass, and tortured metal.

For his part Malino hastily jerked the wheel to the left and hit the brakes. All futile actions, impact occurred as the vehicles moved south at approximately thirty-five miles per hour. The left front tire of the truck hit the police car in the right front quarter panel, shoving it like a toy across the northbound lanes.

After initial contact, the heavier vehicle's tire rode up onto the front bumper and hood of the car, crushing the radiator and battery. Bounced and jostled as the truck's front tire landed back on the asphalt, the unmarked sedan slid partially under the large frame until it made contact with the double tires on the forward rear axle. At this point, the tanker, now headed east, continued into the parking lot of the vacant building. With mass and momentum on its side, the bigger vehicle pushed, pulled, and spun the car before depositing it in the entrance of the parking lot, facing north.

Now stopped and pointed in the opposite direction after enduring what seemed like the spin cycle of a commercial washing machine, Thomas and Jack sat stunned. The violence of their short ride had thrown them laterally about the cabin. Even with partial airbag deployment, each received cuts and bruises to their heads and shoulders.

As his brain cleared, Thomas heard Robby calling to him through the fog. He looked to the right and saw his friend attempting to open the damaged passenger door. To his left, he observed Stan Brown helping Jack out of the car. The smell of radiator fluid permeated his nostrils.

Though Robby yanked and prodded, the crumpled door refused to budge. Finally, able to think, Thomas said, "Robby, stop banging." He rubbed his right temple and added, "I feel a headache coming on."

Without another word, he crawled over the center console, slid over to the driver's seat, and accepted help in exiting through the undamaged driver's door. He stood unsteadily. "You okay?" he asked Malino, noting his bruised and cut face.

"I think it might be broken," the captain grimaced, holding his right arm.

He returned the sentiment as he examined the blood running from Thomas' scalp. "You might wanna get that looked at."

Aware of the small gash above his hairline from the resultant headache, Thomas, nevertheless ignored the suggestion. He began a swift evaluation of the scene. Less than a minute before, he sat in a car driving south on Cameron. Now the hulk of that car sat sideways, essentially barricading the parking lot of the vacant building. The smoke and steam that billowed from the compacted pile of metal reminded him how close they had come to death.

He shuddered as he tore his eyes from the destruction and looked east. Not more than one hundred feet away along the north side of the building sat the idling tanker. The utility box, once securely attached to the frame behind the cab, hung loosely, nearly touching the ground. In addition, one of the rear tires had deflated and torn loose, leaving the shiny silver rim exposed.

Back in police mode, Thomas began to generate a plan. He examined Malino, who still clutched his arm, and queried, "Jack, can you get a perimeter established?"

In obvious pain, but still game, Malino nodded and responded, "I'll have the trooper block off Cameron coming north at Berryhill."

With a look to the north, he noted an HPD marked unit rolling south in the northbound lane. More to himself than Thomas, he stated, "Good, I can use that unit to block traffic coming south at Market. Then I'll clear the traffic that's left behind."

Back on task, he pointed at the tanker and directed his comment to Thomas, "I'm not sure what his game is, but it looks like he's waiting for something." He adjusted his arm before adding, "I'll see where SWAT is, but you may not want to keep him waiting."

As the situation clarified further in his mind, Thomas took in the tanker and the three task force vehicles that now sat haphazardly in the northbound lane, facing south. "Bill and Terry," he ordered, "take one car and go next door to the building on the right. Walk across the gully and take cover along the south side of our vacant building. Get eyes on in case he comes around the back. Unless things go to shit, don't try to move in until we coordinate better."

As they moved out, he turned to Stan and Ronnie and directed, "You guys take another vehicle and do the same behind the building to the north. He'll be able to see you as you pull around back, but that's okay. I don't want him running that way. Just take up a position with good cover."

Down to just Robby and himself, Thomas looked to his comrade and in a resolute, but weary, voice asked, "You ready to make contact?"

In response, Robby popped the trunk to Thomas' car and extracted a compact .556 caliber rifle and 12 gauge pump shotgun. "Now I am," he stated, handing the rifle to Thomas. "What's the plan?"

"Pull the car up over the curb. Everyone should be in place by then."

Within thirty seconds, Robby had eased the black unmarked vehicle diagonally over the curb and around the remains of Captain Malino's sedan. As he and Thomas squatted behind the vehicle, Thomas activated the group talk feature of his phone. "Look, no long speeches," he directed. "First, assume Gutierrez is armed. Second, assume his passenger is still alive. Bill, you guys have eyes and weapons to the south. Stan, you have the same to the north. The hill blocks egress to the back. What I want to do is squeeze in from my end before he has a chance to think too much."

He let the instructions sink in before he continued, "Robby and I'll take my car to a position about twenty-five feet behind the truck and try to establish contact. My intent is to talk him out, if possible. One last thought," he finished, "do not let that truck out of this parking lot. Ensure containment. If we have to, Robby or I'll take out the tires. We'll be firing into the bank. If for some reason you have to fire from one of your sides, be sure of your target and avoid crossfires. Everyone understand?"

Acknowledgements followed. With nothing further to be gained by conversation, a banged and bruised Thomas looked at his friend and declared, "Let's end this game."

Chapter 43

The Rabbit's Warren

After the short, violent ride into the parking lot, Manny sat in the idling truck until the noise in his head subsided to a tolerable din. In the mirror he watched two men stagger from the rubble he had left in his wake. Movement to his right reminded him of his passenger, whom he had once again forgotten. "You all right?" he asked.

Perry, who seemed more excited than scared, answered, "Did we hit something?"

"This'll be over soon," replied Manny without answer. "Promise me something," he said after checking the boy for injury.

The words caused Perry to go quiet. His appearance changed to one of nervousness.

"Promise me you'll tell the policemen everything that's happened to you. Don't leave anything out." He noted a look of curiosity and added, "You asked if I was here to help you. Well, I am. Now promise," he pleaded.

Under Manny's unrelenting stare, Perry went thoughtful and then responded quietly, "I promise."

"Good," Manny breathed. "Now it's time for you to go."

With a sullen look, the little boy made the appeal, "But I don't wanna go yet. I don't want them to hurt you."

Not since his childhood had anyone shown true concern for Manny. He would have liked to explore the feeling, but movement outside the cab diverted his attention. To his left, he saw a car pull into the rear parking lot next door. Then to the right, he spotted headlights. With the adjacent businesses closed at this hour, it could only be the police.

Thrust back into the reality of the moment, he tried to think. Then he saw movement from behind. Another vehicle crept toward him. He had long dreamt and worried about this moment, yet its arrival took on a surreal quality and conjured the return of the sound. Unable to deal with the rapidly changing landscape now obscured by the increasingly loud storm of hooves, Manny reacted as he had earlier: he drove.

Only this time, he had nowhere to go. Foot off the brake, he made a wide slow turn to the right around the building into the back parking lot. He continued his one hundred and eighty degree arc, stopping only when he found himself looking directly at the doors and blocks that formed the rear of the building. Now boxed in, instinct built over millions of years took over. He put the truck into reverse and backed as far away from the danger as possible.

He didn't stop until his rear bumper lightly touched the steep hill to the east. In a reversal of roles, he had become the cornered animal. He cowered from the true predator raised from his dreams. He had lost control.

As he sat fearful and sad, his eyes passed over the loading dock where the asphalt lot dropped so the floors of the trailers sat even with the garage doors. He glanced without comprehension at the steps and the entry door to the right. Not until he cast his eyes into the shadows on the left did he appreciate what he saw. Within the darkness to his front and left, he recognized the oversized brown fiberboard garage door at ground level.

Images of his stepfather being dragged through the brown fiberboard front door of his childhood home came to mind. In that instant he knew that as the wolf of his youth had passed over the threshold, so must he, for he had become the wolf. Only in the darkness could he hope to find redemption.

True to his nature: deficient in deliberations, rash to act, Manny hastily cranked the tanker into drive and mashed the accelerator to the floor. As he began to move forward, he nearly lost his nerve, when, suddenly and unexpectedly, a bright light turned night into day. Fascinated by the vividly lit scene to his front, Manny observed the flimsy garage door loom larger. As if watching television, his gaze remained fixed right up to the point the portal and windshield became one.

The impact woke him from his stupor. As he crashed and bounced over the remains of the door, he paid little attention to the speedometer, which indicated twenty-six miles per hour at the time of contact. His focus remained on controlling the bucking vehicle amidst the sounds of tortured metal and snapping wood. Though it seemed endless, his violent, unconventional entry into the structure took no more than a second.

Now inside, Manny felt like a rabbit returned to the safety of its warren. Of course, the feeling lasted only the time it took to transition from the harsh, accusing light into the soothing darkness. Once enveloped by the familiar shadows, he realized the danger hadn't diminished.

Compelled to flee forward, Manny followed the unbroken beams of his headlights up a slight incline, which provided access to the main storeroom. Now in the warehouse proper, he took note of the obstacles littering the space. Though cognizant of the building's clutter on past visits, it took on new proportions from his vantage point inside the cab of the big truck.

Undaunted, he kept moving. He paid little attention to the debris he shoved to the side. Only the bump of larger objects beneath the wheels penetrated his concentration. Then through the dust, which threatened to further cloud his view, he discerned his way out.

Accelerating, he charged to the left front corner of the space where he stopped next to a large rectangular bin made of concrete block, built against the south wall. He had noticed the area on a prior visit to the building but hadn't taken the time to study its interior. He had always been too busy with other explorations.

Aided by the truck's reflected lights, he examined the space through the veil of dirty air. To his surprise, he saw not one big bin, but four smaller ones, all with their own entry point. Essentially six-foot square silos, they rose to a height of ten feet. Each remained open above with a doorway raised up one course of eight-inch block to keep stored material from spilling out.

Not sure what use the bins had served in their past life, he felt confident one would suit a purpose in his.

As the big diesel continued to clack away, he hopped from the cab. He had a job to do, and he had to be quick. However, when he hit the ground, his legs nearly buckled under his weight. At that moment, he grasped just how tired he had become, not from the past weeks of insomnia but from a lifetime of nightmares.

It took a few seconds and some deep breaths before he regained his mental and physical footing. He had to finish what he now saw as his race for redemption. "One foot in front of the other," he told himself.

As a result, with considerable effort, he first walked and then ran to the box containing the switches and gauges at the rear of the tank. He put his hand against the familiar cold metal faceplate. Reassured, he began to drag the long rubber hose from its reel when the passenger door opened and Perry carefully climbed down.

The boy spoke, but his words couldn't overcome the harsh combination of sounds emanating from the truck and somewhere deep within Manny's brain. Like a deaf man, he wanted to hear, but his auditory system failed him. Only when the boy touched his hand did he find the strength to listen.

Through a thunderous waterfall, the little boy's words reached Manny's ears. With a tug on the sleeve, he looked up with teary eyes and asked, "Is it time for you to go, Oilman?"

"It's time for both of us to go," replied Manny sadly.

They stood motionless for a long moment. Then with a hand on one thin shoulder, Manny guided the boy and the hose around the back of the truck. Once positioned in front of the appropriate block bin, he looked down to meet the little boy's gaze. In the light cast from the tanker, he witnessed a single tear slide down Perry's smooth cheek. With a smile, he patted that same cheek, pulled the trigger on the nozzle, and began to make his final delivery.

Chapter 44

Hell on Earth

In the minutes prior to Manny's mad rush toward the back of the abandoned building, Robby had piloted the black police vehicle alongside the structure with Thomas following on foot. As the tanker crept around the building, he called out from behind the ballistic shield wedged on the dash, "He's moving. What do you want me to do?"

In answer to the muffled voice coming from within the semi-armored vehicle, Thomas responded, "Follow him, but slowly, no aggressive moves."

At the back corner of the building, Thomas hollered, "Robby, stop here and see what he does. If it stabilizes, I'll try to establish contact."

Parked near the northeast corner of the building, Robby exited and joined Thomas. With the wall for cover, they observed the big truck complete a slow semi-circle movement in the rear lot. At first, Thomas suspected the driver intended to charge them.

However, once the vehicle faced them, it stopped and then ominously began to back up.

Its retreat continued until it reached the base of the hill, nearly 150 feet away. When it finally came to rest, Thomas used his cell phone to ask, "Can anyone see what's going on in the cab?"

From the north Stan responded, "Negative."

"I see two people inside, but no detail," replied Bill from the south.

At that moment, a bright white light illuminated the entire back parking lot. High on the bank, Thomas detected someone standing in a backyard off Crescent Street. As the figure, which turned out to be two, moved about, he caught the silhouette of a shoulder-mounted camera. The media had arrived.

He intended to ask Bill Travis to work his way up the hill to "help the reporters to safety," but never got the chance. Center stage, the diesel engine spooled up, and the tanker slowly and ponderously rolled forward. As the spectators watched in disbelief, it moved not toward them and possible escape but directly toward the back of the building.

Powerless, the task force members stared on as the massive vehicle slowly chewed and digested the intervening asphalt. By the time it hit the garage door, the tanker, turned tank, had built sufficient momentum to easily punch an opening in the brittle, old portal. Hit by the forty thousand pound sledge, boards splintered and door rollers ripped from their tracks. Out of sight, the sound from within the building left no doubt the truck continued onward, roaring and plowing into objects inside the warehouse.

Over the clamor, Thomas yelled to Robby, "Inside!"

Each took off for the jagged opening created by the tanker. As they reached the gaping hole, Bill Travis and Terry Hassinger rounded the side of the building closest to the garage door. "Spread out and work forward," Thomas called out.

Behind him, he heard the slap of feet on the asphalt as Stan Brown and Ronnie Sanchez dashed from the north. Over his shoulder, he yelled, "Tell Malino what's going on and try to get someone on each side of the building in case this guy tries to run."

With that, Thomas followed Robby, Bill, and Terry from the artificial light cast from the hill to the darkness within the warehouse. Once inside, he scanned the shadows, observing the pulverized remnants of a bygone era mingled with the rolling cloud of dust. The destruction, along with the smell and sound from the big diesel's spewing, screaming exhaust, seemed like hell on earth.

"Two by two, split the building in half. Focus on the truck," he shouted above the noise.

In accordance with common practice, each of the task force members carried a small tactical flashlight. The odd man out, Terry Hassinger stayed paired with Bill Travis as they began to work their way down the right or north half of the warehouse, while Thomas and Robby moved straight down the left side. They had only reached the halfway point when they observed movement in the dusty air.

Quickly taking cover, Thomas prepared to call out instructions, when he heard an unusual sound join the clatter from the diesel engine. Similar to a barbecue grill lighting, he heard a whoosh and witnessed a blooming light. Heart forced into his throat, he feared they were too late.

Chapter 45

The Truth of Darkness

Manny watched through stinging eyes as Perry moved off through the frenetic dust cloud of light. His right hand continued to grip the nozzle, which spouted dark fluid onto the floor of one of the silos. His left hand reached out as if to wave goodbye. Spellbound, he gazed after the boy until his slight form merged with the shadows.

Snapped from his daze, Manny noted for the first time a drain in the center of the little room allowing the fuel oil to bleed away. Not to be denied this final act in the Greek tragedy of his life, the man, once a boy and now by definition a serial killer, walked back to the cab, still grasping the heavy silver nozzle. He opened the door and reached under the seat with his left hand. His fingers searched amongst the discarded paper, gravel, and dust bunnies until they found what they sought.

As he pulled out the blanket, his mind flashed back to Crystal City, Texas. A yellow blanket covered the body of his mother. In more recent times, the yellow blankets covered the bodies of two young boys. Today it would serve a different, but no less final, purpose.

Without pause, he dragged the thick orange rubber hose back through the doorway of the last bin. Dark and dank, what had originally resembled a farmer's silo, now felt like a tomb. The grey concrete blocks surrounded and closed in on him. Though the noise of the truck's engine and the hum of the tank's pump resonated loudly off the solid interior walls, it barely registered in his ears. Only certain sounds, which others could not hear, possessed the strength to pierce the armor of his mind.

With two long steps, he stood in the middle of the small room. Though it was dark, he could see well enough to remove the round metal, six-inch grate from the floor drain. Into the void, he stuffed the blanket. No longer a cover, the softball sized ball of plastic formed a makeshift plug. Satisfied, he took in a deep breath and went to work.

The tanker's onboard pump responded immediately to his squeeze of the trigger. Set at its highest flow rate, it pushed out fuel oil at a ratio of fifty gallons per minute. As the light petroleum distillate poured from the hose, the fumes began to burn Manny's nose and eyes. In the darkness of the room, he occasionally caught a glimpse of the liquid as it splashed and reflected the weak light coming through the bin's doorway.

Soon the dark fluid covered the floor and began a steady march up the walls. As it rose, it soaked his already wet boots and pants, causing them to feel cold and heavy. Not satisfied, he turned the right angle nozzle slightly and drenched his remaining articles of clothing: his winter coat, sweatshirt, his hat, and gloves.

Glazed in a shiny coat of oil, he not only saw it, tasted it, smelled it, and felt it, but also believed he could hear it. Once identified as the sound of a storm, then as thundering hooves, his faltering mind now distinguished the roar in his head as a great waterfall. But unlike the storm or the horses, he sensed the waterfall would never hurt him. It would only cleanse him of his sins.

Fueled by the increasingly incoherent thoughts racing through his mind, Manny tossed the nozzle out the doorway causing the trigger to release and shut off. He reached into his wet pocket and, with great reverence, pulled out the small, solidly built object he always kept there. Though it remained slippery in his grasp, he felt and pictured the engraving on its side: ducks silently gliding over flowing water.

With a flick of his wrist, he opened the lid of his mother's lighter. He noted with disappointment that he couldn't hear the satisfying click produced by the cam. Undeterred, the man, once a boy as innocent as any other, placed his thumb on the rough wheel, pressed hard, and lit the wick.

He intended to throw the lighter into the oil, but that proved unnecessary. Attracted to the fumes and liquid on his hand and arm, the flame attacked, causing him to drop the lit lighter into the oil pooling around his feet. Engulfed in flame and searing pain, he screamed, not once, but many times.

The fire sucked the oxygen from his lungs. It boiled the vitreous fluid in his eyes.

For the next thirty seconds, he endured the agony that battled the sound in his head for control. It came in waves. It ebbed and flowed. Then slowly, as his nerve endings died off, it began to diminish.

As the pain subsided, Manny felt himself moving away from his body as if floating on a soft cloud. Though not clinically dead yet, the pain had gone, as had the noise. Now nothing existed, save a sense of calm and…the light.

Intense and bright, the light promised to consume him. However, though it radiated power, it didn't elicit fear. He knew he had begun a transition, and this transition offered understanding. Most important, it presented him with the possibility of salvation.

As he drew from the energy surrounding him, Manny experienced, what he considered, a revelation. The first of possibly many to come, he suddenly and absolutely gained understanding into the nature of the light. As with the simplest of plants, he realized light fed man's soul. With light came hope. Darkness, on the other hand, simply represented the absence of light and, transitively, the absent of hope.

In hope there existed endless potential. Conversely, darkness, like most drugs, offered short-term gain but long-term destruction.

More joyous than he could have ever imagined, he seemed to be moving steadily toward the source of the light.

Then, something changed. He no longer had the sensation of gliding through the light, but falling. Dread overcame his previous feeling of calm as he spiraled down toward a small spot that served as a blemish on the otherwise perfectly white landscape. Faster and faster Manny tumbled. Though he had no sense of time or space, he knew he had journeyed an eternity. Though bodiless, he felt bone weary.

The farther he fell, the larger the imperfection became. No longer the antithesis of a distant star in the clear night sky, it now looked like the mouth of some menacing cave as seen from the forest on a bright autumn day. Larger and larger it grew until his world split evenly between the light and the dark. Then as his momentary, but eternal, journey continued and the darkness became a majority, Manny finally received some of the answers for which he had so desperately yearned.

In the instant the darkness began to overcome the light, Manny suddenly and unequivocally realized he never stood a chance of outrunning the shadows, for the shadows had never chased him. Nor had they acted upon him as a virus transmitted from the wolf of his youth. Part of his DNA, they had resided within his body from birth as they live within every human being from the point of conception.

This insight led him to a corollary. If human beings had access to an endless font of evil, they similarly had access to a perpetual fountain of goodness. Aided by his heightened perception, he also understood that life's experiences affected, but didn't control, from which source an individual drew power. Ultimately, the difference between good and bad came down to choices.

As for the wolf, it had never physically existed, at least not in the form of his stepfather or even himself. Each, merely a man, had made depraved and everlastingly poor choices. Conversely, though wrong about the existence of a wolf, he realized with certainty that he had been right to be fearful because other things, much more dangerous, hid among the shadows.

Having now established that men and women exercised control over their own destinies by accepting the premise of a free will, Manny clearly understood that there are monsters out there. Disguised in human form, they hide in plain sight, whimsically traveling from the light into the darkness when it serves their maleficent purposes.

Unfortunately, though the answers to his questions placed Manny at ease, the shadows merely toyed with him. Not in the habit of granting wishes or comforting troubled minds, the darkness simply sought to distract and tease him. It wanted him looking in the other direction because it planned to provide Manny with the answers to questions he had never even considered. About to open his eyes or soul, in this case, to the reality of its nature, the darkness intended to surprise him.

As he continued his fall, the light gradually faded to darker shades of grey, and he slowly sensed his earlier expectation of salvation fading with it. At the same time, the sound to which he had become accustomed returned. It started as a whisper but increased to an unendurable roar.

Truly able to see into the past, present, future, and beyond, he finally understood the source of the noise. Never the sound of an earthly storm, or lawmen's horses, or even flowing water, it heralded something much more ominous.

As the light blinked out and his mortal body ceased to function, Manny Gutierrez got his first clear look into the darkness that would envelope him for eternity.

Had he a voice, he would have screamed. Had he a choice now, he would have chosen differently. But as he understood in that ending moment, some choices are final and infinitely worse than others.

Chapter 46

Fire and Smoke

Concealed behind an I-beam support, Thomas kept his light and rifle sighted on the movement. He waited, finger outside the trigger guard, for the picture to resolve. When it did, he pointed the rifle to the side and yelled, "Robby, cover me. It's the boy."

Without further thought, he dashed from cover, scooped up the child in one arm, and dove behind a pile of machinery. Now safe, he breathed heavily and inquired, "You okay?"

Covered by Thomas' body, the little boy murmured, "I'm fine. I have to keep my promise," he added.

"What's that, buddy?" asked Thomas.

"I promised the Oilman I'd tell you what happened to us."

Confused, Thomas replied, "That might have to wait a few minutes."

Though the boy appeared safe and unharmed, the danger had not been removed. A killer still roamed the shadows. No time to stop or rest, Thomas, yelled, "I have the boy. You three move forward. I'll see what I can learn about Gutierrez."

Back to Perry, Thomas queried, "Is there just the one man?"

"Well sure," Perry answered. "Who else would there be?"

Undaunted, Thomas questioned, "Does he have a weapon?"

"Don't think so."

As the smell of burning fuel reached their nostrils along with the sounds of tortured screaming, Thomas probed, "Perry, do you know what's going on?"

With a look toward the blossoming light, Perry explained how the Oilman had taken the large rubber hose from the tanker to one of the bins. He turned back to Thomas and added, "The Oilman's going home."

Explained in terms of a mathematical property, the scene that unfolded before the investigators would have been described as an inverse relationship. As the sights, sounds, and smells of the conflagration increased, the ear piercing shrieking diminished. Just as Robby reached the stationary tanker, it stopped all together.

Cautiously, he searched for threats, human or otherwise. He paused and listened, but heard nothing over the roar of flames and the idling truck. As he circled the front of the vehicle, Bill worked his way around the back. Shotgun in the lower ready position, Robby snuck a peek inside the first bin.

As he pulled his head back behind the safety of the concrete wall, his mind interpreted the snapshot taken by his eyes. Immediately he lowered his weapon and backed away from the intense heat. He met Bill in front of the third bin. "Hell of a way to go out," he said, hooking a thumb toward the fire.

Curious, Bill took six steps forward, shielded his face, and peered into the fiery mass. Inside the bin, he viewed a crumbled form that appeared to have once been human. Satisfied, he wiped the soot and tears from his stinging eyes and backed away. "At least it's over," he announced.

Given the all-clear sign, Terry Hassinger joined them, moving in for a closer look at the growing inferno. Immediately forced back by the heat, he tripped over the rubber hose lying by the doorway and fell against the front of the truck. Provided a reminder of the thermo retention capacity of metal through his singed fingers, he struck upon an alarming notion.

"We gotta move this thing," he yelled over the clacking engine as he pointed at the flammable liquid sign.

Without another word, he covered his hand with his coat sleeve, grasped the hot door handle, and hopped into the cab. He quickly took stock, rolled down the side window, and shouted, "Bill, reel the hose back into the spool. Then, guide me back."

By the time he saw Bill wave him back, Terry felt sweat rolling down his back and left side. At an agonizingly slow pace, he retreated from the danger. Eventually he stopped the unwieldy vehicle at the midway point in the warehouse. With a sigh of relief, he stepped from the cab and pushed the door closed behind him. Once again singed nerves sent a message to his brain, causing him to yelp, "Son of a bitch. I have to be the stupidest mother...," he cursed before noticing the little boy standing behind Thomas. "Mother lover in the world," he finished with a shake of his hand.

With all eyes now on him and the child, Thomas asked, "Gutierrez?"

Robby first looked to make sure the little boy couldn't see him. Then he drew his finger across his neck in a cutting motion. In further explanation, he nodded his head in the direction of the improvised furnace. Fueled by the oxygen drafting through the doorway, bright flames licked at the concrete walls and dark smoke billowed up and out the opening ten feet above.

Entranced by the fantastic scene, the sounds of sirens and horns from responding fire trucks shook Thomas from his reverie. Alerted by the smoke, those outside must be wondering what had occurred. He extracted his cell phone and contacted Jack Malino, who shouted, "What the hell's going on in there?"

"The boy's safe. Gutierrez's dead."

"What about the smoke?" asked Malino.

Unable to provide a detailed summary of what had occurred near the truck, Thomas responded in general terms, "Right now, we have a pretty hot fire burning inside a small cement silo. It appears self-contained, but we're going to have to get the fire guys in here. Have them come around back, and let's keep an investigator with them so they don't destroy evidence. Here's Robby, he'll explain what happened."

Robby took the phone and the two moved to the side. In less than a minute Robby provided details. He left little out in his description of the sights, sounds, and smells that assaulted him as he neared the truck and the concrete bin. He finished by indicating, "Looks like Gutierrez hosed down the inside of the bin with oil. He must've been standing in the middle when it lit because he's toast."

Tale complete, he handed the phone back to Thomas, who had been watching the black smoke swirl lower and lower. With a sense of urgency, he related, "Jack, we're coming out the back. Can you meet us by the garage door?"

"I'll be there. Which door?"

"You'll know it when you see it," replied Thomas, eyeing the gaping hole. "Hey, and grab Stan and Ronnie," he added before disconnecting.

More than ready to leave the building, he tapped Robby and instructed, "Let's get out of here. Help Terry back the truck out first. Then, we'll follow."

It took Terry a few tries to back the cumbersome vehicle through the remnants of the garage door. By this time, not one, but three local media stations had found a spot on the back hill. The video and still pictures taken in those next few minutes catapulted the story to national and international prominence.

The video of the soot-stained, silver tanker backing through the rolling waves of black smoke, tearing pieces from the smashed garage door, went viral on the internet. The scene of Thomas and Perry Lomax walking out of the building, hand in hand, screened by a well-armed contingent in ash and dirt-covered ballistic armor, became the lead video on most national news broadcasts that next morning.

However, as the cameras captured the drama taking place around the old warehouse, the news crews remained oblivious to the scene transpiring mere feet from them on the hill. Also on the bank were members of the Allison Hill neighborhood, including Clementina Rodriguez and her two remaining children. Attracted by the glare of the TV lights in their backyards, they stood in small groups.

An extremely private person following the death of her son, Clementina had been drawn in by the site of Stan Brown and Ronnie Sanchez. She remembered them from her interview. With a sense the events transpiring below would have meaning to her life, she had watched and waited.

At the sight of the little boy walking unharmed from the building, she suddenly felt...happy. She had nearly forgotten the feeling. In spite of her personal anguish, she now realized she could still feel hope.

The thought caused her to lift her gaze toward heaven. She watched as the black and grey smoke billowed up from the building. Enthralled, she followed its rise until it merged with the obscure night sky. Dissipated into the evening, she believed it to be an evil entity fleeing the earth.

With the tiniest thread of optimism in her voice, Clementina looked to her children and quietly directed, "Let's get back into the house where it's warm."

She paused, thinking back on a comment Ronnie had made during her interview. With a nod in the direction of the female agent, she proclaimed, "I guess your best was good enough. It's over now."

Chapter 47 (The Day After)

Yin Yang

Thomas breathed deeply of the crisp, cool winter air as he left the hospital at 3:00 a.m. the next morning. Robby and Bill strolled leisurely at his side. Each had received treatment for smoke inhalation, while Thomas had the additional good fortune to collect a few staples in his scalp and stitches above his right eye.

Jack Malino, who had broken his arm and separated his shoulder, remained warm and relatively comfortable on the third floor, his pain regulated by a mixture of acetaminophen and codeine. Keeping him company, his wife and Terry Hassinger had both fallen asleep at his bedside, in spite of the uncomfortable hospital chairs in which they reclined.

As the three men quietly crossed the alley to the parking garage, lost to their own thoughts, a car horn blared and a baritone voice shouted, "You boys out for a night on the town, or would you like a ride home?"

Off to his left, Thomas spotted Stan Brown, Ronnie Sanchez, and Doc Patel sitting inside one of the task force vehicles. Fifteen seconds later, the six agents stood on the Chestnut Street sidewalk. Each examined the others, noting the disheveled, but upbeat appearance.

Happy to see his friends no worse for the wear, Stan breathed a sigh of relief and offered, "Thought you guys might need a ride."

"That's probably a good idea, big man," remarked Thomas, realizing just how sore and tired the ordeal had left him. "I appreciate the thought."

At this point, Ronnie, who had been standing in front of Thomas, reached out with her hand and compassionately touched his bruised face. Everyone quieted in anticipation of her comments. She examined his injuries and with contrived disgust stated, "A guy gets scarred and it makes him look more interesting. A woman gets scarred, and she just looks scarred."

She paused and laughed, "Another double standard."

Like a bunch of punch-drunk fighters, they all began to laugh uncontrollably. Thomas allowed the humor a moment to die down before he took on a serious tone and commented, "It's been a busy three days. How're you all doing?" he asked, looking from investigator to investigator.

He left his gaze stay on Ronnie. Without hesitation, she answered, "This is the first time in a long time I've felt good about my work. And about the people I work with," she continued sheepishly. "I think I'll stick around for a while."

Stan enveloped her in a big arm and added his response to Thomas' question, "I can handle whatever they throw at me, 'cause I work with Saint Michael and, through him, God."

Thomas nodded at Stan's statement of unwavering faith and then turned to Doc. The young tech man began to speak in what Bill had taken to calling "Nerdish." Painfully aware of the direction of the conversation, Bill put his hand on their resident geek's arm, interrupting his dissertation, and said simply, "We love our job."

Laughter, now bordering on giddiness, provided the impetus for the team to call it an evening. Though tired and worn, they knew one more important task remained.

Eight quick hours later, they found themselves together again. Just before noon on Thursday, the low clouds hid a grey sky, and an inch of fresh powdered snow covered the ground and trees. A bucolic scene near Steelton, the green tent nestled among the pine trees of the cemetery provided cover for the freshly dug grave and tiny brown casket of Jeffrey Englehart.

Outside the tent, Thomas and the members of the Major Crimes Task Force stood on the periphery as they paid their respects to a little boy whose life had been cut short by the senseless and selfish actions of a caregiver. Though he hadn't died at the hands of the "Cradle Killer," he was no less dead than Jesus and Jamal.

Amongst the lightly falling snow, Thomas pondered the futile nature of his life's work. One day he hunted a budding serial killer, the next a drunken stepfather. The thought caused him trepidation until he reflected upon his knowledge of the Asian philosophy of Yin Yang. It reminded him that the universe required dualities: male and female, dark and light, and good and bad. His mission, the mission of the task force, wasn't to eradicate evil, but to balance it with good.

In the midst of this thought, a familiar scent caressed his nostrils. Carried by a cool gentle breeze, he caught a whiff of lavender, the scent worn by his late wife Lynn. It passed quickly, leaving him feeling lighter.

At that moment, someone gently grasped his gloved right hand. He turned to look onto the bright brown eyes of Breanne O'Malley. "A little birdie told me you might be here," she offered, noting his look of surprise. With a quick glance at Robby, she added, "He said it was important."

As his heart skipped a beat, Thomas uncharacteristically gave her a hug, which didn't go unnoticed by the others. He whispered a quiet, "thank you" in her ear. As he did, he took in her scent. Astonishingly, she smelled of soap, shampoo, and a light perfume. Though intoxicating, it couldn't be mistaken for lavender.

With a squeeze of Breanne's hand, he looked toward the heavens. He imagined Lynn taking in the scene below and smiling, saying to herself, "I finally found someone good enough for you."

Ten minutes later, the priest concluded the funeral service, and the tiny assemblage began to disperse. The members paid their respects to the family and began the walk back to their cars. As they progressed, they engaged in quiet conversation. They hadn't even made it to the vehicles before intrusive, yet well-meaning, inquisitors besieged Thomas and Breanne.

The only member to maintain distance, Maggie stood back and watched the interaction with apprehension. Though not romantically linked to Thomas, she had been the only woman in his life for nearly five years. The sight of him with someone else unsettled her. Though she had always hoped he would find love, she now worried he might find additional heartbreak.

However, her unexpected fear disappeared as quickly as it had come, facilitated by the same fleeting flowery scent carried moments before by the wind. Unable to identify the specific bloom, she, nonetheless, grasped its beauty and the feeling of contentment it instilled. Negative feelings aside, she smiled as she observed the furtive looks and touches exchanged between the couple. With the realization that her wishes for Thomas might be coming true, she gave in and happily joined the crowd.

Immediately enlisting her into the good-natured ribbing, the group's focus remained on Thomas and Breanne until Thomas felt his cell phone vibrating on his belt. He excused himself as he dug inside his heavy winter coat to retrieve the device. A look at the caller ID and he reflexively stood taller. "Good morning, director," he answered.

"Agent Payne," came the unmistakable voice of Director Arnold Greene. "How're you all doing this morning?"

"Pretty well, sir. A little tired. It was a late night," replied Thomas as succinctly as possible.

"Why didn't you take the morning off?" questioned the director.

Enigmatic, Thomas offered, "We had something important to do this morning."

"Well, I'm in the governor's office right now," the director continued, overlooking the evasive response. "He'd like to speak with you. Mind if I put you on speaker?"

Thomas responded in the affirmative, though he sensed the rhetorical nature of the question. The governor's voice then came on the line, "Thomas, I just wanted to thank you and the task force for the fine police work. You and your people solved the murders of three boys in as many days." He paused briefly and then continued, "Director Greene forwarded me your email with the arrest summary from last night, so I have a pretty good handle on the events, but I still have a few questions."

"Yes, sir," replied Thomas."

"I hear the little boy wasn't hurt at all, thanks to you," stated the governor.

"Well, let's just say he wasn't hurt by Gutierrez," clarified Thomas. "As a matter of fact, he thinks Gutierrez came to help him. I'm not really sure what that means yet, but it's clear the poor kid's been physically and mentally abused by a number of his mother's paramours. At this point, he's been removed from the environment, but he's going to be in counseling for some time. As for mom and her boyfriends, we're going to help the city make sure they get what's coming to them."

The comment caused the governor to exhale and concede, "I couldn't do what you do, Thomas. You see and touch the worst our so-called civilization has to offer."

Silence took over until Director Green broke in, "I understand you threatened the deputy secretary for public safety."

Thomas had forgotten about his run-in over the phone with Mark Murphy. He steeled himself for the next words from either the governor or the director.

To his relief, the governor laughed and offered, "The next time he interferes, let us know. I'll butter his phone."

"And," quickly added the director, couching his words, "I'll gladly take it upon myself to find the appropriate orifice into which it should be shoved."

Thomas breathed a sigh of relief at his bosses' willingness to overlook his breach of etiquette. This did not, however, cause him to forget the lessons he had learned over the past few days. In particular, he now recognized that in politics, the most important question would always remain "What have you done for me lately?"

The discussion lasted for another few minutes before the governor ran out of questions. As he signed off, Thomas Payne, commander of Pennsylvania's Major Crimes Task Force, stood for a long moment observing his friends across the snowy lawn. In particular, he noticed Breanne and Maggie quietly talking and smiling. Though he hadn't thought of it until that moment, he now appreciated how much Maggie's approval meant to him. He relaxed when he saw them both laugh and hug each other.

Endorsement apparently given, he ended his contemplation and hurried over to pass along the governor's and director's appreciation. As he closed the distance, his mind stopped on one thought, "If my lot in life is to battle evil, these are the people I want by my side."

Surrounded by friends, not just colleagues, a warm feeling came over him as he realized he no longer stood alone. In fact, the events of the last few days had shown him that he had never really been alone at all.

With this thought in mind, he slid one arm around Breanne's waist and the other around Maggie's shoulder. With a smile on his face, he decided that for today at least, the future looked promising.

Epilogue

In the weeks following the demise of Manny Gutierrez,
investigation by the Harrisburg Police Department and the Major
Crimes Task Force conclusively linked the troubled young man to
the deaths of Jesus Rodriguez and Jamal Wilson. Interviews in
Pennsylvania painted a vague picture of a quiet and introverted
newcomer to the state. The image clarified after Texas authorities
became involved and provided insight into the tragedies of his
formative years.

As Stan Brown would say during one particularly long after-
action meeting, "This guy was physically and mentally abused by a
parental figure as his mother sat idle. His mother was beaten to
death while he sat idle. Last, the system sat idle and failed him. He
had three strikes against him from the start."

Then he paused and added, "But no matter what, he always
had a choice. He chose wrong."

Scientific evidence, further enhancement of the videos
obtained from the plumbing store and bank, as well as more detailed

interviews, proved useful in placing Gutierrez at the first dumpsite and near the vacant building. Additionally, lab personnel documented the consistency between the tread from the brand boot worn by Gutierrez and a print left at the second dump sight.

As the forensic scientist had indicated earlier, the trace evidence on the necks of both young victims tested consistent with cowhide and number two fuel oil. Examination of the gloves utilized by Gutierrez and his company determined their inclusion as possible donors. Further, inquiry of markings and trace evidence on the blankets at both dumpsites linked them to opened packs found in the vehicles used by Gutierrez on the nights both children disappeared.

Unfortunately, investigators never determined the significance of the yellow synthetic blanket in the mind of the killer. A trivial connection at best, they never asked for nor received a copy of the death investigation for Gutierrez' mother. Therefore, Pennsylvania investigators never looked upon the photographs of the woman as she lay in repose with feet crossed and hands on her chest beneath the same type blanket.

While investigators found no diaries, writings, or documentation attributed to Gutierrez, the most damning evidence against him came in the form of the yellow wristband and stick gun found in his locker. Souvenirs of his conquests, these reminders of his power over others turned out to be a significant flaw leading to his undoing. As frequently occurs, strength based in arrogance or perverse sentiment simply disguises weakness.

In regard to the stuffed bunny rabbit also found in the locker, investigators believe it a souvenir from a previous crime, though they could never associate it with a known murder or assault. Reported and probed as an accidental death, the boy's fall into the Texas quarry resulted in only a cursory investigation. Additionally, even if a murder investigation had been conducted, the existence and disappearance of the bunny had gone unnoticed by the young owner's parents. Sadly, they had paid little attention to the child or his activities until the day he died.

As with most criminal investigations, not every question receives an answer. Like an archeological dig, bits and pieces lead to foundations. Eventually, following much painstaking and tedious work, partial reconstruction of the early civilization's infrastructure occurs. Unfortunately, the inevitable decay of brick and stone and the decomposition of wood and ornamentation prevent even the most astute scientist from making the ancient society whole again.

Robby Franklin's observations provide a good example of this concept, "When you deal with someone as abnormal as Gutierrez, even if you could interview him, it would be difficult to understand his answers because his mind works differently from ours. Since he's dead, we're always going to be left guessing about some of the finer points of his actions."

But then, Robby being Robby, he added, "Looking on the bright side, by charcoaling himself, he saved the state the cost of a prosecution and a prison stay. It's a two-for."

As for the task force, the governor and director took advantage of its new-found celebrity. In a formal ceremony, including the press, they christened the state's newest investigative resource. During the dedication, a large sign, approximately five feet square, magically appeared on the poorly lit wall outside the basement door of the task force office. Seen by the politicians as an excellent backdrop for the media on that day, the emblem is shaped like a keystone to represent Pennsylvania's position as the "Keystone State" and overlaid with Lady Justice holding her scales.

Though originally only a temporary measure, the task force members asked that the sign remain as a daily reminder of their ongoing duty: to provide justice to the victims of crime when all else and all others have failed.

THE END

References

Smurfs are a creation of Belgian comics artist Pierre Culliford (Peyo) first utilized in his 1958 comics series *Johan and Peewit.*

The Twilight Zone is a science-fiction/fantasy television anthology series created by Rod Serling and produced by Cayuga Productions, Incorporated and CBS Productions that first aired on CBS from 1959–1964.

The Lone Ranger is a radio adventure series that first premiered on Detroit radio station WXYZ in 1933. Both show owner George W. Trendle and main writer Fran Striker have received credit for its creation.

Groundhog Day is a 1993 Columbia Pictures Corporation film, produced by Trevor Albert, C.O. Erickson, Harold Ramis, and Whitney White, directed by Harold Ramis, and starring Bill Murray and Andie McDowell.

Theodore Samuel "Ted" Williams (1918–2002) was a Major League baseball player, and manager.

Harry Potter is the title character and protagonist in a series of seven fantasy novels written by British author J. K. Rowling and published by Bloomsbury Publishing (UK) and Arthur A. Levine Books (US), an imprint of the Scholastic Corporation.

Catch-22 is a satirical novel written by American writer Joseph Heller and published by Simon and Schuster in 1961.

Dirty Harry is a 1971 Warner Bros film produced by Robert Daley and Carl Pingitore, directed by Don Siegel, and starring Clint Eastwood.

I Love Lucy is a Desilu Productions television sitcom (1951-1957) produced by Jess Oppenheimer, directed by Ralph Levy, Marc Daniels, William Asher, and James V. Kern, distributed by CBS television, and starring Lucille Ball and Desi Arnaz.

Fatal Attraction is a 1987 Paramount Pictures film produced by Stanley R. Jaffe and Sherry Lansing, directed by Adrian Lyne, and starring Michael Douglas and Glenn Close.

More from Jon D. KURTZ

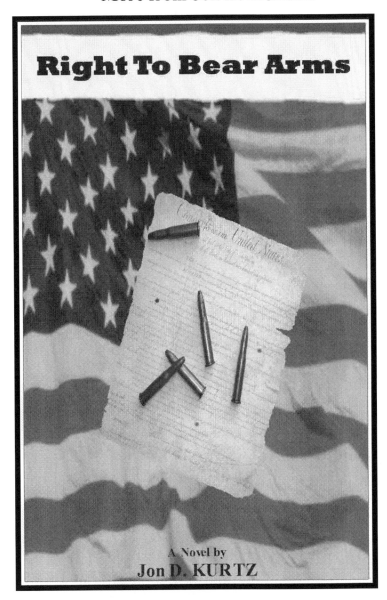

Right To Bear Arms

A Novel by
Jon D. KURTZ

Coming Soon

Author Page

Jon D. Kurtz is a retired Deputy Commissioner for the Pennsylvania State Police, living in Harrisburg, Pennsylvania. Writing what he calls "Pragmatic Police Novels," his goal is to provide the reader with works of fiction that exhibit an authenticity born from experience.

To learn more about the author, provide comment, or to be included in the mailing list announcing new projects, please visit http://www.jondkurtz.com and https://www.facebook.com/authorjondkurtz.

Also, like A Choice of Darkness at https://www.facebook.com/AChoiceofDarkness and don't forget to provide a five-star review at http://www.amazon.com/Choice-Darkness-Major-Crimes-Force-ebook/product-reviews/B00HDPWL0C/ref=dp_top_cm_cr_acr_txt?ie=UTF8&showViewpoints=1.